Praise for Steven F. Havill

Lies Come Easy

Best of the West 2019–3rd Place in 20th- to 21st-Century Western Mystery Fiction by *True West Magazine*

"Havill has again written an engrossing mystery that focuses on the people of Posadas County and the intricate ways in which their personalities and lives intertwine."
— *Reviewing the Evidence*

"This compelling novel contrasts the loving family and community life shared by Reyes-Guzman and her retired mentor, Sheriff Bill Gastner, with the troubled lives led by victims and criminals in the county. Series devotees will eagerly welcome this latest installment."
— *Library Journal*

"Havill's irresistible twenty-third mystery set in tiny Posadas County, NM, combines a police procedural with a complex family saga. Havill's inviting world welcomes newcomers and keeps fans happily coming back for more."
— *Publishers Weekly*

"Master of mystery Steven F. Havill accomplishes that rare and remarkable feat of making each book in his compelling series even better than the one that came before it. With meticulous attention to detail and a warm storytelling style, Havill transforms ordinary people into extraordinary. Evildoers, no matter how twisted and complex, don't stand a chance against hard-working Estella Reyes-Guzman and her legendary mentor, Bill Gastner. If you haven't yet discovered these wonderful mysteries, you are in for a treat!"
— Anne Hillerman, *New York Times* bestselling author

Easy Errors

"Fans of the long-running series will be drawn to the backstory here, which fills in gaps in the stories of both Torrez and Gastner. They will also respond to the qualities that have made this series so appealing over the years: meticulous plotting, multidimensional characters, sharp dialogue, and a vivid sense of place. This is one of the very best entries in a consistently excellent series."

—Booklist, Starred Review

Come Dark

"The twenty-first Posadas mystery is a compelling mix of dusty small-town ambiance, complex plotting, and an authorial voice imbued with compassionate humanity. Each of the Posadas novels plumbs the collective heartbeat of a community. Those beating hearts belong to characters who range from despicable to saintly, but together they make up one of the most vivid worlds in mystery fiction."

—Booklist

"Series regulars, including former undersheriff Bill Gastner, interact with a number of intriguing new characters, including Miles Waddell, the owner and sole funder of *NightZone*. Newcomers will enjoy this entry as much as longtime fans."

—Publishers Weekly

Blood Sweep

"The story line is satisfyingly complex, but the novel's great strength is its well-rendered setting, from the opening description of a silent, motionless antelope to the evocation of a dry riverbed. The concluding note of empathy for the many people trying to cross the border is moving without being heavy-handed."
—*Publishers Weekly*, Starred Review

NightZone

"The nineteenth Posadas County mystery places the focus back on the retired Gastner after a few episodes in which the mysteries revolved around his successor. No matter the protagonist, Havill's work is believable and well plotted, and never, ever includes a character who isn't a viable human being. Another fine book in a terrific series."
—*Booklist*

"Gastner's capabilities are plausible for a septuagenarian, and Havill peoples the book with believable characters."
—*Publishers Weekly*, Starred Review

One Perfect Shot

"Gastner and Reyes complement each other well in an entertaining preview of a decades-long partnership. A welcome entry in an always satisfying series."
—*Booklist*

"Undersheriff Bill Gastner of Posadas County, NM, meets Estelle Reyes, the once-and-future undersheriff, in a welcome, well-wrought prequel... Gastner and Reyes charm from the get-go."

—*Kirkus Reviews*

Double Prey

"Havill is a master at using procedural details to expose the complexities of small-town relationships, but he also excels at drawing meaning from landscape. Like an archaeologist sifting history from the ground, Reyes-Guzman digs clues from the guano-splattered floor of the cave where the jaguar's skull was found. One of the stronger entries in an always-satisfying series."

—*Booklist*

The Fourth Time is Murder

"The Posadas County Mystery series notches its sixteenth with all its signature virtues intact: good writing, an unerring sense of place and a protagonist it's a pleasure to root for."

—*Kirkus Reviews*, Starred Review

"Havill is especially good at showing how connecting facts depends on recognizing relationships within a family or a neighborhood. Arid, harshly beautiful Posadas County turns out to be full of captivating stories."

—*Publishers Weekly*

Final Payment

"Havill takes the reader through an all-terrain investigation to an edge-of-your-seat finale."

—*Publishers Weekly*

Statute of Limitations

"The primary appeal of this series continues to be its evocation of daily life in a small New Mexico town."

—*Booklist*

Convenient Disposal

"As intelligent, carefully plotted, and insightful as its predecessors. The original star of the series, former undersheriff Bill Gastner, drifts in and out of the action these days, but Havill has successfully switched the focus to Reyes-Guzman and her struggle to balance a young family and an all-consuming career. An outstanding series on all levels."

—*Booklist*

"Literate, lively, and sharply observed as ever. Mystery fans who haven't yet made the trip to Posadas County, consider yourselves deprived."

—*Kirkus Reviews*

A Discount for Death

"Interpersonal issues, usually sequestered behind closed doors in insular Posadas County, take center stage in both cases as Reyes-Guzman follows a trail that leads from troubled lives on the edge of despair to her own thriving family. Mystery series too often lose their way when the author attempts to replace an appealing hero. Hats off to Havill for making the transition work smoothly."

—*Booklist*

"Undersheriff Estelle Reyes-Guzman gets her second star turn here, and longtime fans of Posadas County, New Mexico, won't mind a bit... A first-rate police procedural, small-town division. And Estelle's a charmer."

—*Kirkus Reviews*

Scavengers

"Throughout this low-key, character-driven series, Havill has managed as well as anyone in the genre to balance the particulars of cop procedure with the often unspoken emotions at the core of small-town life. The focus on Reyes-Guzman and her family brings a different dynamic to the series, but the human drama remains equally satisfying."

—*Booklist*

"Skilled investigation, happenstance, and cooperation mesh through every phase of the puzzle, ushering the reader along to one satisfying conclusion."

—*Publishers Weekly*

Red, Green, or Murder

"Havill shows us yet again how random bad decisions spur unnecessary tragedy. As always, a fine mix of village drama and carefully rendered police work."

—*Booklist*

"Another highly entertaining entry that shows those unruly New Mexicans doing what they do best. Long may they stay homicidal."

—*Kirkus Reviews*

"Havill's characters have a depth and a clarity that's refined with every new book in the series. It's a pleasure to see them operate not merely as lawmen or suspects or witnesses but as members of a community where flaws and quirks are understood and accepted."

—*Publishers Weekly*

Bag Limit

"The quiet pleasures of small-town life are again at the center of this appealing series as Gastner reaffirms his belief that even the encroaching evils of the modern world can be endured with the help of friends, family, and a properly prepared green-chile burrito."

—*Booklist*

Dead Weight

"Havill is every bit as good at evoking procedural detail as he is at capturing small-town ambience. This series continues to provide a vivid picture of change in rural America: small-town values under siege from within and without as a big-hearted sheriff tries to keep the peace one day at a time. Quiet yet powerful human drama resting comfortably within the procedural formula."

—Booklist

"Nice, easygoing, entirely literate prose, and if the approach is a bit too 'cozy' for some tastes, others will delight in dollops of local color and in Sheriff Bill, of course, who may well be the most endearing small-town lawman ever."

—Kirkus Reviews

Out of Season

"Gastner's calm, experienced leadership guides his staff, as well as FAA officials, through several prickly conflicts with a couple of fiercely independent ranchers. For readers, his considerate, methodical approach will prove a welcome change from the angry, violent paths trod by so many cops in other novels. Full of bright local color and suffused with a compassionate understanding of human motivation, this intelligent, understated mystery deserves a wide and appreciative readership."

—Publishers Weekly, Starred Review

Prolonged Exposure

"Another excellent small-town caper in which common sense, compassion, loyalty, and decency are law enforcement's primary tools against an increasingly brutal world. It's a good thing Gastner has had his heart mended because it may be the biggest in contemporary crime fiction."

—*Booklist*

"Fine storytelling married to a spicy Southwestern setting marks the latest Bill Gastner mystery... Gastner remains a solid center, using his knowledge and experience to good effect as the various cases of burglary, kidnapping, and murder play out."

—*Publishers Weekly*

Privileged to Kill

"The fifth Gastner mystery is a crystalline gem of dusty atmosphere, small-town personalities, and razor-sharp plotting. It also raises questions regarding the law—especially small-town law—and its attitudes toward the indigent, the homeless, and the privileged. Toss in Gastner, one of the most endearing mentors in crime fiction, for a mystery that is disarmingly simple on the surface but ultimately reveals surprising depth."

—*Booklist*

"Havill's fifth quietly continues a project virtually unique in detective fiction: anchoring his tales of crime and punishment as closely as possible in the rhythms of small-town friends, routines, and calamities."

—*Kirkus Reviews*

Before She Dies

"The fourth Gastner case is easily the best, no small feat in a series as strong as this one. Gastner is compassionate, intelligent, bulldog tough, and painfully aware of all his limitations, both physical and emotional. The same inward eye that provides insight into his own soul can quickly swivel outward to discern others' hidden traits. And if what you're hiding is motive, Gastner will ferret it out and do what needs to be done. An outstanding mystery."

—*Booklist*, Starred Review

Twice Buried

"Gastner is an incisive investigator whose two most valuable qualities are compassion and insomnia. Unlike other fictional detectives who approach murder as a personal affront, Gastner sees himself as the victims' advocate, striving to even the scales of justice for those no longer able to do it themselves. This is definitely a series to watch."

—*Booklist*

"Bill and his hardscrabble neighbors—especially Estelle, who seems destined for a return to Posadas next time—are as modestly appealing as ever, and in his third outing, he does his best detective work yet."

—*Kirkus Reviews*

"Havill sensitively explores the area's Mexican-American culture in this increasingly estimable regional series."

—*Publishers Weekly*

Bitter Recoil

"This one's a winner all the way."

—*Washington Times*

"The authentic flavor of the New Mexico locale is so real you'll be tempted to check your shoes for fine red dust."

—*Mystery Scene Magazine*

Heartshot

"Gastner is a unique and endearing protagonist who certainly deserves plenty of encores."

—*Booklist*, Starred Review

"Septuagenarian undersheriff Bill Gastner of Posadas County, NM, is the skeptical, endearing narrator of this mystery debut by a writer of Westerns... If the villain's identity is not surprising, readers still will enjoy this caper and look forward to future appearances of curmudgeonly charmer Gastner."

—*Publishers Weekly*

Also by Steven F. Havill

Heartshot
Bitter Recoil
Twice Buried
Before She Dies
Privileged to Kill
Prolonged Exposure
Out of Season
Dead Weight
Bag Limit
Red, Green, or Murder
Scavengers
A Discount for Death
Convenient Disposal
Statute of Limitations
Final Payment
The Fourth Time is Murder
Double Prey
One Perfect Shot
NightZone
Blood Sweep
Come Dark
Easy Errors
Lies Come Easy

LESS
THAN A
MOMENT

LESS THAN A MOMENT

STEVEN F. HAVILL

A POSADAS COUNTY MYSTERY

Published by Poisoned Pen Press, an imprint of Sourcebooks
P.O. Box 4410, Naperville, Illinois 60567-4410
(630) 961-3900
sourcebooks.com

Library of Congress Cataloging-in-Publication Data

Names: Havill, Steven, author.
Title: Less than a moment / Steven F. Havill
Description: Naperville : Poisoned Pen Press, 2020.
Identifiers: LCCN 2019043383 | (hardcover)
Subjects: LCSH: Sheriffs—Fiction. | Policewomen—Fiction.
Murder—Investigation—Fiction. | New Mexico—Fiction. | GSAFD: Mystery
fiction.
Classification: LCC PS3558.A785 L47 2020 | DDC 813/.54—dc23
LC record available at https://lccn.loc.gov/2019043383

Printed and bound in the United States of America.
SB 10 9 8 7 6 5 4 3 2 1

For Kathleen

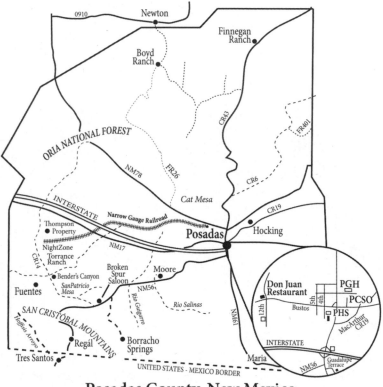

Posadas County, New Mexico

Chapter One

"You're on my shit list, bud," Deputy Edwin Hennesey grumbled as he looked up from his console. The target of the dispatcher's complaint, rookie news reporter Rik Chang, skirted the dispatcher's island and headed for the antiquated "out" basket of police reports perched atop the first of four equally antiquated filing cabinets. Chang, twenty-six years old and with a freshly minted bachelor's degree in journalism from the University of New Mexico, glanced over at Hennesey.

"Yeah, you," the deputy added.

Chang frowned, managing to look equal parts contrite and confused.

"Sir?" The young reporter was likely the only person in Posadas County who referred to Hennesey by that courtesy title. Hennesey took his time closing the *Field and Stream* magazine, pushed it away from himself as if it were an empty dinner plate, and swiveled his chair. For a moment he watched the young man leaf through the report copies.

It had been a quiet Thursday night and predawn Friday. The latest edition of the *Posadas Register* had been on the streets since earlier Thursday afternoon, and any tidbit of news that the rookie reporter might glean from the slender pile of reports would be old news by the next week's edition.

By an edict from the sheriff, routine paperwork generated by deputies was not posted on any department website where it would be available to talented hackers, curious gossips, or criminals seeking to improve their education. Sheriff Robert Torrez personally eschewed computers, preferring to read hard copy reports. He didn't tweet, chat, blog, post, or link in to any of those other supposed necessities of modern life. The number of emails that he might send in any given month could be counted on one hand. He liked hard copy, and although he knew as well as anyone that the workings of the Sheriff's Department were for the most part public record, his attitude was simple: if a "public" wanted to see the paperwork, let them come into the office and ask for it, face-to-face.

What *was* routinely posted on the department's little-used website were nameless statistics reflecting the department's work…the number of violent crimes compared with previous years, the number of clumsy souls arrested for shoplifting, and responses to fires, family disputes, and all the other aggravations of modern life that required a call to law enforcement. A curious web reader could find the number of people ticketed for running stop signs, for speeding, for failure to wear seat belts, for texting while rear-ending another vehicle.

But as far as Sheriff Torrez was concerned, the job of "naming names," if that's what the gossips wanted, was the turf of the local newspaper.

Every morning, regular as clockwork, someone from the weekly *Posadas Register,* either publisher Frank Dayan or more often rookie reporter Rik Chang, stopped by the sheriff's office in hopes of a scoop worthy of a stand-alone story. Staff of the *Register* could have paid a visit to the out-basket once a week, but one never knew. A simple arrest could lead to an interesting story that demanded further investigation.

Most of the paperwork in the wire basket, if not ignored as un-newsworthy, would deserve only a line or two in the standing newspaper column, "Sheriff's Report." As a newly hired cub reporter, Rik Chang had inherited the task of assembling the "Report" each week.

Deputy Hennesey pushed himself to his feet, making an effort to suck in his gut. He always felt a little intimidated by someone as elegantly put together as Rik Chang. Just over six feet tall, with black hair, inscrutable eyes behind frameless glasses, square shoulders, and not the slightest hint of belly flab, Chang moved with assured grace.

Hennesey jerked up his Sam Brown belt so the utility rig's weight rode more easily above his hips. A short, narrow-shouldered man with a pear-shaped body and only a few wisps of graying hair mopped across his shiny skull, Hennesey had spent a long hitch as a security guard at one of the Albuquerque malls before seeking out small-town peace and quiet. The shopping mall's hard, polished tile floors had tortured his knees and inflamed his plantar fasciitis. As a dispatcher for the Posadas County Sheriff's Department, he didn't need to walk miles every night.

Sheriff Robert Torrez was aware of Hennesey's intellectual limitations, but appreciated his work ethic. The man hadn't missed a shift in two years, had never been late, had never scooted for home a few minutes early at the end of the day, Friday or not. A longtime widower, Hennesey embraced the solitude of the graveyard hours. Not a lightning wit, the slow pace suited him perfectly.

At 7:35 this particular Friday morning in late May when Rik Chang dropped by the Sheriff's Department, Deputy Hennesey didn't favor the young man with a smile of greeting. He didn't particularly like the ambitious, athletic, computer-savvy young man, even though Chang was not an immigrant like most of the other people Hennesey disliked.

Instead, the deputy rose, leaned over the counter, and pulled the slender bundle of reports—five days' worth—out of the tray. With stubby thumbs, he sorted through until he found the one he wanted, an arrest report now four days old with a large Post-it note attached. He tossed the rest of the paperwork back in the wire basket.

"When I mark something *not for news,*" he said, brandishing the two-page report in question, "that means just that. You just leave it in the basket. It *don't* go in the newspaper."

Chang pushed his rimless glasses up and regarded the report. "Oh, that one?"

"Ah, that one," Hennesey said, trying his best to mimic Jackie Chan. "Yes, that one."

The young man didn't rise to the mild ethnic slur. "Well, I saw that, sir, but I didn't understand what was so special about it," Chang said. He smiled hopefully at Hennesey.

"Ain't *nothing* special about it," the deputy said. "But now we got this." Hennesey reached across the desk and picked up the latest copy of the local newspaper, barely hours off the press, and folded the pages back to reveal the standing column, "Sheriff's Report," on page six. He jabbed a finger at a paragraph near the end of the column. "This ain't supposed to be here."

Chang looked blank. He didn't need to read the column, since he had written it. "It's just a DUI," the young man said. "It goes into the pot, along with everything else. I thought that's what you wanted. I mean, I don't know *why* you wanted to make sure that story got in, 'cause we'd run it anyway, but sure enough, there it is."

"Hey, wise guy," Hennesey barked. "When I mark something *not for news,* then it's *not* for news. Ain't nothing complicated about *that.*"

Chang lifted the Post-it's corner. "This?"

"Yeah, that."

A slow smile grew across Chang's smooth face. "Ah. My mistake. See, I read it as *note* for news. With the *e,* just the way it's written." He pulled the note free and held it out to Hennesey. "See, I saw this *note*, and I thought that maybe because the DUI was Quentin Torrez, that you wanted to make sure that he made the police blotter." The young man smiled. "Maybe to make sure we weren't playing favorites or something like that? So you marked it *Note* for news. Note, not *not.*"

Unsure whether or not he was being gently mocked, Hennesey's eyes narrowed to slits, then opened wide enough to reflect some misgivings.

"I mean, I know—everybody knows—that Quentin Torrez is the sheriff's what, nephew or something?" Chang asked.

"Something." But it wasn't Deputy Hennesey who spoke. A heavy arm reached past Rik Chang and gently relieved him of the *note for news* Post-it and the report to which it was attached. Sheriff Robert Torrez could ghost his six-foot four-inch, two-hundred-forty-pound frame into a room, more frightening than if he'd stomped in, arms flailing. He loomed over Chang, one hand resting lightly on the reporter's shoulder.

After a moment, he handed the report back without comment, but kept the Post-it. He glanced first at the clock, then at Deputy Hennesey. "Pasquale's twenty?" His voice was scarcely more than a whisper.

Taking a quick moment to mentally switch gears with the sudden non sequitur, Hennesey glanced at the desk log. "He was headed out to 14, checkin' up on that complaint from one of the surveyors up at the Thompsons' place that somebody was jerkin' up surveyor stakes."

For a long moment, the sheriff stood silently, perhaps waiting for some amplification. When none was forthcoming, he repeated, "What's his twenty?"

Hennesey turned and keyed the old-fashioned desk mike, eschewing the modern microphone headset that lay on the shelf in front of him. "Three oh four, PCS, ten twenty?" His delivery was crisply enunciated.

The reply was prompt. "PCS, three oh four is northbound on 56, just passing mile marker twenty-one."

Hennesey acknowledged and turned back to the sheriff, one eyebrow raised in question.

"Have him stop in my office when he comes in," the sheriff said. "When he's finished fueling and workin' his log."

"You got it, Sheriff."

Torrez lifted his hand off Chang's shoulder. "Anything in that basket is public record. Anything, any time. If something is an ongoing investigation that we don't want made public, we don't put it in the basket." He gave Hennesey one of his slow, expressionless looks.

"Yes, sir, I understand," Chang said. "And I was wondering..."

The sheriff looked hard at the young man, as if actually seeing him for the first time.

"Frank has a series planned on county budget matters, and he suggested that I ask about the possibility of doing a ride-along with some of the deputies."

"Any time, any deputy," Torrez said. "Talk with the undersheriff. She's the one who takes care of the waivers. Then talk to the deputies. It's up to them."

"Yes, sir. I'll do that. May I ask about the surveyor stake deal?"

"Keep an eye on the basket."

"Maybe I could do a ride-along with Sergeant Pasquale?"

"Check with the undersheriff for the paperwork. Then check with Pasquale. He's free to say yes or no."

"Yes, sir."

Torrez almost smiled, his heavy-lidded eyes relaxing just a bit. "You spent some time in the military."

"Yes, sir. Four years in the Navy."

"Not a career?"

"I never learned how to swim, sir."

Torrez did smile at that. "Not a whole lot of water in Posadas County." He pointed a finger-pistol at Hennesey. "Don't let Pasquale slip away without seein' me, Eddie."

"You got it, Sheriff."

Sheriff Torrez turned away abruptly and strode down the hallway toward his office. "Note for news," he muttered, and he said it just loud enough that both Hennesey and Chang heard him.

Chapter Two

Sheriff Torrez passed by his own office and leaned against the jamb of the undersheriff's open door.

"Did you sit through the whole meeting yesterday?"

Estelle Reyes-Guzman looked up from her computer keyboard, then leaned back in her chair. A light-framed woman just turned fifty-one but looking closer to thirty-five, she favored tan, tailored pants suits with a pastel blouse—the "uniform" that she'd adopted during twenty-eight years with the Sheriff's Department.

"The entire agonizing thing." She smiled and shook her head. "They're very good at making mountains out of even less than molehills. And by the way, Bobby, I overheard Rik's conversation just now with Hennesey, but I didn't want to interfere." She smiled again. "It's all part of the young man's education. He was also at the county meeting, and it looked as if he's mastered sleeping with his eyes open."

"Huh," Torrez grunted. Estelle knew that Robert Torrez would require a certified, notarized announcement of the earth's imminent destruction before he would attend a county commission meeting.

"I need to work on that talent myself. Nothing came up that would affect us, though, and that's always good news."

"The kids are still here?"

Estelle took the characteristically abrupt change of subject in stride. She knew that the sheriff was referring to her son and daughter-in-law, who, along with Estelle's grandson, William Thomas, were enjoying a vacation from their hectic performance schedule. "They are, working hard on *Padrino*'s house. That's the whole problem, for me, anyway. I'd be over there every minute, given half a chance, but they don't need me breathing down their necks. But as you well know, make-work is deadly boring as well." She swept a hand inches above the paperwork that was spread across her desk.

Torrez's dark face brightened a touch, just enough that a glimpse of his movie-star dentition showed. "I thought hanging out with family was what grandmothers were for, Grandma."

She pointed a pistol finger at the sheriff. "I want my daughter-in-law to smile with some heartfelt greeting when she sees me, not recoil in resignation. 'Oh, God, here she is *again*. What's it been since the last visit, twelve minutes?'"

"Can't see you doin' that."

"Exactly. But waiting on the sidelines is also torture. And speaking of torture, are you getting family flack after your nephew's arrest?"

"Nope." Clearly that topic was not one that the sheriff wished to pursue. "At the county meeting, did this guy Thompson make some presentation?"

"As a matter of fact, he did not. It was on the agenda, but he didn't show. He did pass along a message that he wanted to meet with Miles sometime today. Miles invited me to attend— and Frank Dayan as well, I think. I'm driving out there about 9:00. In just a few minutes." She looked down at the budget papers again. "Get some fresh air and soak up some sun." Miles Waddell's astronomical mesa-top development had made an international name for itself, despite all the naysayers.

"Never met him. This Thompson guy."

"Nor I," Estelle replied. "All we know is that he bought up some of your favorite hunting turf, am I right?"

"Yep. Got to talk to him about that."

"You're welcome to ride out with me."

"Don't think so."

Estelle's phone rang and she picked it up. After listening for a bit, she said, "Sure. Now's a good time. Send him back." She hung up. "Rik Chang wants to talk to me. Anyway, I think a few folks in the audience yesterday were disappointed that they didn't get to argue with Thompson. There's quite a bit of resistance to what he wants to do—at least what everyone seems to *think* he wants to do, and not just from Waddell's people. I haven't actually heard from a reliable source—like from Mr. Thompson himself—what he's planned."

"He bought a lot of acres, is all I heard."

"Yes. Some of Johnny Boyd's property, and maybe some others. My best source is usually Bill," she said, referring to former sheriff Bill Gastner, "but he's in the dark too, which is surprising, since he's spent a lot of hours out on that property. He knew Johnny Boyd as well as anyone in the county."

"Huh." Torrez shrugged. "How's Bill's house project thing comin'? Is that going to work out?"

"I'm sure it will. With an adjustment or two."

Torrez grunted something incomprehensible and shook his head. "Can't imagine." He handed the *Note for News* Post-it to Estelle. "You heard all the ruckus about this. It's a funny story." He turned to go, then stopped abruptly. "It don't matter to me personally one way or another, but I want to find out whose idea that was." He nodded at the note. "If there's somebody puttin' pressure on Hennesey. Even if it's just him brown-nosin', thinkin' it's something I'd want to do."

With the sort of perfect timing that led Estelle to believe that the young reporter had been lurking in the hallway outside her office, Chang appeared behind the sheriff, whose bulk all but blocked the office doorway. The sheriff stepped to one side to let Chang pass.

"Good morning, Rik," Estelle greeted. She rose and offered a hand which Chang pumped eagerly, his smile wide and sincere.

"Catch ya later." Torrez glanced at the young reporter. "Stay safe."

"So what's driving your day?" Estelle asked Chang after the sheriff had left. She gestured toward the chair beside her desk.

He sat with easy grace, at the same time drawing his narrow reporter's notebook from his hip pocket. A good-looking kid, she thought. Maybe a little more slender in build than either of her sons, but close enough in his white polo shirt and new blue jeans to remind her that Francisco, her oldest son, was just a handful of blocks away, caught up in an exciting construction project.

"Frank...Mr. Dayan...was wondering about a ride-along? He says no one from the paper has done that in a while, and with the budget coming up and all, that it might be a good idea. Some good feature material, maybe. Sheriff Torrez said any time, any deputy, but to check with you first for a waiver?"

Estelle pushed her wheeled office chair over and slid the second file drawer open. In a moment, she found the form she wanted, pushed the drawer closed, and slid the paper across the desk toward Chang. "Read carefully and sign," she said. With amusement, she watched Chang scan the simple form—looking at the bottom first, as many people did, then returning his attention to the top line.

"It's worthless, but our county attorney requires it," Estelle said. "As I'm sure you're aware—and I know the county attorney is aware—there's no way we can waive responsibility for you once you're a captive audience in one of our patrol units."

The young man scanned down the document, his heavy black eyebrows arching in amused surprise. "Aw, gee. I don't get to carry a gun?"

"No. There is a shotgun in the vehicle that the deputy will show you how to unlock." At Estelle's comment, Chang glanced up. "For your own protection," she added. "The most important thing is for you to pay attention to any instructions from the deputy. If he or she tells you to stay in the car during a stop, that's what you do. Pay attention. Always pay attention."

Chang nodded eagerly. After another moment reading the few paragraphs, he signed with a precise script that would impress an architectural draftsman. He handed the form back to the undersheriff.

"Did you have any particular time or deputy in mind?"

"I'd like to ride with Sergeant Pasquale on swing, if that works."

Estelle nodded. "Sure. He's volunteered to cover graveyard for Deputy Sutherland until Monday, then Brent will be back, and Pasquale will return to his regular swing shift. Just any time. Most of the deputies enjoy some company, and you'll find that they'll be eager to answer questions and share war stories."

Chang's deep frown etched lines in an otherwise fault-less olive-skinned complexion. "Sergeant Pasquale's wife was involved in an incident years ago, wasn't she? I mean, not with him, but with another deputy, during a ride-along. She was a reporter for the newspaper at the time, Frank says."

Estelle lifted an eyebrow. "That's ancient history, Rik. But, yes, she was riding with one of the deputies." She grimaced. "Sad times. If you want, you can dig through the morgue of old newspapers in your office. The incident involving the shoot-ing of Deputy Enciños and Ms. Real was well covered by the *Register*. Along with all the follow-up."

Chang jotted in his notebook, and when he looked up, Estelle held up the Post-it. "The sheriff tells me that I should ask you about this."

A dark blush moved up the young man's smooth cheeks. "The dispatcher stuck that on one of the reports, ma'am.

Apparently, he meant for me *not* to take it. But when he wrote it, I guess an *E* kinda slipped in there somehow. I didn't know why the note, since I would have picked up on the story anyway, without the dispatcher's encouragement. I was going to check to see if this was a first-time bust or if it's a multiple. But I guess Deputy Hennesey didn't want me going down that route."

"The arrest was Quentin Torrez's third," Estelle said. "It says that on the arrest report, down toward the bottom of the first page." She turned the Post-it this way and that. "So Deputy Hennesey says that this was meant to read '*not* for news.' That's what you two were going on about."

"Apparently so, ma'am."

The undersheriff sighed and slipped the note under a corner of her desk calendar. "Just for future reference, Rik...we don't decide what makes news and what doesn't. That's your turf."

"Yes, ma'am. Sheriff Torrez made that very clear."

"We still use the old-fashioned method. If it's in the basket, it's fair game."

"That's what Pam had told me—how it all works." Pam Gardiner, longtime editor of the *Posadas Register,* was one of Estelle's favorite people: fair, prompt, unfailingly friendly, a genuinely cozy person—as long as she didn't have to stray from her desk.

"While I'm here," Chang continued, "I wanted to ask... what's the deal with the vandalized surveyor's stakes out off County Road 14? Can you tell me about that? The initial complaint that Deputy Miller filed doesn't say much."

"That's because there *isn't* much, Rik. It appears at this time that several dozen flagged stakes were pulled out of the ground and tossed into an arroyo. As far as I know, that's the extent of it."

"On Thompson Development property?"

"Kyle Thompson and Associates. Yes."

"And he was scheduled to present at the county commission

meeting yesterday, right? I know that the clerk received word that he couldn't make it."

"That's correct. Several people are eager to meet him. To hear what he has to say. Myself included. The original land sale went through without much fanfare, and since then, it's been pretty quiet out there."

"The S.O. is investigating the vandalism?"

"Yes."

Chang waited expectantly for explanation or amplification. Estelle smiled pleasantly and said nothing.

"Is there some theory behind all this?" he persisted. "Why would someone bother to pull out a bunch of stakes? I mean, they're pretty easily replaced, I would think."

"A nuisance, for sure. Who knows what goes through some-body's little pea brain when they decide to pull vandalism pranks like that?" She glanced at the clock. "I'll make sure that dispatch has this ride-along waiver posted on active file, so you're all set. Any deputy, any time, as long as the deputy agrees. That's the rule. I don't tell the deputies that they have to take riders. That's entirely up to them. As I said, most of them will be delighted for the company."

"Yes, ma'am."

She tapped her desk for emphasis. "There are some inherent risks, as I'm sure you realize. A civilian will assume, if he doesn't know you, that if you're in company with a deputy, that you're also an officer. The deputy will make every effort to keep you on the periphery, which is why most of the time he'll instruct you to stay in the car during a stop. But circumstances can change in a heartbeat, and you have to be aware of that." She smiled as she pushed her chair back and stood up.

"You pay attention, even in the dullest of moments. You're cleared to ride until you get bored with it, unless for some obscure reason the county attorney objects. I have a meeting in just a few minutes, so if there's nothing else?"

She reached out and shook Chang's hand again, but this time she held on to it in a tight grip. "Be careful out there. *Especially* during the ride-alongs. And I'll say it again…in most cases, the public won't know who you are, and you'll be identified with the officers. If someone gets mad at an officer—and they always do, especially during domestic disputes—they'll also be mad at you. So when the deputy instructs you to remain in the unit, do exactly as the officer says.

"If the officer is in conversation with a subject, you do not participate. You do not record or photograph, you do not discuss the conversation later with anyone except the deputy. As the late Tony Hillerman wrote years ago, you remain a *fly on the wall*."

"Yes, exactly." Chang nodded enthusiastically. "Thank you, ma'am. I need to cover the slo-pitch tourney this evening, but maybe I'll see about a ride-along tomorrow night."

"Whenever suits your schedule, Rik. Fridays and Saturdays are usually the more productive nights." She turned and looked at the duty board on her east wall. "Captain Taber and Deputy Obregón are on tomorrow swing. Both interesting folks. And Tom Pasquale is on at midnight, if you want to ride the dark side."

"Maybe I'll start mid shift with Captain Taber, and then catch Sergeant Pasquale for a while after that. That way I'll hit two of 'em to interview. Maybe it'll be an interesting ride."

"Be careful what you wish for." She smiled. "Give my regards to both Pam and Frank."

"Oh…" Chang said as he started to turn toward the door. "I don't know if I should ask you, or contact your son in person. Do you think that the maestro and/or his wife might give us an interview? Pam told me that he and his wife are in town for a few days, and they say that the two of them might be planning to live here?"

"Ah, *they*. What would we do without *they*?" She laughed and shook her head. "At the moment, he wants to stay under the radar, Rik. But if I get the chance, I'll tell him that you asked."

"I'd appreciate that. It's kinda the talk of the town right now."

"*That's* just what he and Angie need. But that's between Francisco and you. I try very hard not to stick my nose in their business."

Chang ducked his head in appreciation as he started to back out of the office. "Thanks for the waiver, ma'am."

Estelle watched Chang skirt the dispatch island and then pause out in the foyer, his attention drawn to the Wall of Honor, a small section of polished marble, where the framed photo of Deputy Paul Enciños hung in company with several other law enforcement officers who had given their lives in the line of duty.

Her cell phone chimed, and she recognized Miles Waddell's number.

"Good morning, Miles."

"What a gorgeous day," Waddell greeted. "Are you still going to be able to visit with me this morning for a little bit? Or should I check with you when I come into town?"

"I was just heading your way, Miles."

"Oh, good. There were a few things I'd like to run by you. I invited Thompson to stop by as well. He said he had some sort of accident yesterday or the day before, and that maybe his wife would run out instead."

"I have not met her."

"Me neither. Super. I don't know when we're going to see the whites of this Thompson guy's eyes, but I'll keep workin' at it. But we'll see you topside in what...half an hour or so?"

"*Más o menos.*"

"Good. I'll make sure the snack tray is well stocked. And you're a tea drinker, if I remember correctly."

"You do."

"Good. I invited Frank Dayan as well, so everything is going to be public record, on the up-and-up. My director of security is here as well. I'll leave word that you're coming and they'll have the gate open down below. See you in a bit."

Estelle Reyes-Guzman had a minute and a half before her phone rang again; this time the landline console on her desk blinked that it was an internal call.

"Guzman."

Sheriff Torrez's near-whisper gave no hint about whether he was ten steps away in his cubbyhole of an office or out in traffic. "If you get a chance, go ahead and talk to Hennesey and find out what the deal was with the note. I want to know who talked to him."

"His own brainstorm, maybe."

"Could be. If my 'nephew or something' threatened him, I want to know. If Hennesey just thought to head off some gossip, I want to know that, too."

"Have you talked with him?"

"With Hennesey? Nope. He always gets so damn 'yes sir, no sir' with me. Maybe you'll have better luck. Mother him a little."

Estelle laughed. "Yeah, sure. *That's* going to happen. He's gone for the day now. I'll catch him tonight. Will that work?"

"Yeah, there ain't no urgency. Thanks."

She hung up and then sat quietly, her gaze drifting across the large map of Posadas County on the west wall of her office. Miles Waddell's *NightZone* development on top of Torrance Mesa included a large chunk of the western side of the county, and had gained renown largely because of Waddell's vision and daring. Estelle had come to appreciate Waddell's efforts, and held a deep affection for the man. She'd never known him to lie, or to take the easy way out.

Kyle Thompson was at the moment just a name on a piece of paper. Estelle had never met him, but knew from county records only that Thompson had started work to develop a large tract of land a half mile north of Waddell's mesa. She had heard the name *Stella Vista* rumored.

What was Thompson's group after? It was a genuine puzzle, since County Road 14 wasn't on the way to anywhere. A couple of ranchers driving by each day, their stock trailers banging and clattering, wouldn't support a business. A subdivision? Maybe a mall? Truck stop? Not likely. But who knew?

Miles Waddell was well on his way to spending a third of a billion dollars on *NightZone*. It was hard to imagine that Thompson had those kinds of resources.

County Road 14 had once been just a dusty two-track running north and south through the western side of the county. A few ranches, lots of hunters, but not many others pounded along its rough tracks. In time, the county had bladed the road to make it a more comfortable thoroughfare, but it remained a dusty, rural byway, without much tourist traffic other than those who might be lost.

Waddell's enormous investment had proven that a venture could succeed with little natural drive-by traffic by becoming an important attraction on its own. *NightZone* was heavily advertised, even internationally, in all the best magazines, along with consistent television coverage that reached out to a wide variety of interests.

For Thompson's venture, no paperwork had been filed, no legal notices had appeared in the county newspaper. And to the undersheriff's knowledge, Thompson had yet to meet with his immediate neighbors. The rumor mill was working hard.

No matter what was planned, Estelle could appreciate Miles Waddell's anxiety. He'd spent more than two hundred million dollars so far, much of that to guarantee that *NightZone* would remain just that…dark as pitch after sunset, with no light pollution to tint the sky or obscure distant nebulae. As little as a single porch light would be visible from the mesa-top astronomy facility.

Although a single porch light a mile or more away would make no difference to the huge telescopes, the urge to put out that light would be monumental. Lights were like cancer cells. Once there was one, there would be others, with the halo of light pollution blooming.

Chapter Three

Twenty-seven miles of winding State Highway 56 brought Estelle to the Broken Spur Saloon, off-duty haven to the few cattle ranchers who were still able to make a living in Posadas County. As was her habit, she slowed and crunched into the gravel parking lot, checking license plates against the short list of BOLO tabs that she kept posted on the computer screen in the center console. All local, all clean.

One of the cattle trailers behind a well-worn Dodge one-ton carried a license with an expired tag, and the undersheriff made a note of it. She knew the truck, knew the rancher, and would remind him when next she saw him.

She pulled back out onto the highway and continued the quarter mile to the intersection with County Road 14 and headed north. A few miles ahead rose the buttress of the *NightZone* mesa, and from one point near the overgrown two-track that led to her Great-uncle Reuben's homestead, she could look up toward the top of the mesa and see a sliver of white rim, just the tiniest sliver, of the huge radio telescope that shared the mesa top with the other observatory attractions. That was the only hint. Miles Waddell eschewed signs, particularly the huge billboards that touted attractions even as they blocked scenery.

Another eight miles brought her around the end of the mesa and the observatory's parking lot. Estelle slowed her county patrol car as a handsome young fellow ducked out from the low adobe building that nestled among the rocks by the gate. He wore the official *NightZone* summer uniform…lightweight blue windbreaker—with the *NZ* emblem on the left breast—that he would shed as the sun found its way past the rocks, a light-blue shirt also carrying the *NZ* emblem, khaki chino trousers, and black hiking shoes. His black hair, comfortably individual, peeked out in curls from under his dark blue ball cap. Rafael Gonzales looked fit enough to sprint up to the mesa top if called to do so.

"*Buenas dias,* Sheriff," he greeted with an enormous, toothy smile. "It is so good to see you out here today."

"Thank you, Rafael." She switched off the Charger's burbling engine, letting in the quiet of the prairie. "How's your day going?"

He frowned and marked on his clipboard, then the smile returned as he looked up. "You know, we have had some very interesting people visit our park this past week. Very interesting. Right now, there's a large contingent"—he said it as if he had just learned the word and was proud of it—"of birders who are doing the south rim walk. Some of them may be just a little bit elderly for such a thing. But they're from New York City, you know. Indomitable." He emphasized each of the five syllables. "And they enjoyed an early start, before it becomes too hot. Efrin went along with them. He knows where all the shady rest spots are along the rim walk. You know him, I think."

"I do. I'm glad he's working here." Efrin Garcia was one of *NightZone*'s success stories, after coming perilously close to spending the rest of his life in prison after being caught up in some really bad choices, thanks to a bozo for an older brother. The giant mural painted on the wall inside the observatory's auditorium was testimony to Efrin's talents.

Estelle was not surprised that a young man with such an artistic, quick hand with a pen, pencil, or brush would be a good escort for a bunch of less-than-surefooted ornithologists. He could dash off autographed cartoons of them as they lugged their cameras equipped with monstrous lens, along with binocs, water, iPads, and the ubiquitous, much marked-up copies of *Field Guide to Western Birds.*

Rafael stepped closer to the car and turned the iPad that had been resting on his clipboard so that Estelle could see it.

"*Dōmo Arīgatō,*" he said, with a stiff bow. "Except I have no idea how to say it. I don't know what those little bar doohickeys over the letters mean." He pinched the image to enlarge it.

"You're studying Japanese now?"

"You recognized it!" Rafael exclaimed with delight. "I'm studying hard, because next week, there's a trainload of tourists from Tokyo coming for a week's stay. Can you imagine! Thirty in the group. I have to have a few words down, at least."

"Mrs. Burns at the high school can help you. She spent two years in Japan before she was married. I'm sure she'd be delighted."

Rafael's face lit up. "You think?"

"I do. Mrs. Charlie Burns. She's in the book. You knew her as Ms. Stiles, I would guess."

"Ah, that's right," Rafael said, brightening at the revelation. "I almost earned an *F* in her biology class." He grinned. "My fault, though. Thanks for the tip. That'll sure help." He bowed again. "*Dōmo Arīgatō.*"

Estelle laughed. "You're welcome."

He turned and chin-pointed toward the mesa top. "*Señor* Dayan from the newspaper just went up a few moments ago." He nodded and smiled again. "And *Señor* Waddell asked if you would kindly meet him in the admin building. The fastest way is to take the left loop when you break out on top. Or if you prefer, you may park over in staff parking and ride the tram up. Someone will be up-top to greet you."

"I'll drive, thanks." She nodded at the computer terminal that dominated the center console of her vehicle. "I need to have my office with me." She glanced in the rearview mirror at the staff parking facility, a long carport roofed in tan metal, giving ample room for thirty vehicles. Half a dozen SUVs were parked in the shade there.

"Absolutely. I understand completely." He patted the roof of the car just above the window as the Charger rumbled to life. "Be careful going up. Both the deer and the quail are active today, I'm told." He looked thoughtful. "I have to learn how to say that in Japanese. Or 'May you see many birds.' Something like that."

He keyed the small remote that rode on his clipboard, and the massive gate swung inward to allow access to the mesa road—nearly two miles of circuitous, perfectly maintained macadam, with road markings in the European fashion, painted directly on the pavement.

Just beyond the gate, a single discreet road sign announced *No Vehicular Traffic 6 p.m. to 7 a.m.*, one of many efforts aimed at reducing light pollution on top. Estelle knew that the roadway, reaching from the base parking lot to the top of the mesa, had cost Miles Waddell more than nine million dollars before he was satisfied with it. Visitors to the park didn't travel on it, one way to reduce the risk and liability. If they arrived by car, they were directed to park in the lower parking lot, and ride the tram to the top.

The narrow gauge locomotive with its six classy cars, running twenty-six miles from the terminal at the Posadas Municipal Airport just northwest of the village of Posadas to the *NightZone* parking lot at the foot of the mesa, had eaten through almost fifty million dollars. Estelle enjoyed watching the developer's face light up when he either discussed the locomotive with visitors or as he stood by the track, watching it whisper by.

Miles Waddell looked at that venture with the same

enthusiasm that an eight-year-old plays with his new HO gauge train set. The narrow gauge, powered by propane/electric and making six round trips each day, along with extra trips when need arose, was another key part of the effort to keep vehicular traffic off the mesa. On top of that, it was a grand tourist attraction by itself.

Visitors were encouraged to board the train in Posadas, then were thrilled by the excursion through rugged country to the foot of the mesa. She'd ridden the train half a dozen times, her wonder growing each time. During its route, the train would stop to drop off bird-watchers, herpetologists, cactus hunters—any of the naturalists who had adopted the property as their own study area. The three formal stops featured well-marked trails, shaded interpretive kiosks, and most recently added, propane-powered refrigerators filled with a supply of bottled water.

There were even dyed-in-the-wool naturalists who rode out on the midnight run, to sit in the deep quiet of the nighttime desert and listen to the owls converse.

Upon reaching the terminus parking lot, visitors boarded the spectacular tramway to climb the nearly vertical mesa rise to *NightZone*.

Once visitors to the observatory complex reached the mesa top, the reason for the developer's determination that the facility should live up to its name became obvious. The three domes of the four-meter telescopes, the trio capable of working in unison or individually to transmit their images to the large-screened auditorium/theater, dominated the east rim of the mesa, along with the squat administration building, the planetarium, and nearest the rim, the futuristic hotel/restaurant.

Tiny, discreet solar lights at ankle level bled off their energy downward to mark the macadam footpaths at night, but the buildings themselves had no outside lights, and windows were heavily tinted and placed such that interior lights didn't wash outside. The restaurant featured a polycarbonate ceiling whose exterior cover could retract, revealing to diners a stunning view of the heavens.

At night, the mesa top was pitch dark, with no sweep of vehicular headlights, individual flashlights, or camera strobes. Tourists and night creatures loved it, including the rattlesnakes, who had a disconcerting habit of enjoying the lingering heat of the macadam walkways as night settled in.

The newest addition to the facility, a three-meter telescope near the south mesa rim, stared at the sun from rise to set, keeping busy with various solar research projects organized by participating universities. The solar research facility, unconcerned with nighttime lighting, was housed in its own observatory a quarter-mile stroll from the hotel.

A quarter mile to the southwest, essentially untroubled by issues of light pollution or most weather, the enormous radio telescope was fenced artfully to exclude the general public. The radio telescope *listened* to deep space, rather than struggling with the complications of optical equipment. It was a project with combined sponsorship by the California State University system, the National Science Foundation…and the ever-generous Miles Waddell, who made sure the facility's operation lacked for nothing.

Estelle allowed the county car to idle along the narrow roadway, enjoying the bursts of horned larks that careened away as she passed. Miles Waddell had predicted great interest in his project by dedicated birders. He'd been correct. "More birders than stargazers," he would joke, and he was nearly correct.

When the road divided on top, she stayed left, as Rafael had suggested. Looking north beyond the rim rock, she could gaze over several million acres of Posadas County, including the area that the newcomer developer, Kyle Thompson, had allegedly started to survey—land originally owned in part by the late Johnny Boyd, a rancher who had died several years before, but a portion of whose land was still tied up in an estate snarl with his children.

Less than a half mile north of Waddell's *NightZone* parking lot, the first strike by a road grader had marked the prairie just east from County Road 14, a scar that joined the huge collection of two-tracks, ranch roads, woodcutters' swaths, and cattle paths through the prairie scrub. From that single new cut in the dirt, it was impossible to tell exactly what was planned for the property.

At one point several years before, when Boyd had been ailing with the cancer that finally killed him, Miles Waddell had considered buying the property himself and turning it into a cactus preserve—convinced that there were just as many cactus aficionados as there were avid birders. He hadn't moved fast enough.

The undersheriff nosed the Charger into a roundabout in front of the administration building, a structure surprisingly not made of adobe, but instead faced with muted brick, each wall featuring a wide roof overhang so that shade was always available. No spot was marked for parking, so she snugged the car in close to the curb behind two twelve-passenger ATVs, each carrying the *NightZone* logo on the front fender.

The heavily tinted front doors of the administration building slid open, and Miles Waddell appeared, walking with one hand on the shoulder of Clay Simmons. Simmons was dressed casually, an iPad holstered on his hip. His sharply creased khaki trousers were adequate to conceal the ankle holster that Estelle knew he favored. The logo of United Securities embossed the left breast of his mauve polo shirt.

Waddell, as usual, looked as if he'd just left a calf branding operation on his ranch—well-used blue jeans, scuffed boots, white shirt slightly frayed at the cuffs, and the predictable sweat-stained Stetson. Estelle knew that he was equally comfortable attending a Farm Bureau or 4-H meeting as he was in formal conference with his LLC board of directors in Chicago.

Years before, even when he'd been operating a successful cattle operation just north of the Posadas County line, he'd discussed his dreams of an astronomy-based tourist attraction with his widowed mother. When she, a Chicago financier, had retired at age eighty from the rigors of her career in the business world, she'd said to her son, essentially, "Go for it," and bequeathed most of her fortune to Miles.

With a third of a billion in liquid assets, and triple that in real estate and corporate holdings, Miles Waddell had not been overwhelmed. He hadn't bought a yacht, or a year in Paris, or a ticket on the first commercial Earth orbit venture. He hadn't even bought a new pair of boots. Instead, he set about planning *NightZone*, buying property, learning all he could from experts in the field—all of whom found him a fast study.

"You know, I'm really glad you could break away and come down here for a few minutes," Waddell said. He pumped the undersheriff's hand with both of his. His hands were still ranch-work hard, and the rolled-up sleeves of his western-style shirt showed arms bronzed by too much New Mexico sun. "You two know each other, right?"

"You bet." Simmons smiled. His grip was firm, and lingered. "We both attended one of the most uninformative county legislature meetings of current record."

"Oh, sure. That's right," Waddell said. "I wanted to hear what Thompson had to say, but then I got busy, and figured Clay here could report the high spots. And then I learn there *weren't* any high spots. Look, our friends are inside. What say we get ourselves out of the sun? When the Thompson people show up, we can..."

He interrupted himself and pulled his phone out of his back pocket. "Yo, Rafael," he greeted, then frowned as he listened to his gatekeeper. "Sure. Does she want to ride the tram? Well, sure, that's fine. Send her up. Remind her about the dang deer."

He switched off and grinned at Estelle. "I think we're hosting most of the deer in Posadas County on our mesa." He gestured for the undersheriff to enter the admin center, and Estelle felt a twenty-degree drop in ambient air as she did so.

"It's the missus," Waddell added. "Thompson's wife…I'm not sure what her name is, but she's just coming up from the gate. Have you met her? No, you said that you hadn't."

"I've met neither of them," Estelle said.

"Ah. Well, I'm in the same boat, but I think it's time we did. Maybe we can get something done, reach some kind of consensus." He gestured down a hallway to the right. "Let's meet in Pleides. Third double doors down thataway." Turning to Clay Simmons, he added, "Would you meet her out front and bring her in?"

He slipped a hand through Estelle's elbow. "I hate all this." He lowered his voice. "Just hate it. You know, up to this point, zero problems with neighbors. Well, almost zero. And now we have this guy proposing a whole new urban community at my doorstep, if you believe all the rumors."

"Lots of rumors, yes, but I haven't actually heard what he's proposing," Estelle said. "Have you?"

"I *thought* we were going to at yesterday's meeting. It was on the agenda, but who knows? I guess I'm just a natural pessimist, expecting the worst."

Estelle stopped beside a gigantic photo-mosaic of deep space that dominated one wall. "Was there something specific that you wanted from me, Miles? You know, what a developer chooses to do with his property is not the concern of the Sheriff's Department. Unless actual statutes are violated."

Waddell hunched closer and lowered his voice, holding both hands inches apart in front of him. "Almost anything Thompson wants to do," he said, "means a problem for me. You can understand that, I'm sure. Unless he's going to just leave the acreage alone…or maybe run a few head of cattle."

"Yes. Even a simple, conservative subdivision means light pollution. Right on your doorstep. Light and noise both. I understand that."

"Exactly so. Maybe I'm just shouting 'FIRE!' in a crowded

theater. I don't know. I just wanted you to be aware of the situation, every step of the way. And I value your opinion. How you see things going." He grinned sheepishly. "I had to put up with some shenanigans when I first started—you remember that, I'm sure. I don't doubt that the Thompsons will experience the same sort of thing. There's folks out there who don't want *any* kind of development.

"That's not me. I mean, look at this mesa of mine. But on the other hand, come on. How do you design a whole suburbia without exterior lighting? Streetlights, headlights, porch lights, damn storefront lights, neon signs…jeez, it makes me cringe just thinking about that damn rosy glow. And not a damn thing I can do about it."

He smiled painfully. "Nothing that's legal, anyway." He mock-shivered. "And you remember the bozos who were cuttin' down my power poles, way back when? So I want to be proactive. Something happens, I'd rather talk to you than your boss. I guess you can understand that. I mean I like Bob Torrez, but you know what I mean. He's not exactly the most vocal person on the planet."

Estelle smiled gently but tactfully said nothing. Sheriff Robert Torrez struck many people as being rough around the edges—and not overflowing with sympathy about other people's problems. But she could clearly understand Waddell's concerns.

Waddell turned as the silver, older-model Explorer parked directly in front of the double doorway, just behind Estelle's county car. The driver got out and stepped to the curb in front of her SUV, surveying the vaulted architecture of the auditorium. Of medium height and shapely, she wore faded blue jeans with a smudge of something across her left knee and a long-sleeved shirt buttoned to the throat against the sun. She lifted her camo-patterned cap, swept a hand through her short blond hair, shook her head, and resettled the cap.

As if she'd picked up burrs or goatheads on a morning hike through the boonies, she knocked first one work boot and then the other against the concrete curb, and as she turned to do that, Estelle saw the large revolver riding high on the young woman's right hip.

Clay Simmons intercepted her before she'd completed three steps toward the building.

"So wow," Miles Waddell said as he started toward the door. "Calamity Jane. Here I was kinda expecting some hifalutin society lady, with high heels and lots of turquoise."

After a few sentences of conversation, Simmons and the young woman strode up the walkway, but stopped just short of entering. She regarded Waddell coolly as he stepped outside, and then her gaze shifted to Estelle Reyes-Guzman, who had followed Waddell.

"Miss, I'm Miles Waddell. I'm glad you would visit us. Welcome to *NightZone*."

Simmons started to say something, but the young woman beat him to it. "Well, for starters, thank you." Her smile was easy and genuine. "I'm Lydia Thompson, Kyle Thompson's wife. Your new neighbors." She said it as if Thompson Development was planning to build only a single dwelling out in the hills, one with no exterior porch light.

Waddell offered a warm smile. "For heaven's sakes. It's good to meet you."

"Kyle wanted to be here, but he's a little bit sore this morning. He came close to breaking an ankle Wednesday afternoon, and had some therapy on it yesterday. He's kinda gimpy."

"Well, ouch," Waddell said with sympathy.

"He's at the hotel in Posadas, feeling sorry for himself. He's not exactly speedy with the crutches yet."

"This happened out at the site?"

"A little more prosaic than that. He went to hold the door for me at one of the local eateries, and somehow misjudged things when he stepped off the parking lot curb." She smiled and shrugged her shoulders. "One of those silly moments, Mr. Waddell." She turned a somewhat tentative smile on Estelle. "And you must be..."

"Estelle Reyes-Guzman. I'm with the Sheriff's Department."

"Ah. And Dr. Guzman is..."

"My husband."

"Ah. A delightful physician. My husband couldn't have received better care. Just a silly moment at a most inopportune time."

"I hope he mends quickly."

"Oh, he will. This is not his first go-round. And the good news is that we're not really sure it's a fracture. A hairline, at worst." She extended her hand in greeting. "And I spoke with one of your deputies yesterday. Actually, last night." Her handshake was firm. "Apparently, someone is having some fun with our surveyor's markers. You know, we don't need to tell the vandal this, but we're going to reshoot all of our baseline markers, anyway. There are some major changes we're going to make." She turned back to Waddell. "I was up here last night, doing the tourist thing. I have to tell you, I'm *mightily* impressed, sir. I caught the show about Orion in the planetarium. I hope your cameras are ready when Rigel or Betelgeuse goes supernova!"

"Well, thank you." Waddell beamed. "A lot of astronomers are hoping for that. I'm told we can expect that display any time in the next hundred million years or so. And next Tuesday would be fine with me." He flashed another bright smile of nicely capped teeth. "I wish you had let me know that you were visiting. I would have given you the grand tour. Maybe you'll accept an offer of a room for tonight? I mean, we're no Posadas Inn, but..."

"*That's* for sure," the woman said. "Thank you for that. I'll talk to my husband and see how he's feeling. He really wanted to ride the train, but that didn't work out. Maybe he'll feel up to hobbling aboard in the next day or so."

"Well, now, let's make that happen." Waddell extended a hand and beckoned at Frank Dayan. "This is a friend of mine, Frank Dayan. He's publisher of the *Posadas Register* in town."

Lydia Thompson's greeting was civil enough, but Estelle saw the young woman's eyes narrow as she put on the mental brakes. But then Waddell added, "Let's beat the heat and go inside. Maybe you'd like some refreshment of some sort?"

"Actually, no thanks. I need to be running back to town to make sure my husband hasn't tripped in the shower or something equally foolish." She thrust out her hand. "Mr. Waddell, a pleasure. Now I can put a face with the name. I'd like to touch base with you sometime in the next couple of days. When you're free. When you and I and my husband can sit and chat, just the three of us. You've got yourself sort of a crowd here today."

Waddell recovered quickly, with perfect aplomb. "The offer for a complimentary room stands, Mrs. Thompson. Even tonight, if you like. I'll leave word with the front desk right now. Tonight, tomorrow, whenever. Of course, I'll be delighted to talk with you any time. Perhaps over a quiet dinner. We have a great chef."

"Thank you. How can we resist that? I'll see if hubby is feeling better." This time, her smile was a little tight-lipped, and she nodded at both the undersheriff and Frank Dayan.

"Mrs. Thompson..." the newspaperman began, but she shook her head.

"Some other time, perhaps, Mr. Dayan." She extended her hand to Estelle once more. "A pleasure meeting you, ma'am. If we have any other troubles out at the site, I'll know who to call." A final wave of the hand dismissed them all, and Lydia Thompson strode back out to her SUV, and as she turned to slip behind the wheel, Estelle saw that the woman was still smiling.

"I think that went well, don't you?" Miles Waddell said with dry sarcasm.

"She didn't want to talk with me around," Frank Dayan said. "I wonder if she'll wear that gun to the next county meeting."

"Snakes," Estelle said. "It's one of those revolvers that's chambered for both forty-five Colt and four-ten shot shells."

"Your eyes are better than mine. And our neighborhood vandal better watch his step, then," Waddell laughed. "I can see that she's a woman not easily cornered."

"We still don't know what kind of development they're planning," Dayan said. "Some big strip mall, maybe?"

"Nope," Waddell said. "I'd for sure bet against that. With as few drive-by customers as they'd get, that's not likely. Even malls in the middle of Albuquerque have their share of troubles. You got to have traffic flow, that's all there is to it. If she's really lucky, maybe they can make a single dollar store work, once the BLM gets their cave site developed. But I wouldn't hold my breath on even that much."

"Hey," Dayan said with feigned eagerness, "out here in the middle of everywhere, even a dollar store is news."

Waddell reached out a hand to Estelle. "Sorry to haul you out here for nothing."

"The opportunity to meet Lydia Thompson was worthwhile. We all learned something, didn't we?"

"Tough girl," Waddell said. "I wonder who's the boss of her outfit."

"You mean her or her husband? I wouldn't bet either way, Miles."

"And speaking of seeing people," Dayan said, and Estelle accurately guessed what was coming. "I was hoping we could sit down with your son for a few minutes one of these days."

"One of these days," Estelle replied good-naturedly. "Your man Rik asked the same thing. But right at the moment, Francisco is content pretending that the rest of the world doesn't exist. He doesn't have the chance to do that very often, when both of their schedules have a few days' downtime." She reached out and touched Dayan on the forearm. "I'll mention it to him, though. I'm not an official gatekeeper, and he speaks just fine for himself."

"I'm just afraid that the big city boys will find out he's here, and there goes my scoop."

"I'm sure he appreciates that, Frank."

The drive back to Posadas was blissfully quiet—no radio traffic, no phone calls. She drove north along the county road, skirting the perimeter of the Thompson property. Lydia Thompson had driven off this way as well, the light plume of dust from her passing still hanging in the air.

Estelle clearly understood Miles Waddell's concerns, but more than anything else, she wanted to turn the rest of the world off and spend the rest of the day with her son and his wife, the young couple's life—and hers—now enriched by four-week-old William Thomas.

Instead, she returned to the county building. A few moments in the assessor's office armed the undersheriff with land-ownership data, and another opportunity to skillfully field questions about her son's young family without supplying any additional information to encourage the gossip.

Back in her office she used a yellow highlighter to draw neat diagonal lines on a transparent overlay for the huge county wall map. According to the assessor's records, Thompson Development Corp, LLC, had acquired more than 1,000 acres—620 acres of it originally part of the Boyd ranch. The country was marginal scrub in rugged country, with a scatter-ing of bedrock intrusions that looked more formidable than inviting.

In three places, the land adjoined property owned by Miles Waddell, and the various parcels included more than a half mile of frontage on County Road 14, extending north from the prop-erty line with Waddell's *NightZone* parking lot.

Every acre of the Thompson holdings was submarginal ranch land—overgrazed, rocky, and in several spots showing the blackened aftermath of prairie wildfires. Other than the mineral, oil, or gas deposits that might lie subsurface, the land offered two enormous plusses.

First, along a portion of the property's western boundary just across the county road, the developer's holdings joined Bureau of Land Management and state lands. That diminished the likelihood of competing development on the Thompsons' doorstep.

Second, the BLM had been working for years to survey the limestone caves that pocked the country west of the county road, with an eye to future development as a tourist attraction. The federal government moved at glacial speed, with little funding and few staff who could dedicate themselves to the project. But if they succeeded, the cave complex might someday rival the fragile development at Carlsbad.

Estelle stepped back and gazed at the map. So many questions remained. She tried to picture how the Posadas County Sheriff's Department would cope with providing services to a new community on the far side of the county, one that, if rumors could be believed, might see a hundred new homes springing up.

Who would choose to live out there, a minimum of forty-five minutes' drive into the village of Posadas, itself far from being a shopper's paradise? Where would these people shop? Where would they work? Would they be content with a rocky, dusty county dirt road?

Chapter Four

"May I intrude?"

Lydia Thompson stood near the doorway of the under-sheriff's office, her entry politely blocked by Deputy Elwood Ray, who was working day dispatch. That she had appeared so promptly after their first brief meeting suggested to Estelle that the young woman had other issues to discuss. Deputy Ray's big hand rested on the doorjamb, an effective barrier. Estelle nodded.

"Thanks, Woody." She rose and gestured for Lydia to enter the office. "Come in. Have a chair. We didn't have much of a chance to talk today." She noticed that Lydia had shed the snake gun. "How about something cold to drink?"

"I'm fine, thanks. I tell you, out there when I saw that Mr. Newspaper Guy was present, and Mr. Security Guy, and who knows who else inside, I thought"—and she wrinkled her nose in a fetching expression of distaste—"not something I wanted to do." Even as she sat, her eyes drifted over to the wall map. "Interesting stuff."

"How's that?"

Relaxing back, Lydia crossed her legs and folded her hands comfortably in her lap. She pushed her cap back like a rancher preparing for an over-the-fence chat. "We purchased some property, true enough. You have it outlined pretty accurately there on your map. But we haven't applied to do *anything* with it. We haven't applied to the state engineer to drill even a single domestic well, we haven't talked to the county about a subdivision variance; we haven't met with anyone from the state. I'd love to know how all these rumors start. I'd love to track what fertilizes the old grapevine."

"The sale of property is public record with the county assessor," Estelle pointed out. "A sale that involves so many acres, in that particular location, is going to generate lots of curiosity. Not to mention the purchase price. The same thing happened when Miles Waddell first started to organize what became *NightZone*."

"The assessor broadcasts recent sales?"

"No, I don't believe that he does. If it were up to the staff in his office, facts and figures would never leave the filing cabinet. But there are people who keep constant track of real estate activity. Not surprisingly, most Realtors do, as I'm sure someone in your position already knows. I'm sure that a fair handful of folks knows exactly what you purchased, and how much it cost you...Frank Dayan included."

"Hmmm." For a moment, Lydia studied the map. "I guess Kyle and I are well aware of all that." She shrugged and her eyes narrowed as she focused on the county's western boundaries. "It surprises me to see this map on your wall, Sheriff Guzman. Is that just being proactive?"

"That's exactly what it is. As you've no doubt heard, when Miles Waddell first started his project, there was considerable resistance. Some bad times. We even had a fatality when some punks decided to chainsaw down a few power poles. And now, with your purchase right on his doorstep, there are people who are concerned—and perhaps rightfully so. The *NightZone* development has created lots of jobs, and it has put lots of money into lots of pockets." Estelle leaned back in her chair, hands folded across her stomach. "Lots of vested interest, so to speak. Now that they have it in their backyards, with all its contributions to the local economy, folks tend to be defensive."

For a long moment, Lydia Thompson sat silently, gazing at the wall map. "There's no zoning in Posadas County. That's one good thing."

"Correct. There is no formal zoning in the county. Some folks would argue that's a good thing, some would argue the opposite. There are building codes in the village itself. Blair Edgewood over in the village clerk's office can give you the details, if you haven't already explored that avenue."

Lydia waved an impatient hand. "What the village does or doesn't do isn't my concern, at least for this project."

Estelle let the silence hang for a moment, then prompted with a *why-are-you-here?* gesture. "May I ask what is?"

"We're way out *there.*" Lydia waved a hand at the left-hand edge of the map. "Remember that Kevin Costner movie about putting a baseball diamond in a cornfield? This is also one of those 'if you build it' situations." The young woman sighed. "Buying that property was my husband's idea. He's a developer by nature, more than a little bit of a risk-taker, quite an accomplished dreamer. He's super impressed with Mr. Waddell's baseball field, if you will."

She smiled ruefully. "You know, a *speculator* might be a more accurate description in my husband's case. He just made out like a bandit with a big commercial property sale up in Albuquerque, and this all was just too interesting to pass up. And kind of on the other end of the spectrum. The Albuquerque sale was metro, with lots of strings attached, lots of hoops to jump through. This is the boonies, where anything goes…or so it seems.

"With both Mr. Waddell's development, and the BLM's activities across the road, it's clear that there might be some opportunities out there. Miles Waddell obviously has found his niche. My husband certainly thinks so."

"Mr. Waddell is an interesting case," Estelle observed. She hesitated, not wishing to intrude on Miles Waddell's privacy. "If I understand him correctly, and this is just my own opinion, you understand, *NightZone* really has nothing to do with the urge to develop, or even to make money as a primary reason for being. Astronomy is his passion, what started out as first a hobby, and then a *consuming* hobby, and now this. He's developed the perfect spot for it. Stargazing, and everything that goes along with it, to make it a comfortable adventure."

"Interesting case is right," Lydia agreed. "I couldn't believe what I was seeing when I prowled around up there last night. I think I gained ten pounds just reading the restaurant's menu." She frowned for a moment, then said, "My husband and I saw the chance to buy and didn't hesitate. Well, *Kyle* didn't hesitate. But here's the thing."

She leaned forward, resting her elbows on her knees. "We...I...absolutely do not want to develop in a way that jeopardizes the ambiance of Waddell's holdings. It's pretty clear to me that what's good for his venture could be good for us as well. If we play our cards right. I think Kyle agrees with me, up to a point."

"Waddell will be happy to hear that."

"I mean it. That's the way I see it. I admit to being a little flustered when I saw Mr. Dayan up there today, and you'll forgive me if I acted like a little pill, turning my back on everybody and huffing off. But it was sort of like Mr. Waddell was marshalling all his forces. My husband thinks that at this stage, the community will make every effort to protect what Mr. Waddell has built. And that's what I hear you suggesting, too. Does that sound like a fair assessment?"

"Yes. It wasn't always that way, believe me. Miles Waddell had more than his share of naysayers who believed he was going off the deep end. And I suppose there are still some that think his astronomy park is a colossal waste of money...folks who never look up at the night sky."

"Which camp are you in?"

Estelle smiled. "Neutral, I hope. I have no axe to grind one way or another. How Miles chooses to spend his money is entirely his affair. I *will* say that we've seen more and more interesting folks, from all over the world, coming here to visit. We're a little village without much in the way of economy since the mines closed. The infusion of tourist money has been a plus. I'm delighted with his success."

Lydia Thompson shrugged. "And with more people come drawbacks as well. It must be hard to maintain your distance," she said. "Kyle and I talked long and late last night until the Tylenol put him to sleep. We need to revisit our plans, and make sure that they dovetail with Mr. Waddell's development. I think I've convinced Kyle of that approach."

She held up an index finger. "We agree on that, sure enough. But that doesn't mean that we're going to let Mr. Waddell decide for us how to proceed. He doesn't get to dictate what happens on the private property around him. But we can work together."

"Fair enough. As I said, he'll be happy to hear that."

"I didn't say that up topside today because the newspaper guy was there. I didn't want it blared all over the front page. Because who knows? We may…do *nothing*."

"All right."

Lydia Thompson smiled at Estelle's cryptic response. "Any suggestions?"

"Mrs. Thompson…"

"Lydia, please."

"Lydia, I can tell you what the law is, but I think you know perfectly well what your legal rights are." Estelle ticked them off on her fingers. "You can't drill water wells without approval from the state engineer. Even a permit for a single, simple domestic well for one family goes through his office. You can't establish a subdivision without state and county approval. You can't install a public water system or a sewer system without state environmental approval, or without certified operators. And on and on.

"This may not be the big city, but you still have an impressive number of hoops to jump through, nevertheless." She smiled. "The long fingers of the state reach out, even in Posadas County. But you're already aware of that."

She shrugged. "But Frank? Frank Dayan is an interesting guy. Pam Gardiner is his editor, and she runs a tight operation over there. Now, were I in your shoes, Lydia, and had I decided what I wanted to do with the land, I would do my best to make Frank Dayan and Pam Gardiner my allies...if you and your husband are aiming for a commercial venture. Those two, and their newspaper, are staunch defenders of Posadas County and our way of life. I firmly believe the same can be said for Miles Waddell."

"That's pretty obvious," Lydia said. "I know that I was a little precipitous walking out of our little meeting up there, but it didn't feel right. It felt like stacked odds."

"I understand that. But Frank Dayan is an intelligent man, and a fair one. If after talking with you he thinks you and your husband have a good thing going out there, what he says in his paper will reflect that. That helps quell the rumors."

"You gotta love small towns."

"Human beings everywhere," Estelle offered. "There are some people whom you'll never convince. They'll do what they can to stop you, and within the bounds of the law, that's their right. This county is home to a pretty substantial flock of conspiracy theorists...sometimes I think more than its share. Believe them, and you'll believe that Waddell's radio telescope is eavesdropping on his neighbors. When you put shovel to ground, I have no doubt that you'll hear from the crazies. You'll be under constant scrutiny."

Lydia Thompson's eyes narrowed. It looked as if she was

calculating odds. "Maybe we'll put twelve steers on the acreage and call it done. That's about all the land will support."

"There is that."

"Or drill some exploratory oil or gas wells."

"That too."

"You probably think we're out of our minds to get into this."

"No. As I said before, I suppose that most people thought Miles Waddell was off his rocker for throwing money at his dream. But he's making it work. His visitation traffic grows every week, and it's traffic from all over the world. What *you* do with your money is your business."

Lydia pushed herself to her feet. "Time to go back to the motel and check on hubby. Then we might take Mr. Waddell up on his offer of a hotel room on the mesa. Not that there's anything basically wrong with the Posadas Inn, mind you." She grimaced and raised one eyebrow.

Estelle laughed. "It's a great place he's designed up there on the mesa top. Five-star all the way. He was being modest when he said their food is good. It's incredible."

"Maybe we'll do that." She thrust out her hand. "Thanks for taking the time to talk with me."

"Any time."

"I want you to know that I appreciate your discretion, Sheriff Guzman. I really do." Her smile grew radiant. "I have two of your son's DVDs, by the way." Her smile widened. "When I took my lame husband in for treatment, one of the ER nurses made sure I knew about your hometown celebrities."

The sudden change of subject took Estelle by surprise. "I'm delighted to hear that. About the recordings." She resisted the temptation to ask which nurse had taken such delight in blabbing the news.

Lydia regarded Estelle for a long moment. "I read the article in *Rolling Stone* about them a few months ago. That must be quite a challenge, being mother to someone like that."

"It has its moments."

"I'll bet. Is he planning any local concerts in the near future? I'd love to see him in person. Both him and his wife."

Francisco Guzman, live at Posadas High School Gym. Estelle smiled at the thought. That had happened once, years before, when the youngster was a fifteen-year-old prodigy, fulfilling a conservatory requirement.

"He's at Lincoln Center in September. In New York." She did not add, *he's also five blocks away at this very moment, coping along with his wife and their new son with the trials and tribulations of building a new home.* She did not mention that Miles Waddell had lobbied Francisco Guzman's agent long and hard for a concert in the *NightZone* auditorium.

"Oh, I envy your going to New York. Do you know yet what he's going to be performing?"

"No, I don't." That came out a little more abrupt than Estelle intended, and she added, "He's a busy young man. And September is a long way off."

"Oh, I'm sure he is. He has that seven-disc DVD set coming out covering the Beethoven tribute festival in Munich that he did last winter. I preordered it. I can't wait." She waved a hand. "Listen to me. I get so caught up." She lowered her voice. "My husband listens to blues. Saxophone and steel guitar...it all sounds the same to me. Not that I'd ever tell him that."

Deputy Ray appeared in the doorway. "Ma'am, there's an elderly gentleman who wants to talk to you," he said with a straight face. "He's making a nuisance of himself out in dispatch."

Estelle rose and accepted Lydia Thompson's offered hand. "Good luck with your project, Lydia. If there's anything that the Posadas County Sheriff's Department can do for you, don't hesitate to contact us."

The young woman's footsteps past dispatch to the entry foyer were quick, and at one point, Estelle heard Lydia Thompson chortle as she walked out, "Oh, wow."

Chapter Five

"What's 'oh wow'?" Bill Gastner asked. The former sheriff of Posadas County rested against the dispatch island counter, both hands locked on his skeleton-framed walker. "That was the lady developer, wasn't it? Thompson?"

"It was. Lydia Thompson. It turns out that she's a big fan of my son's music." Estelle reached an arm across Gastner's broad shoulders and gave him a hug. The shoulders that once had been heavy mounds of muscle were now angular and bony—some of the old man's weight-loss by choice, some by his various battles with so many birthdays.

"I can't imagine why," Gastner said. "Anyway, are you ready for lunch? I've got some interesting news for you...also in the 'oh wow' category. Or are you going home to see what the kids are up to?"

"As a matter of fact, I am ready for lunch, and no...I'm trying my hardest to stay out of their way. So your timing is perfect, *Padrino*. Where are we eating?"

"You don't usually ask silly questions."

She caught the dispatcher's eye. "I'll be at the Don Juan, Woody."

Gastner's walker slid silently over the tiles, demonstrating that he clearly didn't need its steadying assistance. Once out-side, he folded the walker onto the backseat of Estelle's patrol car. Two minutes later, when they reached the Don Juan, he left it there. He walked slowly but steadily, taking advantage of handholds when he reached them, but making an obvious effort to keep his spine straight and erect. In a few minutes they were comfortably seated in Gastner's favorite booth, deep in the shadows near the back of the restaurant behind the waitresses' service island.

The retired sheriff, who had recently and grudgingly cel-ebrated his eighty-fifth birthday anniversary, looked nifty in a plaid shirt and new corduroys. He had carried a large manila envelope in from the car and now laid it carefully on the table, well out of range of his coffee cup.

"Anything new in Waddell's world that I need to worry about?" he asked. From day one of the *NightZone* project, Gastner had been a consultant and advisor to Miles Waddell. He still spent considerable time on the mesa, almost always rid-ing the train out to the site the moment it became operational.

"*He's* worried, maybe. He doesn't know what the Thompsons are up to yet."

"I don't think anyone else does either. A subdivision seems a likely bet if you're among the brain-dead."

"Time will tell. They're changing their minds, apparently. From whatever their original plan was when they bought the property."

"Huh. Well, so be it. Maybe they'll decide to put in one of those commercial rocket places, and launch space shuttles full of tourists out into orbit. New Mexico already has one of those, and as we all know, one is never enough."

He leaned back as the waitress appeared. "I'm so excited that I gotta eat." He beamed at the attractive young woman, holding a hand out toward her. "This is Rosita Mirales in person. She started here just this week."

Gastner swung his hand over to present the rest of the introduction. "Rosita, this is the undersheriff of Posadas County, Estelle Reyes-Guzman. A better person you'll never meet." He let out a sigh, not bothering to open the menu. "A burrito grande for me, with all the fixin's, *por favor.*" He waved a dismissive hand. "Yeah, I know. I'm on a strict diet. But today, to hell with it."

"Red or green?" Rosita asked gently. Her husky voice was self-conscious, not much more than a whisper.

"Just remind Fernando that it's for me and he'll do it right. He'll decide."

Rosita nodded, her thick black eyebrows converging as she wrote the order's instructions. She then glanced across at Estelle, a little uneasy.

"I'd like the chicken tostadas plate, please, Rosita. Green, with a to-go box. And iced tea."

"Coffee, black, with water, Rosita," Gastner added.

The girl nodded her thanks, her smile needing work.

"You remember her?" Gastner asked when Rosita had vanished toward the kitchen.

"I do. She was a lot younger then."

"Yup. And her brother is *still* in jail."

"Yes, he is." She took a deep breath. "One of the joys of a small town. We get to meet our clientele over and over and over again." She shrugged with resignation. "It's good that Fernando gave her a job here at the restaurant, though. I hope she does well."

After a moment, she added, "So. What's happening in your life, *Padrino*? Last Sunday when you came over for dinner, you were not your usual ebullient self."

"Ebullient? I'm ever *ebullient?*"

"On occasion, yes."

"I'll work on that, then. I think it was just because the kids weren't here yet, and I was having an attack of the lonelies, struggling with the anticipation. That happens now and then. Now I'm concentrating on just staying out of the way."

"Me too."

He leaned forward and lowered his voice. "Sweetheart, I can absolutely guarantee that Francisco and Angie would like to see more of you. And I don't mean just to provide free babysitting services."

"They haven't found a *nana* yet."

"They will, in due time. Anyway, you and the good doctor are coming over for dinner tonight? Francisco asked me to remind you. He and Angie are cooking some weird thing that they learned about in Munich. Probably something awful with Brussels sprouts or fermented cabbage. But on a brighter note…"

He opened the envelope with care and pulled out a letter protected in a glassine cover. The rampant Colt logo of the historic Colt Firearms Company was prominent on the letterhead. "And this is a good place to start, speaking of *ebullient*. You remember this?"

"I do remember." She scanned the brief letter from the Connecticut firearms company's archivist. Gastner had discovered the rusted remains of a Colt revolver seven years before, on land just north of Miles Waddell's astronomical park—land now owned by the Thompsons.

The old man had worked patiently with oil and the finest brass wool until he could piece together the serial number from the three locations where it was stamped on the revolver's rusted frame. That number told a tantalizing story, according to the company's archivist. Manufactured in 1889, the gun was part of a shipment of two sent to Rosenblum and Sons' Mercantile in Silver City, New Mexico Territory.

When Gastner had found the gun, it was a rusted hulk, a relic apparently lost more than a century before among the rocks out in the bleak prairie. It still held three unfired cartridges in its six-shot cylinder, along with two empty shell casings.

Estelle looked up and saw the twinkle that lit Gastner's face. "And as I recall, you received this response to your inquiry to Colt about…how long ago?" She looked at the date. "Six years. And as I recall, at the time it was a dead end."

"Yep. Since then, I've tracked a few things down, being the talented sleuth that I am. Rosenblum started his Silver City business in 1878, and went bust in 1891. Just thirteen years in business. But…" he opened the envelope again and pulled out the rest of the paperwork. "It's not a common name."

He handed a photocopy of a small newspaper clipping to Estelle. "Came across this not long ago, and it got my juices started again." His jowly face broke into a smile. "I think your kids coming to live with me was a master stroke. I feel twenty years younger, all motivated and stuff."

"And stuff." She looked at the paper. Dated March 30, 1917, the clipping from the Silver City newspaper announced that Michael Rosenblum had been lost in fierce fighting near a tiny village in southern France. Gastner waited until Estelle looked up from reading the clipping.

"Michael was the son of Jules and Mary Rosenblum," he said.

"And Jules was…"

"The son of Richard Rosenblum himself, the store's founder. One of Richard's sons, anyway. There were three." Gastner waved a hand and sat back to give the waitress room to maneuver his plate. "I don't know what happened to the other Rosenblum boys. Quiet lives and faded away, I guess. Anyway, the name to remember is *Mary* Rosenblum.

"The store closed in 1891, shortly after Richard Rosenblum, the original founder, was killed in a freight wagon accident. Jules, Richard's son and Mary's husband, tried to take over after his father's death, but died the next year from an infected tooth." He grinned and sampled his burrito. "You following all this?"

"So far." She stirred her salad. "Richard the elder owned the merc with his sons. He died in a wagon accident. One of the sons,

Jules, died of a bad tooth about the time that the store closed. He and his wife had a son who was killed in France twenty-six years later. He was no boy soldier, then. This all sounds like one tragedy after another."

"Yep. Not much in the good luck department." Gastner savored the rich flavors of the chile and cheese. "Mary is the name to remember, though. Ever the good daughter-in-law, she kept the books for the mercantile when it was in business."

"You've seen them?"

"No. I'm not sure they exist anymore. Mary died in 1943, in Santa Fe. She might have kept the ledgers after the store closed, and maybe not." He spread the fingers of both hands out, fan-like. "The family went this way and that. The obit in the Santa Fe paper says that Mary was survived by four children and a gaggle of grandkids, great grandkids, and so forth. I don't know if all four of her children were from her husband Jules, or if she married again."

"The four children, then. One of them might have kept her mother's souvenirs."

"Might have. *If* she kept them. Some folks get a real kick out of old artifacts like that. Some couldn't care less. Just dust-collectors. I have the kids' names from Mary's obit. Son Michael, of course, died in the war. As of 1943, the surviving siblings were Irving…" Gastner put down his fork and counted on his fingers, eyes half closed. "Irving of Ratón; Gladys Tupperson of Amarillo, Texas; Rosie Rosenblum of Merced, Oregon; and Glenndon of Miami Beach." He shrugged and dug another generous mouthful of his burrito. "How hard can it be? Except…"

"Except 1943 is a long time ago, *Padrino*."

"A mere three quarters of a century. Hell, I'm older than that. So I'm looking at the next generation."

"*Ay*."

"One of the joys of this being eighty-five business is that naps are often *much* more important to me than doing any kind of challenging work. But on occasion, I get lucky.

"The way I figure it, several things could have happened. The sales record book might well have been destroyed...and I gotta be realistic. It probably was. Or maybe Mary kept it for sentimental reasons. Maybe before she died she gave it to a historical society somewhere. Maybe one of her children got it, and it's now in the possession of one of *their* kids. Maybe, maybe. I mean, if I'd had it, *I* would have kept it. Journals like that are fun reading. Somebody pays twelve cents for a can of peaches, a dollar fifty for a shovel. That sort of thing. It appeals to historians."

"At least you know the gun's shipping history after it left the factory."

Gastner grimaced. "Yeah, but I want to know who purchased it from Rosenblum *originally*. I want to know who plunked down their seventeen dollars or whatever it was to buy it, all shiny and new. Because, see, I also want to know what it was doing out there on the prairie, dropped in the rocks of Bennett's Trail, lost for all these years. I want to know what life it led between 1889, when it left the factory all bright and shiny, and when it was lost. I mean, people don't go around just casually dropping Colt revolvers. Only in the movies. Why didn't the owner pick it up again after he dropped it? That's a month's wages, after all. That's a pretty simple question. And the titillating thing is that Josiah Bennett himself was supposedly murdered down in that country."

"Supposedly by someone he knew, his skull cleaved with an axe," Estelle offered. "Right around 1890."

Gastner looked sideways at her. "I've bored you with his story before."

"Not bored. But having his skull split with an axe would sure explain why he dropped the gun and didn't pick it up, if the gun was his. My question is who or what was the target of the two fired cartridges?"

The old man chewed thoughtfully. "So you see. The gun is from the appropriate era, found in landscape coincidental with Bennett's last cattle drive and his death." He sipped his coffee. "Inquiring minds need to know. I mean, if it was *Bennett's* gun, and he was murdered while trying to bring it into action, then we know why it was never picked up, right? And that marks the actual site of the murder, which has never been accurately pinpointed."

Estelle smiled. "It's nice to see you so occupied with this project."

"Yeah, well. The dead ends are a frustration, and I don't give it the time I should. Naps, you know."

"What's your next step with it?"

"I'll see which of any of the four kids is still alive…doubtful, but maybe. Maybe the obits can shed some light on the next generation. The good thing is that as the journal ages, it seems like a more and more valuable relic. I have to hope that the current generation thinks so."

He shrugged, worked a large portion of dripping, smothered burrito into his mouth, and after a moment of blissful noshing, changed the subject. "So the 'oh wow' lady didn't give you any hints about what they're planning up top?"

Estelle shook her head. "She said that they're rethinking."

"Good for them, then. They dropped a chunk of money on that land. And *my* trail, Bennett's Trail, goes right through the middle of it. I found that gun on what is now their property, or close thereto."

"Who knows?" Estelle said.

Gastner laughed. "You're just not nosy enough, sweetheart." He pointed an unloaded fork at her. "You going to stop by this afternoon in time to see how the house project is coming before we get busy over dinner? Hell, they even recruited me."

"To make what?"

"Don't say it like that. I've been cooking for years. I know my way around the kitchen."

"Or at least the most direct route over to the Don Juan. What are you making?"

"The coffee."

"Excellent," she laughed. "We'll come over a little early, but not too. I'd like to spend all afternoon there, but as I said, I'm trying not to be a hovering grandmother."

"Hover away, I say." He swabbed up the last of the chile. "The contractor tells me that he'll likely be punching through that east wall next week. When I first saw that music room foundation being laid out for pouring, I thought Christ almighty, that addition's going to be a monstrosity. But now that I see the way Carlos designed it all, it just *flows*. That kid's got a touch."

He tucked the papers away. "All this activity motivates me, sweetheart. The kids are always asking my advice or my input on this and that, but what the hell can *I* tell 'em except 'go for it'? Little brother's design is super, the contractor knows his stuff, what more could we ask?"

Estelle smiled broadly. "That their two-month stay turns into forever. That's all I can ask."

"And you're a dreamer, sweetheart. The rest of the world is not all that eager to share their hold on the *maestro* and his beautiful and talented wife."

Chapter Six

"Rosanna wants me to fly to New York to confab with Ernie Gneice," Francisco Guzman said as he returned to the dining table. He pronounced the last name of the New York producer with a hard *G*, even though the letter was normally silent. Francisco had been secluded in the back of the house, in a phone conference that had interrupted their dinner. "I don't think so."

"The great man has summoned you?" Angie grinned and shifted the slumbering William Thomas, a movement that earned a contented little gurgle from the infant. "I thought you didn't like him."

Francisco grimaced and shook his head. "I don't. Not even a little bit. The problem is that he loves me way too much." He poured himself a third of a glass of merlot and offered the bottle first to his mother, who put her hand over her glass, and then to his father, who slid his own glass within convenient reach. "Every time I've talked with Gaa-neice in person, I always feel as if I need to wash my hands really well."

Francisco lowered his voice in imitation of the producer's Brooklyn growl. "We would be *honored* to have you record *blah, blah, blah*, so come to our office and we'll hash out the details." He grinned. "Ordinarily, I might go, because there are always a lot of dollar signs attached. But right now, I have this teeny little window of time to enjoy my world here. So they can either wait, or they can jump a convenient jet and fly out to talk to me while I hammer nails."

"I thought it was Rosanna's job to hash out details for you," Estelle asked. "That's why she's your agent."

"And that's because you're logical, Ma," her son said. "Rosanna Wilcox Stein sees the dollar signs, and that's about all. She's aghast that Angie and I are planning a residence in New Mexico. 'New *where?*' she's fond of complaining. 'Can you buy fresh milk for the baby out there?' And then she always ends up saying something like, 'I've never heard of *Posado.*'" He draped an affectionate arm over his wife's shoulder. "No matter what we do, it's expected that we'll bow and scrape to the captains of the industry, so to speak. *Bleah.*"

Francisco took a long sip of the merlot and shrugged. "Ms. Stein is trying her best to convince me that part of the deal is that I have to pay my dues, you see. Both Angie and me. We do homage to the powers-that-be at the top of the music industry. Or so producers like Gneice think. And maybe I will. Just not today. Not tomorrow. Maybe not next week. Maybe not next month.

"Anyway, Angie and I have this other project that takes precedence." He set his wineglass down and reached over to settle his hand on top of William Thomas's head, stroking the infant's silky black hair. "And we want to be here when my brother and Tasha visit." He looked across at Bill Gastner, who sat like an aging Buddha, hands folded comfortably on his belly. "You're still sure about all this company descending on you, *Padrino?* Disturbing all your peace and quiet?"

"Very sure." Gastner added nothing to mitigate his blunt response.

"The deal is, if *both* of us travel in different directions, it makes it awkward," Francisco said. "Angie has that concert and recording session this next week in Oahu that has been head-lined into a festival since last year. So I get to go along and play in the surf with William Thomas."

"*Ay,* next week?" Estelle tried to keep the bleat out of her voice. "How'd I miss that on the calendar?"

"Calm, calm, Ma. We leave Thursday, record on Friday, con-cert Saturday evening, home on Sunday."

"Jetting from here? From Posadas?"

"Sure. Nothing else makes sense." Francisco looked puzzled. "You're thinking what?"

"I'm thinking that I can't keep track of you two."

"The trick is to remember that you don't have to," her son said kindly. "If we forget, Rosanna, aka Ms. Stein, will remind us."

For a long moment, Estelle argued with herself, then settled for, "I worry about everything, *hijo.* I worry about this little guy on a plane for umpty-ump hours, even a comfortable private jet. I worry about the noise. The airport congestion. The crowds. The traffic. Especially the *surf.* The *undertow.* Worry, worry." She managed a smile. "I mean, in New Mexico, we don't have undertows. Or sharks." She reached across and tucked Angie's right hand in her own. "That's what grandmothers *do,* I guess."

"You want to come along?" Angie looked over at Gastner and quickly amended. "The three of you?"

"I don't know," the old man said abruptly. "What're you play-ing?" Then he grinned before Angie had a chance to answer. "It won't matter. Every time you touch a string, it's heaven. But no…thanks, but no thanks. I don't do Hawaii. Too many differ-ent time zones to confuse me. Besides, when you guys practice and rehearse, it's either Angie on the cello right here in the living room, or over on Twelfth Street, where the piano is. *That's* my kind of convenient. If you're gone for too long, I can pop in a DVD and watch you."

"But you're taking the baby?" Estelle persisted. "To Hawaii."

"Worry, worry, Ma. It's either that or find a child seat that fits in your county car." Francisco grinned at his father. "Or one that attaches to the counter of the nurses' station at the hospital."

"You don't want him in a hospital," Dr. Francis Guzman said. "Way, way too many sick people hovering around. Or some doting nurse would steal him and not want to give him back."

"I could retire tomorrow." Estelle kept her expression sober. She wasn't sure if she was joking or not. "Then I'd be free to babysit any time."

"*That's* going to happen," Francisco laughed, and walked around the table to hug his mother from behind. "I think most of us *wish* it would happen. You have more than your twenty-five in. But Big Bad Bobby wouldn't know what to do with himself if you retired. Of course, he's got more years in than you do. *He* could retire as well and be free to hunt twenty-four/seven."

"You know, Posadas County is lucky in that respect," Gastner observed. "We have a whole handful of cops who'd be happy to be top dog, and who'd probably do a good job. Jackie Taber, Tom Mears, Tom Pasquale…"

"This is a conspiracy." Estelle held out both hands in appeal and her daughter-in-law passed the bundle that was the snoozing infant to her. She stroked the blanket to one side and regarded the tiny, dark face looking up from the cradle of her arms. William Thomas's eyes opened drowsily, the irises almost a deep indigo. He smiled at the face hovering over his. "Tell me what *you* think," she cooed.

"Right now, eat, piss, shit, and sleep is what he thinks, Ma," Francisco said. "I've been trying to get him to practice basic chord patterns on the keyboard, but all he does is spit up."

Estelle bent so that her face was just inches from the infant's. "William Thomas, tell me your father isn't Leopold Mozart reincarnated," she whispered.

Francisco clutched his chest in mock agony. "Owwww. That

hurt, Ma." William Thomas responded with a mighty yawn and then smacked his gums in contentment.

Estelle looked up at her daughter-in-law. "If I retire and go with you guys to Hawaii, may I hold William Thomas the whole way?"

Angie started to say something, but Francisco was quicker on the draw.

"Remember, eats, pisses, shits, spits up..."

Estelle looked over at her eldest son. "*Ay*, you think *you* didn't, *hijo?*"

"Don't pass this on, Mamá, but he still does," Angie laughed.

Chapter Seven

Estelle didn't hear the phone ring. Instead, her husband's warm hand on her shoulder gently shook her awake. Through blurry eyes she read 11:02 p.m. on the bedside clock. She'd been dead to the world for a scant fifteen minutes, slugged by too much good food and company.

"Dispatch," Dr. Guzman said, and handed her the phone.

She fumbled the receiver, finally oriented it upright, and managed her name.

"You awake?" Swing shift dispatcher Ernie Wheeler's tone was sharp.

"Yes." She swung her legs over the side of the bed and sat up, feet flat on the floor. Her husband was already out in the kitchen. "What's going on, Ernie?"

"We have a multiple shooting at the *Register*. At the newspaper? Captain Taber is responding and wants you there. Obregón is inbound, but ETA thirty minutes."

"The shooting is at the *Register?* The newspaper?"

"Yep. Right across the street. Everyone else is rolling, including the sheriff." He paused for a fraction of a second. "You awake?"

"Yes. I'm on it." Even as she hung up, she heard the nasal wail of her husband's beeper, followed by his voice confirmation. She couldn't hear what he said, but the tone of his voice was urgent.

"Nobody gets sleep tonight," her husband said as he hustled back into the bedroom. Socks, soft-soled loafers, a set of clean scrubs, and he was headed for the door, all in a matter of seconds. "Hey?" He paused just long enough for her to plant a kiss.

"They think two." He held two fingers in front of her face as if checking her for a concussion. "They're not sure yet," he said. Then he was gone.

In simple chinos and a black sweatshirt, she took a moment to make sure her badge was in place on her belt along with cuffs and radio, and that the Glock's slip-on holster was secure.

Outside, the air was clear and calm, the sky of late May black with the first quarter moon partly obscured by fleecy clouds. The Charger started with its low, guttural grumble, its console and computer lighting the cab. Her stomach grumbled in concert as it tried to recover from the assault earlier in the evening of *käsespätzle* and *maultaschen*, heavy on the cheese and pork—souvenir recipes of her son and daughter-in-law's Christmas tour in Germany the previous year.

"PCS, three oh two, three ten is rolling."

"Three ten, PCS. Ten four." But no response from Captain Taber. Estelle sat quietly for just a moment, playing catch-up. Then she pulled the car into gear. Turning from Twelfth Street to Bustos, she accelerated hard past the Don Juan. Despite the hour, the restaurant's parking lot was still moderately full of patrons taking advantage of the soft spring night. Any day now, the blast furnace of early summer would light.

From the Don Juan, she could look east ahead twelve blocks and see the wink of emergency lights in front of the *Posadas Register* building on the corner of Bustos and Grande, kitty-corner across Bustos from the county building.

Taber had parked her county Expedition crosswise, blocking Bustos traffic from the west. Even as she slowed, Estelle saw Sheriff Bob Torrez's unmarked unit pull out of McArthur two blocks east. A small group of people had gathered on the sidewalk across the street from the *Register,* including county commission Chairman Dr. Arnie Gray, who lived an easy stroll south on Rincon Avenue.

The lights blazed in the front room of the *Register,* and even as she palmed the mike to alert dispatch of her arrival on scene, Estelle saw Captain Taber inside the building. Taber straightened up into view, then crouched again. Estelle parked across Bustos. She exited the Charger and heard the first ambulance screaming south on Grande toward them.

The *Posadas Register* was housed in a single-story concrete block building plastered tan to look like adobe, the front of the building including huge tinted windows that stretched from thirty-six inches above the sidewalk to just below the eaves. The bottom two feet of the windows were doubly tinted in dark metallic. In a graceful arc, *Posadas Register* was spelled out in frontier-style twelve-inch gold lettering on the windows to the left of the glass door.

Pockmarks, their small fracture lines radiating out in spiderwebs, scarred the windows. The small holes walked across the name of the newspaper and then the door, the last three chipping the plaster on the west end of the building.

Estelle palmed her radio. "PCS, three ten. Is Linda rolling?"

"Affirmative, three ten."

Taber appeared in the doorway as Estelle approached.

"Two to transport," she said, keeping her voice down. She immediately turned back inside.

The room was divided with the ad staff and composing room taking the east end in a clutter dominated by two large surplus drafting tables, lower shelves weighted with massive clip-art collections. The cramped home of the news staff at the west end included filing cabinets, morgue racks, and a welter of photographic equipment plugged into chargers.

Register editor Pam Gardiner sat at her ancient wooden desk, her eyes wide. A towel had been wrapped around her left arm above the elbow, and she held another under her chin. She waved her right hand at Estelle.

"Take care of him," she croaked and pointed. "Him" was Rik Chang, who sat on the floor near the doorway to the restroom, his back against the wall. Taber knelt beside him.

"It just aches a little," Chang said. He looked up, saw Estelle, and grinned nervously. "I didn't even need to do a ride-along to get into trouble."

The pad that he held against his upper left chest was his own wadded up polo shirt, and Jackie Taber stripped the sterile packaging from a large gauze pad to replace the shirt. Estelle drew Chang's hand away, and she could feel him shaking. The ragged dark dimple of the wound three inches above his left nipple was small, barely oozing blood.

"No exit," Taber said quietly. "No clue where it tracked."

The young man started to shift, leaning weight on his right arm as if wanting to push himself up. "Just sit quiet, Rik. Captain Taber will stay with you. You're going to be fine. The ambulance is here now." She placed the gauze pad tightly against his chest and guided his hand in place. "Hold this for me." She turned to Taber. "Make sure that shirt gets bagged, Jackie."

"You bet."

She rose quickly and as she crossed to Pam Gardiner's desk, she heard the crunch of broken glass under her feet.

"Is he going to be all right?" Pam's voice was hoarse.

"He'll be fine. Let's worry about you."

The *Register's* longtime editor was a morbidly obese woman of fine editorial talents, as long as she didn't have to move from her throne-like chair. Publisher Frank Dayan was peripatetic enough for both of them, concentrating most of his efforts on advertising, but never hesitant to leap into the editorial fray to cover a story.

"I was reaching over there for some papers," and Pam nodded at the stack on the right-hand wing of her desk. "And all of a sudden, I hear this racket, there's glass breaking, and as I turn a little, I felt something tug at my arm and kind of a little sting at my throat."

"Let me," Estelle said, and gently moved the woman's clenched left hand and the wad of tissue she held under her chin. The projectile had raked across Pam's enormous throat wattle, inflicting a gouge that at first had bled profusely but then had quickly clotted to a slight ooze.

Either the woman had been struck by two separate projectiles, or one had done the damage, passing first through her arm and then grazing her neck. The flesh hung from the back of Pam's arms like great curtains. Moving the towel pad that Pam held with her right hand, Estelle saw the small wounds on the upper left arm, what would be an entry on the outside of her arm, with the exit on the inside of the curtain of fat. It too bled little. Both wounds were far below the line of bone.

"Here's the ambulance," Pam said. "I don't think I can do that."

"Just let them tend you, young lady," Estelle said. "They'll decide what's what."

"I can get up," she heard Rik Chang say across the room.

"Just relax," Taber instructed.

Pam Gardiner twisted a little in her chair. "Is he hurt badly?"

"I don't know, Pam. But we'll take care of him. Francis will be at the hospital already, so no worries."

Jason Finnegan appeared in the doorway and Estelle pointed toward Rik Chang. "Check him," she said. Finnegan looped the stethoscope from around his neck and crossed the room even as his partner, Emily Baca, appeared with the wheeled gurney.

Behind Baca, Sergeant Tom Pasquale appeared, followed by his wife, Linda, who served as the department photographer. Her Sony was already unlimbered and quietly snicking away.

Moving quickly to stay out of the EMTs' way, she shot dozens of photos of the two victims and their surroundings.

It was no challenge to position Rik Chang on the first gurney, where his wound was field-dressed and an IV started. By that time, the second ambulance had arrived.

"Oh, just let me waddle on out," Pam said, trying for a brave smile.

Finnegan put his arm around her shoulders as he draped her with a warm blanket. "You don't do anything except just sit quietly," and he patted the edge of the gurney, "and we'll do the rest."

The vast woman overflowed the gurney as they coaxed her onto her back. Remarkably, with some adjustment, the restraining belts were long enough, and she was wheeled out to the sidewalk where the two EMTs, along with Tom Pasquale and Jackie Taber, managed to lift the gurney into the ambulance.

"I'll ride with her," Taber said. "Taylor?" The captain beckoned to Deputy Taylor Obregón, who had just arrived from prowling the western side of the county. "Take a ride with Unit One there and secure as much of a statement from Mr. Chang as you can."

Chapter Eight

"A dark sedan."

"A red SUV."

"He stopped twice."

"He never stopped."

"They fired at least a dozen times."

"Oh, fifty times, at least."

"It had to have been a suppressor…I could hardly hear it."

"Probably a twenty-two."

"Enough noise to make *me* jump."

The witness reports went on and on, contradicting, supporting, weaving a story with a dozen variations. No one had actually witnessed the shooting, but at least four people had heard what they thought was gunfire.

Retired chiropractor and longtime county commissioner Arnie Gray, who lived in one of a dozen stately downtown quasi-Victorians built during an early mining boom in the 1800s, had been in his front yard waiting for his aging Pomeranian to relieve its plumbing.

"That little old guy is as bad as a geezer with a blown prostate," he told officers. Waiting on his dog, he'd heard "a couple dozen rounds, at least, but on the other side of the building so

I couldn't see anything." The vehicle had sped off to the west, sounding "powerful but quiet."

Estelle stood in the street, the area now taped off, all the spectators gone except for a handful that included Arnie Gray and County Manager Leona Spears. Jackie Taber had returned from the hospital with word that Pam Gardiner's wounds were as superficial as they appeared. She'd been cleaned up, bandaged, pumped full of antibiotics, and put to bed for twenty-four hours of observation before they would release her. Had she been twenty years younger and two hundred and fifty pounds lighter, they would have sent her home.

"Rik saw the vehicle," Taber continued. She kept her voice down, her back to the spectators. "Most likely a Ford Expedition, most likely dark blue or red, maybe black. He said he heard the first rounds hit the glass and turned…he was standing in the doorway to the restroom. He says he was looking back at Pam, who had just asked him a question.

"He heard the shots, just little pops, he said, and he turned to his *right*. He had time to see five or six rounds actually hit, and says that it was an even cadence. *Pop, pop, pop, pop*. Not a rapid-fire burst." Jackie poked an index finger against her own chest. "So when the bullet hit him, it tracked upward and toward his left. The X-ray shows that it's lodged in the muscle of his left shoulder, just to the median side of his rotator cuff. Rik says that he never felt it hit him."

"Obregón is staying at the hospital for a bit?" Estelle asked.

Taber nodded. "Until Rik is out of surgery and everything is stable. It shouldn't be long."

Sheriff Torrez stood behind Linda Pasquale as she documented each bullet-strike, and he glanced over his shoulder at Estelle, beckoning her with a crook of his finger.

"Everybody is on the road," Taber added. "We'll go with Chang's description of the vehicle until we learn otherwise."

"Twenty-five," Torrez said as his undersheriff and chief

deputy approached. He held his hands a foot apart. "Spaced pretty even. No up and down, so we ain't talkin' much recoil."

"Like maybe a twenty-two?" Estelle asked.

"Lookin' like it. Some of 'em didn't go much of anywhere. We got one stuck in the metal doorframe over there, and it's lookin' like we can match up some of the window strikes with the damage to the far wall inside. But it ain't going to tell us what we don't already know. Car full of punks havin' a good time."

"Kids, you think?"

"Yep." The sheriff sounded as if he had no shadow of doubt. "When they ran out of window, they just kept shootin'. They hit the building a few times there at the end." He swung his arm horizontally, indicating the straight line of bullet strikes.

"You know any local kids who drive a dark Expedition?"

Torrez frowned. "Is that what Chang and Pam say?"

"Chang saw it. A dark-colored Expedition. And Arnie Gray claims he heard it driving off to the west. He didn't see it, but he heard it. That doesn't sound so much like kids, Bobby. Nobody heard laughter, or shouts, and they didn't circle back."

Torrez gazed at the riddled building. He shook his head a couple of times, then asked, "Who's on the road, then?"

"Everybody we have. We were lucky to have a couple of state guys concentrating on the interstate east-west. The Border Patrol is covering 56 down toward Regál. We have Obregón at the hospital, with Miller, Vasquez, and Sutherland staying central."

"Where's Dayan? He ain't workin' tonight?"

"I'll find him." Taber slipped her phone out of her pocket.

"He might still be out at *NightZone*," Estelle said. "He was there earlier today, and I know that he's working up a feature on their latest planetarium show. That, and trying to catch the Thompsons. Waddell invited them to stay out there, and there's a possibility Frank managed to get his interview after all."

"In the middle of the night?" Torrez muttered.

"That's the way that place works," Estelle said. "And if it was a swank dinner meeting, it'd take a while."

But the simplest answer was the correct one. In a moment, Taber was breaking the news to the newspaper publisher, who up to that point had been enjoying a peaceful night's sleep home in his own bed.

"He'll meet someone at the hospital," Taber said.

"I'll go talk with him," Estelle said. "He'll want to come down here to see the damage after he checks up on Rik and Pam."

Estelle guided the Charger into the slot marked in orange as "Official Parking Only," and when she entered the hospital was greeted by the same aromas that were brought home each day on her husband's clothing. Betty Dugan, gray-wigged and wrinkled of face, sat behind the desk in the receptionist's corner, working her way through a thick puzzle book...her defense against a job that most of the time was crushingly boring. She glanced up, saw Estelle, and smiled sympathetically. She lifted a hand and one bent, arthritic finger pointed down the hall to her left.

"The gang's thataway," she croaked in a voice scarred by sixty years of smoking. "But I guess you know as well as anybody, better'n most."

"Thanks, Bets," the undersheriff replied. "Tough night."

"Dawn brings a new day." She smiled the prim, contented smile of someone who knows just how everything works.

Down the wide hallway past dark offices, through an intersection offering myriad choices that included a large red-and-black arrow that pointed toward the emergency room, Estelle rounded a corner and saw Frank Dayan leaning against the tiled wall under the sign for radiology. He looked up, his expression brightening. A small, dapper man, he usually managed a ready smile for everyone.

"They're going to be all right." The newspaper publisher looked haggard, his "Nixonian beard," as he was fond of calling his swarthy complexion, at its grubbiest. "Rik took the worst of it, but your husband said that the surgery went well. They were able to remove the bullet intact. Dr. Guzman said it missed the major brachial artery by just a fraction." He held two fingers a slight pinch apart. "Also missed the lung. They're going to keep him for a day or two just to be sure."

"He's a fortunate young man," Estelle said.

"Boy, ain't that the truth? But I'm worried about Pam, Estelle. The stress of the whole thing is *really* hard on her. She doesn't have the constitution for all of this."

"Maybe she's tougher than we think."

"Maybe she is, but I still worry. She's a med popper, you know." Dayan held up his hands in frustration. "She's got a whole damn drawerful at the office. Who knows what she has stashed at home? Diet root beer and popcorn. That's her idea of a balanced meal."

"I'll mention your concerns to my husband, but I'm sure he's talking to her already."

"And to me." Dayan shrugged helplessly. "She's been with me for a lot of years, Estelle."

"And a lot more to come."

"Let's hope so." He took a deep breath. "God knows, she can be exasperating. But a shrewd mind. A shrewd mind. She keeps me on the straight and narrow." He heaved a mighty sigh, and his right hand patted his shirt pocket. "It's at times like this that I wish I still smoked."

"A stiff shot of brandy might be more productive."

Dayan laughed weakly. "I'm thinking there will be a lot of that. Look, nobody tells me much, and as soon as it looks clear to break away here, I'll go over to the office to see for myself. This looks like just a drive-by? How many shots were fired?"

"Twenty-five. Despite that, we think it was a single gunman. There were several people who heard the shots, but their statements are varied."

"I know how that goes. But a *single* shooter, with twenty-five rounds fired? How do you know that?"

"It's looking that way. The holes are spaced in a neat line. Not just a spray effort, not like multiple shooters going at it." She poked imaginary dots in the air from left to right. "The sheriff is over at the newspaper office. When you get the chance to run over there, he'll want to talk with you."

Dayan ran a hand through his thick thatch of curly black hair, now liberally flecked with gray. "Well, of course. But I heard Rik and Pam were hurt, so I wanted to be here. I mean, hell. *We're* the newspaper, Pam and Rik and I, not some old musty building. A few windows and some holes in Sheetrock are easily fixed." He glanced over at Estelle again. "Besides, I don't do blood well. Tell Bobby that if he gets in a swivet to talk to me, he knows where I am."

"You'll be fine."

A trace of a smile tugged at the crow's-feet at the corners of his eyes. "For years I've always kidded you guys, trying to get you to break your big news on Mondays or Tuesdays so we can scoop the metro papers. And here we go, on a Friday night." He shook his head. "Some long nights ahead just to get the paper out."

"Pam will be up and around by tomorrow, Frank."

"God, I hope so. You know…" He hesitated, looking off down the hall. "The *Register* is her life."

"I understand that. She's been with the paper for as long as I can remember. You have a jewel there."

He nodded vigorously. "I do. I do."

"Now the challenge is to figure out who you pissed off, Frank. To do this kind of damage, we've got somebody with a serious vendetta. Give some thought about that."

"Would the shooter have known that Pam and Rik were both there, working late? Did the shooter even *know* someone was in the office? Or is this just a random violence sort of thing? Some damn drive-by doofus stoned high on marijuana."

"The office lights were on…"

"They're always on," Dayan interrupted.

"I know they are, Frank. What I was going to say was that Rik would have been in clear view. Although he was in the back of the room, so maybe they didn't see him. Pam was sitting down, obscured by the window's tint line. It's possible, I suppose, that the shooter just didn't notice, caught up in the excitement of the moment. Late at night like that, he might have thought he was leaving a message for all to see come morning. Like painting with graffiti. But *unlike* graffiti, he can't linger. Even late as it was, the gunshots are going to attract attention. "

"Machine gun, you think?"

"I doubt that. Bobby would be the one to talk to, though. His first guess was a semi-auto twenty-two. The damage is pretty limited."

"Yeah," Dayan snorted. "Tell Pam and Rik that."

"Of course. And as far as that goes, it may well be lucky for them that it *was* small caliber."

Dayan frowned. "If the shooter *knew* that my guys were working late, if they *knew* Pam and Rik were there, if they could see 'em, if they were shooting at them intentionally, then it's a whole different ball game, am I right?"

"Yes. That is absolutely correct."

He waited a moment for Estelle to amplify, and when she didn't, he nodded abruptly. "I gotta get in to see the guys."

"We'll keep you posted, Frank."

"I hope so." His smile was determined as he sought to lighten the mood. "And you know…I appreciate anything you can do, especially if it's before our last deadline at Wednesday noon."

Chapter Nine

Pam Gardiner was lying flat on her back, and from the concentration of her expression, it appeared to Estelle that the newspaper editor was counting rows of ceiling tiles. Her various monitors hummed and clicked, amplified by the hushed quiet of the hospital in the middle of the night.

Her eyes flicked down past the rise of her vast body and brightened at the sight of Estelle Reyes-Guzman. "You know," she said, her voice husky, "regardless of what they say, this is not the least bit restful. I just *hate* trying to sleep on my back. But who can move with all this junk?" She lifted the IV tube in one hand and the EKG wiring in the other. "Have you had a minute to talk with Frank?"

"I did, just now out in the hall."

"He's a worrywart."

"Maybe with good cause, Pam. He's headed over to the office right now, probably after he looks in on Rik."

"Oh, my. I'm so upset about that poor boy."

"He'll be all right. The surgery went well."

"You're sure? They won't talk to me, you know." She closed her eyes. "I'm just supposed to lie here and relax and rest and… oh, my, how can I do that? I looked across the newsroom and saw him sitting there, with the blood and all…"

"He's lucky," Estelle said. "The way he was turned? The bullet hit him here," and she touched high on her left chest, "and angled off to the left, stopping just shy of his rotator cuff. They removed the bullet, patched him up, and got him flooded with antibiotics. He'll be out in a day or so."

"That's what Frank told me. But still…" She shifted position a little, grimacing with the effort. "Any leads?" Her amazing violet eyes locked on Estelle's.

"I need to go back over and talk with Bobby. We've got a BOLO for the vehicle, but without a positive ID, that's going to be a long shot. We have everyone we have out on the road. State, Border Patrol, even the Game and Fish. They'll stop any vehicle they see."

"You know, I never saw it. Maybe Rik did."

"Dark and big, like a Suburban or Expedition. We're doing our best to cover the county. Anything that moves gets a hard look."

"Good luck with that," Pam said skeptically. Her eyes narrowed, as if accusing Estelle of keeping secrets. "Your kids are home now, I heard."

Even violently removed from her news desk, Pam Gardiner was still close to the pulse of things, loath to let a good story slip by.

"Francisco, Angie, and the baby are here, for a little while."

"You think one or both will hold still for an interview? We like to follow their schedule, you know."

"I know you would, and we appreciate it. You've been wonderful. I'll twist Francisco's arm. They're working on the addition to Bill's old adobe, and that's a consuming process." She reached out and gently rocked Pam's right ankle. "I'll see what I can do."

"Before the metro papers find him. That addition that they're building to Bill's house—the music room and everything— that's really quite a story. Choosing a little town like this to settle in? My goodness. You and Francis must be so thrilled by it all."

"Absolutely."

Pam frowned with vexation. "My big-city brethren are going to hear about this business, too. I mean, shooting up a newspaper office? What is this, Syria or something? The metro news jocks will be crawling all over the place." She lifted her right hand and lightly touched her throat bandages. "Haven't had a sore throat like this since I was a kid with the strep. It's a good thing I can't sleep, though. My snoring would wake the dead."

Estelle's phone vibrated and she retrieved it from her pocket. "Let me take this."

"Of course."

"Guzman."

Captain Taber's clipped delivery wasted no time with pleasantries. "They found the truck. It's parked in the superintendent's space over at the school. At Central Office. It's his."

"It's Archer's vehicle? They're sure? Who's on it?"

"Sutherland found it. Engine's still warm, keys are in the center console."

"Is Brent sure that the superintendent isn't inside the building? Like in his office doing some late-night budget work? That's a habit of his, working when he's not going to get any interruptions."

"As a matter of fact…that's exactly where he is. He heard nothing, saw nothing. The good news is that when the deputy opened the driver's door, he saw that the inside of the vehicle is splattered with spent twenty-two shell casings. He shut it up tight."

"I'll be there in a few minutes." She rang off. "Stranger and stranger."

"I heard most of that. What I need right now is a pad and pencil."

"I'll tell the nurse to hunt one up for you."

"I just knew that after that last editorial about substitute teacher pay, Glenn would be gunning for me." She smiled grimly, her hand still touching her sore throat. "Except this all sounds like the work of someone with few or no brain cells."

"I think you're probably right."

Pam lifted an index finger, monitor wires and all. "I take this as a warning, undersheriff. A sign. From now on, expect to see a new me. A new, svelte me. A less-of-a target me." She cracked a smile. "Of course, on hospital food, it's not hard to diet."

Estelle's phone vibrated again, and she reached out and took Pam's hand. "I need to go, but I'll keep you posted. Take care of yourself."

"I have no choice. Thanks, luv."

Chapter Ten

Sheriff Torrez's phone call prompted her directly back to the scene of the shooting, adding the recovered truck's location at the high school to her list of curiosities to be explored. The superintendent's own vehicle? That could mean that the shooter most likely was still in town—and that narrowed the field of suspects down to a thousand or so.

"I'm thinkin' this is interesting." Torrez held his left index finger over the first hole in the *Posadas Register's* window.

Mr. Patience, Estelle thought. Two in the hospital, the assailant's vehicle in custody, and Torrez moved methodically, examining bullet holes as if he'd never seen one before.

Without moving his left hand, he reached to his right and placed his right index finger over the next hole. For a full minute, he stood like that, then turned to Estelle, expectant. When she said nothing, he prompted, "It's about twelve inches."

Leaving the sheriff with his fingers in place on the glass, Estelle took three steps back, looking westward down the row of riddled windowpanes. Torrez nodded and shifted his hands to the span between the second and third holes. "That's pretty close to twelve inches." He shifted again and repeated the measurement for the next set. "All the way down the line, mostly. Not much up, not much down."

"Pretty steady trigger finger," Estelle said.

"That's what I'm thinkin.' There's thirteen holes, bam, bam, bam, spaced real even. Then a space of more'n six feet with no holes. Then all the rest, just like the first. Another twelve." He jabbed the air with an index finger.

"Maybe he had to change magazines. And if he did, then he's a nimble-fingered little rodent."

"Yup." The sheriff looked both thoughtful and perturbed. "And bullet damage tells me that the shooter didn't shift the gun much. Maybe he had it resting firm on the windowsill of the vehicle. " Torrez sighed. "Other ways it could happen, I guess. But we got twenty-five bullet holes, and that's kinda an awkward number for a twenty-two rifle. Banana magazine, maybe. They can be had easy enough. Or, like you said, two magazines."

He stroked the glass near one of the holes. "A *kid* with a gun bein' that steady would surprise me. I mean, think about that. Kids playin' like they're shootin' a tommy gun? Blam, blam, blam. You'd have a mess of holes, splattered all over. *Two* shooters keepin' pace would surprise me even more. I mean, look at this." He nodded down the row of holes. "Look at that spacing. Whoever done this had some trigger discipline."

Estelle nodded, not in the least surprised by Bobby Torrez's interesting phraseology. The easiest way to jerk the taciturn sheriff's interest chains was to present him with a ballistics puzzle. "Trigger discipline."

"Yup. We'll run string from each hole to what we think is the impact point. I don't know if that's gonna tell us anything or not." He shrugged. "Maybe. Maybe not." He nodded at Linda Pasquale, who was still photo-documenting the scene. "Give her something to do."

Captain Jackie Taber appeared in the newspaper office doorway. "Enough completes or fragments to make seventeen," she announced, and held up a shallow cardboard box in which were nestled a file of plastic evidence bags. "Counting the one recovered from Rik Chang's shoulder, that makes eighteen."

"So seven to go," Torrez said. "We'll keep takin' this place apart until we got 'em all."

"You might have trouble with the last few that hit the outside of the building," Taber said. "It looks as if one or two of them skipped off."

"And maybe now from the recovered truck a collection of spent casings to go with them," Estelle said. "I'm surprised the shooters left the empties behind."

"Yup, me too. You headin' over that way?" Torrez said to Estelle. "I got Mears and Sutherland workin' that up."

"I want to talk with some neighbors," Estelle said. "We're assuming that the shooter took and returned that truck without Glenn Archer's knowing it. Someone had to see *something.*"

"Don't bet on it," Torrez muttered. "You know what I think?"

"What?"

"They took Archer's truck because it was at the school. No nosy neighbors right there. They look inside, see the keys in the console, and know they can get it started. Might even have one of those push-button remote things. They could take it, and use it, and return it, no one's the wiser. There's what, no more than half a dozen houses within shouting distance of the school's front driveway? Most of 'em in that neighborhood are older. The adobe's thick. They ain't going to hear nothing."

"You're giving the shooters credit for a lot of thinking, Bobby."

The sheriff almost smiled. "You ever seen that ship that Archer drives? It'd make a primo shooting rest. Main thing I don't like is the coincidences."

"As in…" Taber asked.

"Who's the last person we know that might give a shit about what was in the newspaper? Maybe barkin' to Hennesey about how if the story got printed, he'd lose his job and all that? Be just like him to pull a prank like this."

"Quentin has the hardware to do this?" Estelle watched the sheriff carefully as the glare from the streetlight played on the planes of his face.

"Yep." He once again gestured down the length of the building. "Good enough to make this work. I ain't real fond of coincidences."

"You want me to roust him?" Taber asked.

"He ain't goin' nowhere. Let's wait and see what Archer's truck tells us. Give him a little rope and he might hang himself."

As Estelle expected, a cavalcade of cars surrounded Glenn Archer's black Lincoln Navigator. Every door of the big SUV hung open, its rear door/tailgate lifted high. A pair of flood-lights, their cables snaking to the generator in the back of Lieutenant Tom Mears's Crew Cab Ram, provided brilliant light that cast hard shadows through the trees lining the school's front parking lot.

In enough light to earn him a tan, the superintendent of schools sat on one of the cast-iron benches bolted to con-crete pads along the bus stop. He was sitting with his head down, hands folded between his knees as Estelle approached, looking more like an eighth grader sent to the office for class-room tomfoolery than the chief executive officer of Posadas Central Schools. Dressed in dark blue sweats and running shoes, he wore a battered baseball cap with the leaping Posadas Jaguars logo.

He looked up at Estelle and offered a wan smile. "I'm never going to be able to trust this truck again. I turn my back, and it's gone, out vandalizing the village, then it sneaks home, right under my nose." His expression turned serious. "I'm hearing that Pam and young Chang were hurt."

"Yes."

"They'll be all right?"

"We hope so." She glanced at her watch. "You're working very late."

"That's when it's quiet. Or at least it *used* to be." He waved a hand at the big SUV. "And that's what makes this all the more puzzling. Although," he added with a touch of pride, "that Lincoln is so darn quiet, who's to notice? I was inside, nose buried in computer printouts when Lieutenant Mears raps on my door. I about jumped out of my skin."

"What time did you drive down here, sir?"

"Oh, I guess it was ten o'clock or so. Clare is in New Hampshire, visiting our daughter and her family, so I'm a forlorn bachelor for a few days. I couldn't sleep, and the district has a tangle or two in the proposed budget that I wanted to unsnarl. I figured I might be able to get the PILT mess with the Forest Service straightened out if I spent an all-nighter on it." He frowned when he looked at his own watch. "And here it is going on two a.m., and do I know where my car has been? No." He rubbed the reddish stubble on his chin. "I'm hoping they don't have to tear it apart. I've only owned it a couple of weeks. Still smells new."

"We'll be as gentle as we can, sir." She started to turn away, and the superintendent reached out to touch her on the shoulder.

"I hear your oldest and his wife are visiting."

"Yes. A little time to decompress."

He grinned at that. "Terrific. I got a kick out of seeing their story in *People* magazine."

"Mixed blessings," Estelle said, and let it go at that. Lieutenant Mears was waiting for her at the driver's door.

"Twenty-five," he said as the undersheriff approached. "Every one of 'em. The shooter made no effort to collect his brass. Shooting in the dark like that, he probably didn't even know where they all went."

"Prints?"

"It's going to take some doing to separate out Mr. Archer's.

I mean, all over the steering wheel, the windowsill, the center console. My suspicion right now is that the shooter wore gloves. *Maybe* wore gloves. I mean, that would make sense."

"We need the gun."

"Indeed we do." Mears straightened up and held the baggie of small .22 cartridge cases out to Estelle. "Generic high-velocity Winchester stuff. Jackie tells me they managed to recover most of the bullets, some intact."

"Most, if not all."

"Harder'n hell to get a good ballistics match with twenty-twos. Lead's soft, usually deforms easily so there's not much left to match. They recovered the one that struck Rik Chang?"

Estelle nodded. "Much deformed."

"I'd think so." He sighed. "We're about to wrap this up. The only thing hiding under the seats is a stray popcorn or two. They didn't track any crap inside." He shook his head and patted the door frame. "Nice ride, this."

"I'm sure the shooter enjoyed it. One to drive, one to shoot, you think?"

The lieutenant grimaced. "I wish I could tell you. If we knew the gun, we might be able to guess about the trajectory of the ejected empties. That *might* help tell us whether the shooter sat in front or behind the driver. Maybe. All the casings were on the right side of the vehicle, most down in front of the passenger seat, so I'm guessing the shooter was the driver. He's got the rifle resting on the windowsill, kinda like tucked under his arm, drives with his left and shoots with his right. No recoil to speak of, and a good brace for the gun. There's a couple tiny black marks where casings might have hit the roof liner, but that's pretty iffy."

"No powder burns?"

"No. If the barrel is sticking out the window, nothing is going to show. That's what leads me to believe it was a rifle, not a pistol. A gun with a barrel long enough to put the muzzle well outside the window. And most twenty-twos kick their empties out and to the right rear. A few eject straight down, but not many."

"Something," Estelle said. "There's got to be something. You can't take a truck on a joyride, fire a rifle or pistol out of it a couple dozen times, then return it—all without leaving a trace. I mean, *something*. A hair or two. Fibers from a coat. Distinctive dirt from the soles of his shoes. *Something.*"

"I'm thinking we need to impound this vehicle so we can do this right."

Estelle held up a hand as her phone vibrated. She flipped it open. "Guzman." For a long moment, she listened without comment. "Give me five minutes," she said. Then to Mears, she added, "Impound the truck. I'll be at the hospital."

Chapter Eleven

Dr. Francis Guzman touched the image, tracing a small circle with his index finger. "MRI shows significant cerebral leakage. My guess is that she's been growing that aneurysm back here in the occipital region of the brain for a long time." He pursed his lips and exhaled loudly. "The odd thing is that I don't think that the aneurysm itself is leaking, at least not where we can see. If that thing pops, she's gone, just like that." He snapped his fingers. "What I think has happened is a smaller artery hidden behind the bulk of the aneurysm itself is the culprit. It's pretty crowded plumbing in there."

"Still serious," Estelle whispered.

"Oh, absolutely it's serious as can be. As soon as we can patch together transport, she's off to Albuquerque. Dennie Holloway is the neurologist who's best at this, and he's ready to dive in." He looked over at the wall clock. "We'll be transporting in just a few minutes."

"Is she awake? Alert?"

"Heavily sedated, *Querida*." He watched his wife's face for a moment. "It's not good, something like this. At the very least, we're talking about deep brain surgery, and you know what comes with that."

"Her chances?"

Dr. Guzman shrugged. "*¿Quien sabe?* There's no putting a number to it. Had the shooting incident *not* occurred, she might have keeled over at her desk while downloading the week's recipe. Aneurysms are like that—silent killers when they finally decide to pop. The attack, her own wounds…none of that can be dismissed as minor. All of that stress contributes, especially for a woman with her health history."

"But…"

"First things first. First, she has to survive transport. Then we see what surgeons in Albuquerque say."

"We can be hopeful."

"Always that." He enveloped her in a powerful hug. "We'll do our best."

"I know you will," she said. "I don't doubt that for a minute."

They stood quietly for a moment. "You're thinking it was some juvenile delinquent on a vandalism kick, or are we looking at something else? Some revenge kind of thing?"

"Nothing fits, *Oso*. At this point, nothing fits. We have a *methodical* shooter, one who doesn't fit the profile of some young punk who just wants to spray a building because it's fun to do."

"Folks get mad at their community newspaper all the time for some imagined slight or another. Usually, they just cancel their subscription."

"Exactly." She sighed and reached up to gently tug her husband's tightly clipped beard. "Some little thing. That's all we need."

"What's Frank have to say?"

"I haven't had the chance to talk to him at any length. If he has ideas about who the trigger man is, he hasn't mentioned it to either me or Bobby. The 'why' of all this is frustrating. What good do broken windows do anyone, other than assuring a vindictive newspaper in response?"

Her husband snorted a little chuckle and shook his head. "I'm not sure vandals think much about the 'why' of things, *Querida*. I mean, they protest in the streets and burn their own cars, for Pete's sake." He looked at the clock again. "See you for dinner with the contractors? It'd be nice to have a repeat of last night."

She grimaced. "I'll try my best. Especially if we don't have to *eat* like we did last night." She pinched her husband's left biceps. "And there's *another* worry. Francisco and Angie's fingers near hammers and saws and other sharp things? I'd like to have a restraining order slapped on that project that requires them to watch from a distance."

"I think they're just watching cement harden right now. *That's* pretty safe."

"Getting fingers caught between the cement chute sections. Tripping over rebar. Choking on cement dust. I could go on."

Dr. Guzman held her face firmly between his large hands. "Concentrate on finding your shooter," he said. "And send lots of positive vibes Pam Gardiner's way. She needs 'em."

Hours later, with the newspaper editor in the hands of Albuquerque brain surgeons, and Glenn Archer's truck safely stored in the Sheriff's Department impound at the county bone-yard, Estelle returned home, shed her hardware, and crawled into bed. Sometime later—she didn't have the energy to look at the clock—she heard her husband in the shower. When she awoke again, it was to the popping of the metal roof expanding under harsh morning sun and bright light seeping around the edges of the thick curtain.

Chapter Twelve

"Well, you know, they take one little thing and blow it up into somethin' it ain't." Deputy Edwin Hennesey's expression suggested that his analysis was the final explanation of the events leading up to the strafing of the *Posadas Register* office.

Estelle relaxed back in her chair, one hand fisted under her chin. She had managed to return to the office just before the graveyard shift dispatcher left for the day, and had taken that opportunity to hear his side of the *note for news* tale.

"Who asked you to put the note on that particular report, Eddie?"

"What do you mean, 'asked me'? I don't let anybody come in here and tell me what to do with the reports and such. It ain't nobody's business but the department's."

"So you decided to mark that particular story, out of all the others?"

"'All the others?' Weren't but half a dozen in the basket at the time."

"But you marked just the one."

Hennesey pulled his face into an exaggerated grimace, and combined that with a huge shrug of the shoulders.

"Just this one," Estelle repeated patiently.

"Hey, you don't like the way I run dispatch, then you're free to make any changes you want." For the first time, Hennesey looked directly at Estelle, as if daring her to engage in a pissing contest with him.

Ignoring his obvious pique and damaged ego, she leaned forward, both hands folded on the desk calendar in front of her. It would be a simple matter to write Hennesey off, but Estelle was loath to go that route. In most instances, Edwin Hennesey was reasonably good at his job...a job that she knew full well was, ninety-eight percent of the time, one of crushing boredom. Short-staffed as the department was, Estelle had no one—no one with the required skills, anyway—waiting in the wings to move into dispatch.

"Here's the deal, Eddie. We don't know yet what direction this investigation of the *Register* shooting is headed. When the call for the medivac went out to take Pam Gardiner to Albuquerque, you handled dispatch."

"Yep."

"Then you know that Pam Gardiner has a brain aneurysm, a dangerous one. If she dies, then this isn't just an investigation into malicious vandalism. Because Pam and Rik were inside the office at the time, it's assault with a deadly weapon. If she dies, it becomes a murder investigation. A death occurs during the commission of crime..." She leaned back and spread her hands. Eddie Hennesey's eyes darted this way and that before settling again on Estelle's.

She gestured toward the nearest and most comfortable chair. "Have a seat for a minute."

"I'm good."

"If you want to stonewall this thing, that's your privilege, Deputy Hennesey. Both the sheriff and I hope you'll cooperate with us."

"Never said I wouldn't. I'm here, ain't I?"

"Then sit down and relax."

He grudgingly sat, making a show of relaxing his arms on the arms of the chair.

"Every little detail, every one, will come under scrutiny, Deputy Hennesey. The when, the why, the who...*every* one. If anywhere along the line," and she leaned forward and made a chopping motion across her desk, "there's a question, an inconsistency, a missing piece—then that's the direction we go."

Hennesey was not a stupid man, and he immediately seized upon the connection. "That's just what I'm sayin', *under*sheriff. I didn't think we were done with that particular arrest. Now you're sayin' that Quentin Torrez shot up the newspaper office because his name was in the paper?"

"Do you think that could happen? Would he do that?"

"How the hell do I know?"

"He never called you after he was ticketed? Never spoke to you about it?"

"Nope. Maybe he did with Wheeler, 'cause Wheeler was workin' day dispatch when the kid was processed through here. Maybe he bitched to Sarge about it. I don't know. He was the arresting officer."

"But you wrote the *not for news* message, not Ernie Wheeler or Sergeant Pasquale."

"Yeah, well."

With effort, Estelle kept her irritation in check. Pushed into what he might perceive as a corner, Hennesey was not about to become everybody's cooperative friend.

"How did that come to pass? What prompted you to do that?"

Hennesey took a long, deep breath to show how patient he was, then said, "I just figured that in this case, it would be better to wait and see what happened during his arraignment, that's all. I know—" Hennesey paused. "I know that there was some issue with how the arrest went down. *You* know about that, him being a three-time offender and all. I just thought it was better not to jump the gun and splash this all over the paper, without really *knowing.*"

He held up both hands. "Hey, call it what you want. Call it a favor to the sheriff's family. Whatever you want. I just thought it best to wait a little bit and see what comes down before goin' public with it."

He shifted in his chair, knocking hardware against the woodwork. "Now we've had troubles with deputies before, sitting outside bars, waitin' for patrons to come on out and drive away. 'Course they're going to be violations. 'Course they are."

Hennesey shifted position again and crossed his legs, leaning hard on his left elbow. "You might recall some of the flack with Torrez and Victor Sanchez years ago, down to the Broken Spur Saloon, back when the sheriff was just a flatfoot deputy. He'd park right across the road from the saloon in one of those two tracks, and when someone came out of the saloon, he'd nail 'em. Old Victor, him, and Bill Gastner went round and round about that.

"You look at Pasquale's report, and you'll see about the same thing. 'Course, Pasquale didn't say nothing about it to me when he put the report in the basket. But sittin' dispatch, I know what goes on. I knew where Pasquale was parked, and I know where the traffic stop took place." Hennesey shook his head in disgust. "This kid...the sheriff's nephew...you two think he's involved in shooting up the newspaper?"

"No. I'm not saying that. We have no evidence that's what happened. But think on this, deputy. Suppose it becomes clear that the attack was because of the newspaper article." She held up a hand to forestall Hennesey's response. "Just suppose. And suppose further that it comes out that you, as dispatcher and keeper of the records for that shift at the Sheriff's Department, tried to protect the assailant by keeping his name out of the paper. But somehow his name appears anyway, and the kid is pissed. He decides to leave a message, peppered all over the front of the newspaper office. Two people are seriously hurt."

Hennesey's face was an interesting mix of flushed and pale. "Yeah, yeah, I know. I'd be in a world of shit. But I wasn't *protecting* the kid. He *didn't* ask me to keep it out of the paper. And he didn't ask Ernie, far as I know. I mean, Ernie never mentioned." He rested a *mea culpa* hand on his chest. "I just did it because it seemed to me that some aspect of his case…" and he chopped the air with his hand. "Might not be just right. I was thinkin' that maybe Sarge was a little premature puttin' the report in the basket."

"Then why not just take it *out* of the basket and leave it in the sergeant's 'pending' file? Or double-check with Sergeant Pasquale if you were concerned?"

"Coulda done that."

"Yes."

"But Sergeant Pasquale himself put the report in the basket. Who am I to second-guess what he done?"

"But that's exactly what your *note for news* did, isn't it? You're deciding what's news and what isn't."

The room fell silent. She watched Hennesey's jaw muscles twitch as he examined the edge of her desk. Finally, he shrugged. "Are you bringing this Torrez kid in for questioning?"

"He's on the list, for sure. I'm giving the sheriff some time to decide what he wants to do."

"I don't see what choice he's got."

"We build a file of evidence. Then we see what our choices are. So tell me—" She relaxed back, hands folded over her stomach. "What was there about the Torrez boy's DUI arrest that bothered you? I mean other than the issue of possible entrapment."

Hennesey looked uncomfortable. "It ain't my place."

Estelle gave him a few seconds of think time, and when nothing more was forthcoming, she said, "Eddie, I appreciate your discretion. And I'm sure that Sergeant Pasquale does as well."

"Have you talked to Sarge yet?"

"No."

"You going to?"

She smiled at the dispatcher without much humor and didn't answer.

Hennesey eased forward in his chair, hands clamped on the arms as if about to push himself upright. "I'll just say this much, even though it ain't none of my business. If that kid is in any way protected from what he done, *whatever* he done, then it's going to come back and bite the sheriff right on his ass. I mean, that was Quentin's *third* arrest for DWI. You see what I mean?"

"I'm sure you'll make any concerns you might have clear to Sheriff Torrez at your first opportunity." Hennesey correctly read her glacial expression, and arose with a deferential nod. "You need me for anything else, ma'am?"

"Thanks for coming in, Deputy. We appreciate the work you do." She watched him as he left the office, the man obviously having difficulty deciding which stride to use. Bluff? Obsequious? I-showed-her? Over-casual? Angry at the world? Estelle sighed. It was always easier to talk with folks who didn't lug along a world's worth of excess baggage.

Chapter Thirteen

Linda Real Pasquale was anchored to her computer, her desk and an additional side table covered with an array of finely detailed photos. Her husband, Sergeant Thomas Pasquale, sat beside her, one arm resting across the back of her chair. Both looked up when Estelle appeared in the doorway. Linda's chubby but pretty, dark face broke into a radiant smile of greeting.

"You want pictures of bullet holes?" She held out both hands, indicating the assortment. "We got bullet holes." She lowered her voice conspiratorially. "I'm not sure why B-Cube wants a separate picture of each hole through the glass, but there we are. Whatever he wants, he gets."

Unlike Edwin Hennesey, Linda Pasquale was completely comfortable in her skin, and wonderfully adept at allowing others their own private foibles…with the possible exception of Sheriff Robert Torrez, aka "Big Bad Bobby," or "B-Cube," whom she teased without mercy. It was a tribute to her skills that the sheriff took her kidding in stride.

"They're good for comparison work, though," her husband added. "Working with the angles."

"God, you're as bad as he is," Linda laughed. "A hole is a hole when you're talking about plate-glass windows. What do you think, my boss?"

"I think you're doing marvelous work. And you're right. If the sheriff asked you for separate portraits of each bullet hole, that's what he gets. He always has a reason for what he wants." She was about to turn to leave, but added, "I'm sure the sheriff didn't ask, but I will, since you're both here. How are the twins?"

"Still entirely innocent," Linda bubbled. "Most of the time, they're about eleven on the ten-point cute scale. I'll be done here in a few minutes, and then Thomas and I will head home and pretend we're attentive parents. Tom's mama won't want to give them up, but there you are."

Her face crinkled into a frown as she pulled a set of photos sealed in plastic evidence wraps. "This, however is *not* in the least bit cute. Another inch or two to his right, and young and handsome Rik Chang would have been in deep caca." She lined up the two photos of Pam Gardiner's arm and neck wound with the portrait of Chang's punctured shoulder. "And equally ugly. They both are sooooo lucky."

"Not as lucky as they should have been," Estelle said.

"Oh, I know. And I heard that Pam was in route to UNMH with complications. Soooo sad." She looked up pleadingly at Estelle. "So if a bazillion photos of holes in glass helps to corral whoever did this, that's just fine with me."

Tom Pasquale pushed himself upright, the leather of his Sam Brown belt creaking. He towered over Estelle, and a few years of married bliss had tucked a few extra pounds here and there on his broad, burly frame. Creeping up on middle age, he still rode mountain bikes with passion and abandon, despite the resultant bruises and missing patches of skin.

"Did you need to talk to me?" he asked deferentially. "The sheriff said you might."

"My ears are soooo plugged," Linda quipped, rocking her head with a hand over each ear.

Estelle made no effort to draw Pasquale out of his wife's hearing. "I'm curious about what Quentin Torrez said to you, or to Eddie Hennesey, after you arrested him last week for his third DWI offense."

"You mean, like maybe threat-wise?"

"Like anything at all."

Pasquale's forehead wrinkled in thought, drawing his closely cropped ginger-colored hair forward.

"At first, he wanted to fight me, but I talked him out of that. He's into that kung fu stuff, but he was too drunk to make use of it. Then he didn't want to be cuffed, but I didn't give him much choice in the matter, and he became increasingly profane."

"Such language you've never heard before," Linda said. Estelle rested a hand on the young woman's shoulder. "Sorry, boss."

"Tell me about the arrest," Estelle said.

"Well, nothing special. He and one of his buds and his girl-friend came out of the Don Juan just as I was driving by. Quentin was behind the wheel of his truck, and he damn near piled into me as he pulled onto Bustos."

"So you stopped him right there."

"About a hundred yards east. Just before you get to that con-struction they got going on there. He got himself all tangled up in the traffic cones."

"Who was with him?"

"Rolando Ortega. Both of 'em were soused, although Quentin was the worst. He blew a one point six. Rolando was right on the verge with a point eight five. And Esmeralda Lucero, she was with them, riding in the little jump seat in the back. She blew clean. I don't know where they got the booze, and they wouldn't say. Maddy Lucero was embarrassed as hell."

"There were three of them, then, including the one female. Did you call in for backup?"

"Uh, no, but Captain Taber was about a minute behind me,

and she took Maddy in her unit while I took the two bozos. They were both thinkin' of their karate moves, but I cuffed 'em both and put 'em both in the back seat of my unit, then I called Stub to come pick up Quentin's truck." He shrugged. "Lots of blah, blah, blah, none of which I listened to. When we got back to the office, Hennesey keeps giving me looks like, 'well you're in trouble with the sheriff now,' but Quentin being arrested isn't exactly a new story. And I'm sure Sheriff Torrez would have chewed me a new one if I had let his nephew slide."

"And with good reason," Estelle said.

"He was goin' at it all the way back here to the office. At one point he tried to kick out a window of my unit. No luck there. Maddy blew clean, so we let her go with a ticket for not being belted in. Mears and I booked both Quentin and Rolando in, and Quentin's mouth is still yammering away. He cussed at Eddie, he cussed at me, and when the captain happened by, he cussed at her. He cussed at Ernie Wheeler. He made a mess of his fingerprint card, and we had to redo that. When the cell door clanged shut, he was blubbering that we were ruining his life, and that the whole town would be laughing at him."

"Any threats?"

"Not really. I mean nothing that we don't hear all the time. He said that he didn't want his name in the paper. That it was going to screw up his job possibilities. Said it wasn't fair, us confiscating his truck. I told him he could pick it up after his arraignment, and after he sobered up, if Judge Talbot lets him keep his license. And he said *that* wasn't fair. Then he took off on a rant that his uncle was going to fire me, fire Eddie, fire Cap, fire everybody if we didn't just let him go."

"*That* sounds like something Mr. Robert would do, all right." Linda glanced back over her shoulder at her husband.

"And all this time, what did his buddy say? Rolando?"

"Nothing. Well, a couple of times, he'd say, 'Quentin, just shut up.' Good advice that Quentin didn't take." He looked hard at Estelle. "You're thinking Quentin had a hand in the shooting at the newspaper office? I mean, when he was yelling at us, he was pretty well sauced. I figured after he sobered up and had a chance to think…"

"Ah, *think*," Linda interjected.

"We don't know yet. It's clear that Glenn Archer's Navigator was used in the incident, almost certainly without the super-intendent's knowledge. At least let's hope it was without his knowledge. That's why we put it in impound…so Lieutenant Mears can head up a really thorough investigation."

"You're bringing Quentin in for questioning?"

"Not yet. We have no more reason to suspect him of this shooting than any of our other resident punks."

"Except for his latest arrest winding up in the newspaper. He couldn't take it out on us, so maybe trashing the newspaper building was next best."

"That may be what the sheriff thinks," Estelle mused. "The *Register* includes every infraction and violation in their col-umn. It's equal opportunity publicity, whether people like it or not."

"Somebody didn't like *something*," Pasquale said.

"Or just impulse. You know how it is with kids."

"For sure I do."

"Having been one himself once upon a time," Linda observed.

"Although at nineteen," Estelle said, "Quentin Torrez isn't exactly a kid anymore. The Don Juan doesn't sell anything stronger than iced tea, so they're off the hook for illegal sales. Did you find anything in the truck?"

"Not a thing."

"So partying somewhere else, then."

"He said they were on the way to drop Maddy off at home. He didn't say from where. He'd just say, 'I plead the fifth.' They thought that was clever as hell."

"Eddie seemed to suggest that maybe the arrest was made at

the Broken Spur, or some other watering hole. That you were lying in wait."

"Uh, no. He's about thirty miles off in that wild-hare guess. Quentin was drinkin' at his girlfriend's house, then maybe some more at the Don Juan, is what makes sense to me. Are you going to talk to Quentin?"

"Yes. The sheriff suggested that I do. And Maddy. And Rolando, for that matter."

"Yeah, well," and Pasquale laughed. "The sheriff would be just as happy to whup his nephew upside the head as talk to him. Not too many warm fuzzies between those two."

"But there's no reason to suspect that Quentin had anything to do with the newspaper assault. Other than the tiff, if there was one, over the arrest publicity. There's no reason to be turning the young man's world upside down. Unless."

"Unless," Pasquale nodded.

The computer's printer pushed out an image, and Linda slipped the print into a labeled glassine envelope and added it to the pile.

"Twenty-five," she announced with satisfaction. She tapped the pile into order. "Cap wanted these. She's working up the schematic for the shooting site."

Captain Jackie Taber's fine art skills would make sense of all the measurements, and with added computer graphics it would be the next best thing to having a video of the episode from start to finish. It was a start, Estelle knew, but nothing in the evidence pile hinted about whose finger had been on the trigger.

Chapter Fourteen

"Hey." Sheriff Robert Torrez rapped a knuckle on the roof of Estelle's car as she pulled the Charger to a halt by the department fuel island. He waited until she'd shut down and ducked out of the car. "Got a minute?"

"Of course."

"When you're caught up here, stop by my office. Got something to show you." Nothing in his tone revealed excitement, confusion, or anxiety. "And we got somebody to talk to." He walked off without waiting for a reply.

In a few minutes, with the gas tank filled and her log sheet caught up, she parked in the reserved spot and went inside. She skirted dispatch and continued down the hall to the sheriff's office, a small room that made it easy to imagine the stark, metallic and concrete, uninviting offices of the lower-echelon military. Even the sheriff's desk was a metallic gray cast-off. Gray filing cabinets, two metal folding chairs, and a map rack served as his decorations, along with a huge, laminated county map compliments of the assessor, similar to the one in Estelle's office.

Incongruously, the only nonutilitarian decoration was a large framed photo of Gayle Sedillos Torrez and the couple's young son, Gabe—a carefully posed portrait taken by the department photographer, Linda Pasquale. The portrait had played to the beautiful Gayle's strongest features—vibrant black hair so long that it flowed over her shoulders and disappeared down her back, the shadows of her elegant cheekbones in high relief, and most startling of all, the bottomless wells of her dark brown eyes drinking in the innocent face of her three year-old son as he snuggled on her lap.

The photo, mounted professionally with a satin black frame and dark gray matting, stood beside one of the teddy bears from the same batch that rode in most of the department's patrol units. One of the bear's paws rested lightly on the edge of the picture frame as if standing guard. No one else would have expected such a subtle display of whimsy from Robert Torrez, but Estelle was quietly amused at the various mellow spots that surfaced in the man's character now and then.

"I was thinkin' to find Quentin and talk with him," Torrez said by way of greeting. "You want to come along?"

Estelle settled into one of the metal chairs. "That's probably a good idea."

The sheriff opened a folder near his left elbow and drew out a plastic evidence bag. "From Archer's truck." He handed it to Estelle without further explanation.

Holding the bag so she could stretch it out against the light, Estelle could see a couple of heavy, black hairs.

"Five of 'em in there. All from around the driver's seat headrest."

"Without bothering with a microscope or a lab opinion, we can eliminate some names. Glenn Archer has what's left of a short buzz cut, now a nice uniform gray. His wife has a pixie cut, dyed blond."

"And my nephew's is black." Torrez paused. "So is his girlfriend's."

"Maddy?"

"Yup."

Estelle laid the evidence bag on Torrez's desk and leaned forward so she could rest both elbows on the desk edge, resting her chin in her hands. She dropped her voice. "Lots of people have black hair in this part of the world, Bobby."

"Yup."

"But?"

"Shooter with black hair, shootin' from the driver's seat."

Both of them fell silent. "On the basis of black hair you want to go after your nephew? That puts him in a club with about half the people we arrest...including you and me, my friend. Or go after him because he shot off his mouth when he was half-lit after his arrest? That's standard, too. They're always right, we're always wrong."

She shrugged. "No one saw him in the area. No one saw him drive by in that lowrider Chevy truck of his, and no one has reported seeing him take Glenn Archer's fancy new rig. No one ran NAA tests to see if he fired a gun recently, although considering your nephew's habits, he'd flunk that test just about any day of the week. As far as we know, he doesn't have a personal grudge against the *Register* or the folks who work there.

"So..." She straightened up a little and spread her hands out. "What do we have? Not much. We can tie things up for weeks with a DNA analysis of the hairs found...maybe."

"How's it going to hurt to talk to the kid?"

Estelle looked at the sheriff for a long moment. "Your relationship with that particular nephew isn't the best, Bobby. To harass him without probable cause isn't going to help that relationship any."

"I ain't worried about that."

"But if he's innocent, you should be. We need to be on firm footing."

"Christ, now you sound like my mother."

"I take that as a compliment."

Torrez huffed something that might have been a laugh. "You going along when we talk to Quentin might stop some of the tongues from waggin."

"What, from thinking you're likely to cut your nephew some slack? What they're more apt to think—and not that it matters what anybody thinks, Bobby—is that you're apt to be a whole lot tougher on Quentin than you might be otherwise."

"We got two people shot. It ain't no time to cut anybody no slack." He looked hard at her. "So you should go. Yeah, we don't got a whole truckload of evidence. Not yet, we don't. So the thing to do is stir the pot a little. And if the kid don't like it, tough shit."

"I'll ride out with you, sure."

The sheriff opened the folder again, laid the evidence envelope containing the hair sample inside, and drew out a single sheet that he passed across the desk. "Not a lot there." Estelle glanced down the inventory of evidence found in Superintendent Glenn Archer's Navigator.

"Every one," she mused, reading the note that listed twenty-five empty twenty-two caliber shell casings. "Now why didn't they scrounge those up, rather than leaving them behind?"

"Dumb shits."

"But your nephew isn't dumb, Robert."

"No, he ain't, but he ain't got the common sense God gave a toad, neither."

"Middle of the night like that, maybe they just didn't think about the casings. They got in a hurry...afraid to keep the Navigator too long for their harebrained stunt, afraid to linger around the school, afraid that Archer might come out and see his truck gone and call the cops. Or maybe they thought that there wasn't much we could do with twenty-two casings. They're small, hard to hang onto, and won't provide much surface for prints."

She scanned on down the miserably brief list. "A few strands of black hair from the headrest. Some gravel on the floor mat that matches what's in the school's parking lot, and could just as easily have been tracked into the vehicle by its owner. But…" She stopped and looked across at the sheriff. "…no latents other than Glenn and his wife."

"Gloves," Torrez said. "Maybe smart enough to do that."

She handed the inventory list back. "We don't have much."

"Nope."

"Quentin would be at work now."

"He ain't. He was workin' at Leland's Auto Repair. That didn't last long before he was shit-canned."

"He was fired?"

"Yep. Got mouthy with a customer."

"When did this happen?"

"Same day Pasquale arrested him for DUI. Celebratin', I guess. He mouthed off to this guy, then he mouthed off to Pasquale and anyone else who would listen. He's what we got, and we need to follow it along a little."

As they walked outside, the sheriff gestured toward his truck, parked in a far corner of the department parking lot. "Let's take mine," Torrez said, and Estelle groaned a little at that suggestion. Torrez actually smiled. "Hey, it's a good truck. I coulda been driving the one your son sold me." The thought of riding through town in the convertible troop carrier—a whim purchase by Francisco that turned into a whim gift for the sheriff—made her groan again.

His aging Chevrolet was what he referred to as his "undercover unit," even though anyone in Posadas County who'd been the least bit awake knew that the 1970 three-quarter ton was his. A combination of primer gray, flat black, and traces of the original Forest Service green offered a certain panache.

Estelle climbed up on the running board and then inside. Slung under the heater controls was a police radio, the microphone hung from the lip of the coin-choked ashtray. An archaeologist would have had a good time sorting through the various levels of litter on the floor, the dashboard, and on and under the seat. An Ithaca pump shotgun nestled in the rear window gun rack.

"Your side don't have one," Torrez said when he saw Estelle searching for the seat belt.

The big V-8 fired up promptly, a waft of oil fumes making their way through the firewall. Estelle reached for the window crank, and saw only a serrated stub projecting from the door. "Your side don't work." Torrez smiled again. "Makes for better security. And we ain't goin' that far."

"That far" was a small, older mobile home on North McArthur just before the intersection with County Road 19. One of three rental units, the trailer slumped among the surrounding tumbleweeds that were packed tightly enough to provide trailer skirting of sorts.

"He moved out of his mom's place about a year ago." Torrez maneuvered his truck into the narrow driveway. "Turned eighteen and moves out." The sheriff's sister, Quentin's mother Mariana, was the second youngest of the vast Torrez brood, earning something of a family reputation by having Quentin when she was only fifteen. Tight-lipped for a teenager, Mariana had never revealed who the father might be—and had never married, either him or anyone else.

The door of the trailer opened, and Quentin appeared, wearing nothing but a towel wrapped around his middle. "I just stepped out of the shower." He pushed a thatch of wet, black hair off his forehead. The family gene pool was evident—broad through the shoulders like his Uncle Robert, still trim at the waist, and at six feet three in his bare feet, just an inch shy of his uncle. Fate had not cared that Quentin Torrez was movie star handsome, articulate, and intelligent. His life had not been an easy one, despite the head start his good looks had given him. Estelle knew that the boy had a quick temper, and loved a good fight almost as much as he loved the various controlled substances with which he had experimented.

"Yeah, well, go get dressed," Torrez replied.

"Madame Undersheriff, how are you doing?" Quentin's smile was bright, white, and just a little seductive, Estelle thought, his gaze drifting down her figure all the way to her shoes. Without waiting for an answer, he added, "Just give me a minute."

He went back inside without inviting them in, not bothering to wait until he was completely out of sight before whipping off the towel. In less than two minutes he returned, wearing old sneakers without socks, veteran jeans, and a T-shirt with a clever three-dimensional rendering of a snarling pit bull, the graphics making the animal appear as if he were vaulting out of Quentin's body.

Estelle's dealing with Quentin Torrez had been infrequent, and she noted that the nineteen-year-old was growing into a bruiser. Still, he wasn't a dullard. Even drunk, he'd had the self-control not to take on Sergeant Pasquale.

"You guys want some coffee or something? I can make some."

"Nope."

"I mean, it's no trouble."

"Nope." Sheriff Torrez reached out and tweaked the pit bull's nose. "Cute."

"Yeah." Quentin took a half step back and smoothed the pinched fabric against his chest. "Maddy gave it to me. Kinda gross, but I like it. You oughta get a little one for Gabe."

"Don't think so," the sheriff said. "Look, do you still got that twenty-two rifle you used to have? That Ruger bunny buster I gave you?"

Estelle looked sharply at the sheriff. This was the first mention of what was on his mind—fueling the suspicion that placed his nephew at the newspaper shooting.

Quentin slid his hands into his back pockets. "'Course I got it." He nodded toward the house. "It's in the house now, thanks to you guys takin' my truck."

"Get it for me."

"What, you lose your own?"

Torrez balled his right fist and with no wind-up jabbed the young man square in the pit bull with the flat of his knuckles, his hand instantly recoiling back and his index finger becoming an aggressive pointer inches from Quentin's nose.

"Hey." Quentin managed an engaging smile at the same time. "Don't be doing that, now." He rubbed the spot on his chest.

"I want to see that gun." He took Quentin by the arm, but the young man resisted, still smiling. "Sure. And speakin' of that, when am I going to get my wheels back? I mean, what do they expect me to do, ride my bike to work?"

"I heard you ain't workin.' That the garage fired your sorry ass."

For a long moment, Quentin regarded his uncle, jaw muscles working as he considered his choices. Then he glanced at Estelle and his eyebrows knit together as if to ask, "Is this guy with you?"

He thrust his hands back in his hip pockets. Estelle suspected that the young man, faced by his angry, intimidating uncle, was making more of an effort to rein himself in than he would with anyone else. He turned a little bit and smiled first at Estelle and then at his uncle. "What is it you two actually want with me?"

"I want to look at that twenty-two, is what I want."

"I got a right to have it, as you well know, since you're the one who gave it to me. I mean it's just a damn twenty-two."

"Didn't say you couldn't have it. What were you doin' Friday night?" Torrez snapped.

Quentin looked puzzled as he turned back. "You mean just yesterday?"

"Yup."

The young man turned again to look toward his trailer. "Couple beers, stayed in and watched television. Had a fight with my girl, but she won't stay mad at me long." He grinned with self-confidence.

Sheriff Torrez regarded his nephew for a long moment. "You going to invite us in?"

Quentin started to nod, started to say something, but thought better of it. He made no move toward the small three-step stoop. "Are you asking as my Uncle Bobby, or as Sheriff Torrez? 'Cause if it's as the sheriff, you can come in when you got a warrant." Light dawned behind his dark eyes. "You're thinking I had something to do with that shooting at the newspaper office on Friday?"

"The thought crossed my mind. You got the gun, and I *know* you got the skills."

"Yeah, well, you taught me good. But sorry to disappoint. I didn't. I don't read that rag, and I don't give a shit what they print. They screwed me out of a job, but what the hell. There's others."

"You spent enough time shooting off your mouth about what you were going to do if your arrest ended up in the newspaper."

"Yeah, well."

"Yeah, well, what?"

"That was the beer talkin'. You know I've had some trouble that way."

"And still do."

Quentin flushed with anger. His hands pushed hard into his back pockets. "Nobody's got a perfect life around this town."

"You don't work at it much," the sheriff said.

"We don't need to come in, Quentin," Estelle said. "But if you let us check that rifle, it relieves a lot of the suspicion."

"How long is *that* going to be locked up in your evidence room? If you get your hands on it, I mean."

"A hell of a lot longer if you force us to bother with a warrant," Torrez snapped.

"Yeah, well." He shrugged with resignation. "Hell, you gave it to me, so I guess you can have it back. Just a minute." He went back inside, giving the dilapidated door an extra nudge with his foot.

"You gave it to him?" Estelle asked.

"Yup. Sixteenth birthday. He was all hot to hunt back then."

The young man returned with a plastic rifle case, swung it horizontal and rested it on the hood of his uncle's truck. He popped the latches, but paused with both hands resting on the case.

"You promise I'll get this back?"

"Don't promise nothing," Torrez said.

Quentin shook his head in disgust. "And I don't get my truck, either. You're something else, Uncle Bobby."

"Tune up that bike, Quent," Torrez said. "You went down for the third time, so it might be a while." He started to turn away, then stopped. "What ammo was you usin'?"

"What do you mean by that? I wasn't. Last time I went shooting was I don't know when. I guess it was a couple of weeks ago. Me and Rolly went to that prairie dog town over by McInerney's gravel pit. North of there."

"With a twenty-two?"

"Sure. Why not? It's not like we were shooting at five hundred yards or something. You can get close out there."

"What ammo?"

Quentin held his hands cupped to indicate a box the size of a softball. "That bulk Remington stuff. Used to be cheap." He looked philosophical. "Used to be. What's left of the box is in the case there. That and the magazines."

"And that's all you got, what's in here?"

"Yes."

"You sure?"

"I'm sure."

"Quentin, Maddy's not home now?" Estelle asked. "I mean, not *here*?"

"She went off to work." He grinned. "Went off *mad* to work."

"Up at *NightZone*?"

Quentin nodded. "She got a job in the restaurant." He turned and extended a hand to the west. "She loves ridin' that train. They got one that runs back here just after midnight, when she's finished her shift. Then she rides her motorbike home from the airport terminal. In this good weather, that works just fine."

"She's still staying with her parents?"

"Not no more. She's got that little apartment, over by the school?" He paused and a slow grin—a grin of embarrassment, Estelle thought—touched his face. "That's what we were fighting about. I want her to move in here, she don't want no part of it." He turned and regarded the modest, aging trailer. "Not good enough for her, I guess."

He made a face. "That's the trouble with workin' topside. Fancy-schmancy place like that, maybe she don't want to come home to this. She likes that little apartment of hers better. But, hey, whatever floats her boat, right?"

"Maybe it'll work out, Quentin," Estelle said gently.

"Yeah, well. I *thought* I had me a job workin' on the train as an apprentice, sort of. They were all eager, until that business came out in the paper. That killed that." He snapped his fingers. "Went from 'yes' to 'no' just like that, overnight."

Torrez grunted something incomprehensible and popped the latches on the rifle case. He stood silently for a moment, staring at the rifle. Finally, without turning his head, he said to Quentin, "What the hell's this?"

"That would be my rifle, Sheriff."

"This ain't the one I gave you."

"Well, it is. I've done a lot of work to it. I always wanted one of those thumb-hole stocks, so I made one. I bought one of those ninety percent finished ones on the internet, and I'm about to finish it. Couple more coats of oil, and it'll be ready. That and the heavy barrel make a nice set-up."

Estelle could see that Torrez didn't believe his nephew, but the sheriff huffed something without pursuing the matter and snapped the rifle case closed, and then slid it off the hood of the truck. As the sheriff stowed the case in the truck, Quentin extended a hand to Estelle. "Thanks for comin' by with him," he said quietly. "Somebody needs to buy him some happy pills."

"If you think of something we should know, will you give me a call?"

"Sure. Don't know what that might be, but sure." He stood on the stoop of the trailer and watched them back out of the narrow driveway.

"Tough times for that young man," Estelle observed, but Torrez didn't reply.

Chapter Fifteen

Late afternoon sun glinted off the silver finish of the propane-electric locomotive as it backed along the platform that marked the eastern terminus of its run. Its four cars carried a fair assortment of tourists, as well as several day-shift *NightZone* employees coming home at the end of the day.

Estelle waited in the shade of the platform's portico. To her left, a small gaggle of senior citizens gathered, lugging cameras and binoculars—and at least half of them glued to their phones, either stroking the screens or engaged in dialogue with someone maybe half a continent away.

In a moment, Hank Quintana appeared and made his way carefully down from the locomotive. As he stepped off onto the platform, he consulted his watch, then looked up and grinned at Estelle.

"I got about five minutes, young lady," he announced, and thrust out his hand. A short, powerfully built man, he wore the "uniform" that tourists might expect: clean bib overalls, dark blue denim shirt with the *NightZone* logo on the left breast, and a striped engineer's cap topping his bald head. "It seems like every day, our passenger manifest grows just a little." He glanced down the train's length. "Walk with me?"

"Sure."

His attention never left the locomotive and its train of four cars. "Don't ask me how," he said, "but last week we had a coyote caught up in one of Sadie's axles." He reached out a hand and patted the passenger car, third in line. "This is Sadie. Kind of a silly name for a railroad car." He shrugged. "But that's what the boss wants."

He stepped back away from the track, pointing at each car in turn as he recited the names. "Susie, Bea, Sadie, and Henri. Cute, huh? Bernard and Hortense are over in the barn."

"Very cute. And Bernard?"

"Yep. I'm told the car was named after a cousin of Mr. Waddell's mother."

"And Hortense? That's another old-fashioned name."

"Yep. Anyway, tell me how a coyote manages getting caught up like that. All mangled up, and took us a while to clean the mess. I mean, we don't exactly go careening down the tracks with this rig." He looked back at Estelle as if expecting an answer. "Apparently that dog was not from the fastest part of the gene pool. Anyway, yak, yak, yak. You said you needed to talk to me."

"Yes, sir. I understand that Quentin Torrez applied for a job with you. Is that correct?"

Hank Quintana stopped and turned to face Estelle, his attention finally drawn away from the cars and their couplings, brake lines, and truck mechanics. "He did apply. And I was all set to recommend to Mr. Waddell that we take him on. He's big, strong, agile, and smart." He grimaced and shook his head. "Well, in *some* ways he's smart. In others…" He shrugged. "Dumb as a post. He drinks like a damn fish. His application never mentioned his interesting history with the law, but one of my people saw the clipping in the *Register.* Third arrest for DWI. Is he going to see some jail time?"

"Not likely."

"Well…that's between him and our lenient judges, I guess.

But on this rig? We can't be running that kind of risk. Every member of the crew takes random urine samples, and we pay attention to the old pilot's adage, 'eight hours between bottle and throttle.' That goes from the chief engineer," and he smiled tightly as he rested a hand on his chest, "to any of our part-timers in customer service. That's one of my headaches. I guess you would know better 'n most how hard it is to find employees who stay clean?"

"Yes, I do." She knew that if she spooled down through the entire roster of the Sheriff's Department employees, there would be at least one who could keep Quentin Torrez good company, sharing the bottle. "What position had Quentin applied for?"

"On his application, he wrote down, 'Any shift, any position.' I liked that. Shows he knows he's getting in down on the ground floor. But he said to me that he'd like to be an engineer someday. See, I like that, too. Young fellow wants in on the job early, wants to work his way up. Hey, we got us enough old geezers like me on board. We *need* some young blood. But like I said, this day and age, it's hard. The drugs, the booze." He shook his head. "We got the same problem the trucking companies do with this young crop. Damn shame, too. I was ready to hand him a job when that article in the paper came out." He looked hard at Estelle. "Turns out that's not the first time, either. So he lied on his application on top of everything else. You can imagine the shit we'd be in if we hired him on, and then something happened. Drunk or stoned on the job or something."

"Yes, sir."

His inspection reached the final car, and he stepped back and wiped imaginary grease from his hands. "Sweet rig, this. She don't have the power that a proper diesel-electric would have, but sure enough plenty for the light loads we run. No big grades, things like that."

"How many crew total?"

He ticked them off on his fingers. "Engineer, fireman—that's

more a historic title than a factual one, as I'm sure you know—
brakeman, conductor, and depending on the run, a steward or
two. Don't need a crowd, but you know what makes it hard?" He
didn't wait for Estelle's answer. "The hours. Mr. Waddell wants
us to run anytime there's folks that want to come or go. We try
to keep a strict schedule, but nighttime is big for us. And there
are extra runs—sometimes we don't get much notice."

"You can't be the only engineer, then."

"There's two of everybody, just about." He held up both
hands. "Richard Wells works three days a week, Monday on to
Wednesdays. I take the weekends."

"What was Quentin's reaction when you broke the news to
him?"

Quintana grimaced. "Oh, a few choice words that I'm not
going to repeat. But he was pissed. I mean, I could tell that he
really wanted that job with us. And like I said, a shame. He's personable, would have been good with the public, as long as you
don't step on his toes."

"Maybe so." Estelle didn't remind Quintana that Quentin
Torrez had been fired from a garage job for mouthing off to
a customer—and whether it was the alcohol speaking or a
moment of inherited rudeness didn't matter.

The engineer thrust out his hand, and his grip was warm
and just shy of crushing. "Did he get himself mixed up in that
deal the other night? Over at the newspaper office? Damnedest
thing I ever heard."

"We don't know yet who's responsible, sir."

He grinned without much humor. "Yet."

"Yes, sir."

"That sheriff of yours has a little pit bull in him, doesn't he?"
Estelle wondered if Quentin had worn his dog shirt to his job
interview.

"That's a good way to put it, sir."

"Best of luck to you. Ride with us when you get the chance."

"Thank you. I have, and I will."

The train was, at best, sedate. With three stops to drop off and pick up hikers and bird-watchers, it finally hove into view fifteen minutes after Estelle had arrived and found a viewing spot on one of the overlooks behind the *NightZone* auditorium. The train snaked through the trees and around picturesque outcroppings, looking like a large worm prowling the prairie.

Estelle watched it sigh to a stop at the terminal behind the parking lot. Twelve passengers got off, seven got on. A cheap tour bus or van would have delivered tourists for a hundredth the price of operating the locomotive…maybe even less than that. But Miles Waddell was right: What was exciting about a tour bus? During the train's run, only briefly was it ever within view of a highway, giving the excited passengers the idea that they were out in the middle of the western wilderness.

She turned away and headed for the restaurant, the spectacular wing on the north side of the auditorium/planetarium. The heavily tinted doors slid open silently, and the tiniest aisle lights marked the path toward the maître d's desk. A handsome woman, dressed entirely in a blue so deep and rich it mirrored what might be expected in outer space, greeted Estelle.

"Well, how delightful to see you," Carmine Quintana said. "Business or pleasure?" She hooked an errant strand of silver hair behind her ear and looked at Estelle expectantly.

"Some of both, I think. I just spoke with Hank a little bit ago, just before the last run with the train."

"Isn't that thing just so marvelous? Hank just loves every nut and bolt."

"Yes, it is. Is there someplace where we might talk for just a few minutes?"

"Most certainly. How about a cup of coffee to perk things up?"

"No, thank you."

"Water? Tea? Wine?"

"No, really."

"Then let's slip into my office. It's quiet this time of day, and if we have guests, Maddy can take care of them." She glanced at the faint, almost ghostly face of the clock that seemed to hang suspended, like a silver moon, from the rich tapestry of the wall.

The first door to the right led to three rooms, one of which was Carmine Quintana's office. She closed the solid door and touched a rheostat. "Tell me when you're comfortable," she explained. "We get used to living in the dark, but many people are uneasy...at least at first." She turned the rheostat until Estelle could see the defined contours of the woman's face.

"That's fine." Without windows, even with the high-tech lighting, the room seemed claustrophobic.

"Please...have a seat." The furniture was curiously utilitarian in appearance—stout, but with heavily rounded corners. Estelle settled into the padded leather that was anything but utilitarian. "Now then, what can I do for you?"

"Esmeralda Lucero." Estelle nodded toward the door. "Maddy, I think she goes by."

"Oh, what a doll," Carmine said eagerly. "She's been with us for just a month, but my, how she's come along. Just a delight." She looked concerned. "I hope there's no problem."

"I just need to speak with her for a moment or two."

Carmine looked at her watch. "She comes in at five, and as far as I know, she always rides the train in from Posadas. So..." She stopped abruptly at the sound of a burst of feminine laughter from the restaurant. "She's here now. I recognize the voice." Rising quickly, Carmine reached for the door. "You'd like to see her now?"

"If I might."

"Certainly. One moment." She slipped through the door, closing it behind her. Estelle turned in her chair, surveying the office. With only one heavily shuttered window, the room could have felt stuffy, but the plethora of space art—photos both large and small, dominated by an enormous portrait of Saturn—gave the impression that the room's occupants were floating in space. On the wall opposite Saturn was the famous print of Earthrise, showing the home planet just appearing over the lunar horizon.

Carmine Quintana's desk was home port for a fleet of silver framed photographs, all of them a younger generation of relatives, along with a single portrait of engineer Hank Quintana, standing with one hand affectionately on the *NightZone* locomotive's broad flank.

Estelle turned back as the door opened.

"Maddy, this is Undersheriff Estelle Reyes-Guzman. She would like a few minutes of your time."

Esmeralda Lucero was indeed a beauty, with jet-black hair wrapped into a tight bun secured with a simple silver and turquoise clasp. Her widely set eyes were so dark that her pupils were invisible. She offered up a smile that struck Estelle as a little too nervous, and her hands fluttered, smoothing imaginary wrinkles in her black skirt.

Estelle smiled warmly, trying to put the girl at ease. "Do you have a few minutes?"

"Sure. I mean, I guess." Maddy glanced at Carmine, who nodded her assurance.

"You two make yourselves comfortable. I'll be out on the floor if I'm needed."

"Carmine, thank you." Estelle gestured toward one of the leather chairs, and Esmeralda sat down on the very front edge of the cushion, as if poised to flee. "This is an incredible place, isn't it?" Estelle said.

"Yes, ma'am."

"Weren't you with the telephone company before coming here?"

"Yes, ma'am." The girl squirmed, then settled a little as her nerves composed. She folded her hands in her lap. "I worked in customer service and billing."

"And now you're getting used to working in the dark." Estelle offered a warm smile. "That's a big change."

"You know, I thought at first it would be hard to get used to, but it's really not. I guess the eyes get adjusted. And..." she leaned forward conspiratorially, "the tips are just *great*. I mean, usually."

"I'm happy for you." Elbow on the chair arm, Estelle rested her chin on her left fist, regarding the girl. "How long have you known Quentin Torrez?"

"Quentin?"

Estelle nodded.

"Well, just forever. I mean, we went to school together since, like first grade?"

"You see each other socially now?"

"Sure. Sometimes. I..."

Estelle remained silent, watching the parade of emotions flow across the girl's face.

"I was hoping that he'd get on with this place. I mean, I know that he applied to work with the train, and that'd be good for him. But then he screwed up and got arrested." She shrugged helplessly, and glanced quickly at Estelle before dropping her gaze. "And he just lost his other job with Leland's Auto. I mean, he has a temper, but still." She looked up quickly. "Is he in trouble again?"

"When was the last time you spoke with him?"

"This past week, I saw him. I mean, it's hard to keep track. We went out Monday night, I know that. And..." She hesitated, unsure of how to proceed. "We had a fight." The girl took a deep breath. "About his drinking. I mean, it's like he can't just have a beer or two. He has to keep on until he's wasted. And he won't quit driving when he's like that."

"Was that when you, Quent and Rolly were out? When you were stopped by Deputy Pasquale?"

Maddy puffed out her cheeks, and her eyes shifted to Estelle briefly, as if trying to decide whether to tell a believable yarn. "Yes."

"Where had you guys been?"

She shrugged. "Just hanging out."

"Were you with him later in the week? "

Esmeralda drew in a sharp breath. "Is this about that newspaper deal? I *heard* about that. Somebody shot up the newspaper office? I mean, like *riddled* the place. A couple people were hurt? Do you think Quentin had something to do with that?"

"Do you think so?"

"He *couldn't.*"

"Even when he's been drinking too much?"

Esmeralda shook her head vehemently. "He just wouldn't. Couldn't." Her eyes started to tear. "I know we argue all the time, but Quentin is really a good guy, Sheriff. He would never do something like that...a stupid drive-by? That would be so... so completely unlike him. I mean, when Quentin gets mad, he'll get right in your face. There's nothing sneaky about him. He wouldn't just drive by like some gangster."

"He's gotten in your face a time or two?"

"Sure."

"What sets him off, usually?"

Maddy fell silent, but then finally said, "He gets all jealous way too easy."

"Does he have reason to be jealous, Esmeralda?"

"No. But I know that he doesn't like me working here. I mean, I *have* to be nice with people here, with customers. I can't be all standoffish and stuff. And please...call me Maddy."

"All right. But Quentin doesn't understand that? That your job requires some hospitality?"

Maddy hunched her shoulders. "He thinks I'm surrounded by all kinds of people hitting on me. That's ridiculous. And 'cause I work five nights a week, and he doesn't like *that*. And it just goes on and on. We had a big fight this week 'cause I wouldn't live with him in that ratty little trailer of his."

"But you have your own apartment now."

"My folks helped me with that."

She lifted a hand. "And that's another thing Quent and I fought about. He wants to help me choose where to live. I mean, what's with that? It's *my* apartment, so why wouldn't I make that decision?"

"It sounds as if Quentin is a little bit more controlling than you'd like, Maddy."

"Yeah, I guess that's what it is. That's kind of a guy thing, is what I think." She smiled ruefully. "And I don't control so good." She laughed and dabbed at one eye. "I think he wants me wrapped around his little finger. And maybe…maybe I'm the one who wants to do the wrapping."

"Boys are complicated, no?"

"Is *that* ever right."

"What hours do you work here, then?"

"Tuesday through Saturday, from four to midnight, unless there's a special early morning star show. Then I shift around and sometimes, if there are lots of people, I work all night. The kitchen has this special pre-dawn menu, they call it. It sounds awkward, but Mr. Waddell and Carmine are *really* great people to work for.

"They know the hours are killers, and they work hard to make it up to us. You know, there are days now and then when hardly anyone comes up here. We might serve some meals to staff, but otherwise, the place is empty. We still draw our full pay, though. And like I said, when there *are* tourists, the tips are humongous."

"You're enjoying the challenge, aren't you?"

"Yes, ma'am. I'm studying hard to get better at it."

"Studying what?"

"Oh, astronomy, and all that. See, Mr. Waddell expects us to be able to answer questions that tourists might have. I mean, he doesn't want us to be all know-it-alls, because lots of the visitors are astronomers themselves. Mr. Waddell says that's the art… to know when to let a tourist educate *us*. To know when to let *them* talk and be all excited. He talks about that all the time in our training sessions. How to be what he likes to call a 'human sponge.' And I know he's right. I mean, imagine a tourist asks me a simple question, and I'm all 'Well, duh, I don't know…'"

"Tell me about a typical shift…this past Wednesday, for instance."

For the first time, Estelle saw a hint of uncertainty in the girl's eyes, a little dodge right to left. "Wednesday?"

"Sure. Wednesday, Thursday, Friday…just a typical day."

"Wednesday was a usual day," Maddy said. "Had a good dinner hour with a group from Japan. There were twelve of them, and they're fun, 'cause it seems like they just enjoy everything so much. They finished dinner about eight thirty, and went over to the planetarium.

"Then Mr. Waddell himself came in with five other guys. They looked like they could be businessmen—I guess that's what they were. They were busy talking, not bubbling about all the attractions or the star show." She held up a hand. "See, that's what I mean. That's a good time for the waitstaff to do our best to blend in with the furniture."

"And that was it for the evening?"

"Oh, gosh no. But other than those two groups, it was just sort of a constant trickle of singles and couples, mostly."

"And you finally finished by when?"

"Midnight, if I'm lucky. When things are really slow, I can use the staff lounge if I want. But I don't do naps very well. I always wake up feeling like somebody slugged me. Sometimes, Quentin comes up and keeps me company. See, that's why he was hoping for a job with the train, or maybe the tramway. A lot of his friends work here now, and they like to hang out."

"In a manner of speaking," Estelle said.

"Well, yeah. I mean, they all went to school together."

"'They' being..."

"Well, you know. Efrin, Rolando, Rafael...who else. Oh, Efrin is trying to go out with Stacy Jensen. She's working over at the planetarium."

Estelle knew Rafael Gonzales at the gate, and Efrin Garcia, the mural artist, as well as Stacy Jensen, whose mother Amelda Jensen worked as a media specialist at the high school. "All local crew," Estelle said. "And Rolando? How about him?"

Maddy lowered her voice to just above a whisper. "Rolando Ortega? He's the hunk who works with the maintenance crew. He's maybe a year or two older? His dad worked for Mr. Waddell's ranch, before all this."

"Ah. *That* Rolando." Estelle remembered Rolando Ortega as a skinny little twerp whose sole passion in life appeared to be rodeos, until a cranky bull broke one too many of his bones and changed the boy's mind.

When Miles Waddell had promised to hire locally as much as possible, he'd kept his word—and it seemed as if he favored bringing lost souls on board. Efrin Garcia's older brother was in prison on a murder charge, and Efrin himself had narrowly avoided going down as an accessory, thanks to a skilled defense attorney.

Rolando, the alleged hunk, had been a young rodeo has-been without much of a future.

Rafael Gonzales, working day shifts at the gate, had tried one semester of college, then returned home where little opportunity was awaiting him—until Miles Waddell realized his fantastic dream. Now the kid was studying Japanese.

Even Maddy Lucero had wandered a bit before deciding to follow her mother's career in the billing department of the telephone company...and then had thought better of it, coming to Waddell's mesa to try her hand at something a bit more unusual.

And then there was Quentin Torrez—one of those unfortunate souls with his own challenges, and overshadowed by his taciturn uncle, Sheriff Robert Torrez, a man not exactly overflowing with sympathy or compassion.

"When was the last time Quentin was up here with you?"

Maddy thought for a moment, staring down at the dark, red carpet. "I really don't keep track. I *know* he was here Monday, 'cause he helped us move in a new freezer. I thought maybe he was going to ask Mr. Waddell for a job, but he didn't. And he and I had dinner together. I guess that was Wednesday." She nodded abruptly. "It was Wednesday."

"And then you had the fight."

"Yep." She smiled, took a deep breath, and looked forcibly cheerful. "He'll get over it."

"We can hope so. Look," Estelle said, pushing herself out of the too-comfortable chair, "I've taken enough of your time."

"Is Quentin in trouble?" Maddy sat forward, her hands on the arm of the chair, not quite ready to push herself upright.

"We don't know yet *who's* in trouble, Maddy."

The girl shook her head. "I guess I'm not supposed to ask questions about what happened?" she said.

"You can always ask," the undersheriff said with a pleasant smile. "But there's not much I can tell you at this point."

"Is Rik Chang going to be all right? Him and Ms. Gardiner?"

"We hope so."

"Rik's been up here several times." She smiled warmly. "A neat guy."

"He's a talented young man."

"And then the whole community will know, won't they? I mean when it comes out who the shooter is."

"That's the way small towns work, Maddy."

Chapter Sixteen

To give herself a little more secluded time to think, Estelle took the long way home—north on County Road 14 to State 76, passing through the northern third of the county, past the airport, and south into the village.

The temptation was too great. Before another call might interrupt, she drove into the village and swung south, passing under the interstate and turning into the sparsely shaded Escondido Lane. Just after the trailer park, she swung onto the short spur of Guadalupe Terrace.

She braked hard and stopped the car in the middle of the road. A power wheelchair headed directly toward her, taking its half out of the middle of the street. The contraption featured aggressively lugged tires and a slightly wider stance than a normal chair for the handicapped.

The grin on her son's face was ear to ear. He turned abruptly and ran onto the grassy verge along the macadam, the chair effortlessly navigating the rough surface. He stopped within reach of the Charger's driver's side door.

"He's letting me take it for a spin," Francisco announced.

She knew perfectly well who the "he" was, but she frowned sternly anyway and said, "And the 'he' being…"

Her son took a moment to flip a switch on the small control arm, and stepped away from the power chair. "*Padrino's* new life," he said, and leaned down, forearm on the windowsill of the Charger. "How's your day going? We haven't seen much of you."

"Chasing bad guys," she said, and smiled up at her son.

"They don't stand a chance."

"Would that were true. Is this that outdoorsman's contraption that *Padrino's* been talking about?"

"Just delivered. And it's *amazing.* You need to try it."

"Because I should be looking ahead to the day…"

He reached in and shook her by the shoulder. "Come on. You'll love it."

"*Padrino* has been aboard?"

"Oh, for sure. He's had it in and out of his van, and prowled the neighborhood. He's hoping that when my brother gets here, Carlos can do a few adjustments to get some more speed out of it."

"That's just what he needs." The chair was indeed impressive, with four large wheels instead of the usual two-and-two arrangement of a standard chair. A fifth wheel, much smaller in diameter, projected on an axle from the center rear, like that on the back of a dragster to prevent it from doing backflips.

Francisco laughed. "You're such a worrywart, Ma."

"That's why they pay me the big bucks. To worry about all you crazy people." She glanced in the rearview mirror. "Let me move out of the street before somebody comes along and rear-ends me."

"Are you going to take time to come see the progress on the house?"

"Of course." She watched him swing on board the chair, and just as she said, "Be careful with that thing," he hit the joystick and turned it in its own length, its aggressively lugged tires throwing gravel. The machine whined off down Guadalupe toward Bill Gastner's driveway. For just a moment, she sat quietly, then took a deep breath. All right, she *was* a worrywart. And that wasn't going to change.

Gastner had found a spot in his yard awash in dappled sun, and he relaxed on the padded chaise. On a small picnic table at his elbow was a large mug of coffee. He watched Estelle slide out of the car and beckoned.

"Is this the life, or what?" He waved at what appeared to be a completely poured foundation. "They just finished with the pour. Now we get to sit here and wait." He grinned. "I told 'em that I don't buy green bananas anymore, but I'm told that the fresh concrete can't be rushed." He shrugged. "I knew that." Francisco appeared carrying two lawn chairs, one of which he opened for his mother.

Gastner sipped his coffee and made a face. Francisco interpreted the expression correctly and stretched out a hand. "How about a refill of some hot stuff? And Ma, what would you like?"

"Nothing, thanks."

"Well, that's easy. But Angie made some green iced tea that's pretty fine. How about some of that?"

"Thank you. Just a small glass."

The old man watched his godson skirt the construction zone, headed for the kitchen. "Amazing kid, that one," he said. "If it's not politically incorrect to call a twenty-six-year-old a 'kid.'"

"I think he's a keeper."

Gastner nodded. "What's the news on the drive-by? Any progress?"

"Rik is going to be fine. Pam is a worry."

"No results on her surgery yet?"

"Not yet."

"This whole thing reeks of *kid*, you know. Steal a fancy truck, use it in a drive-by styled after some Chicago gangland thing out of the thirties, and then don't even bother to clean up the truck afterward. What's with that?"

"I'm thinking that they wore gloves, *Padrino*. Mears is checking the shell casings for prints, but that's a tough go."

Gastner made a thumbing motion with his right hand, holding an imaginary rifle magazine with his left. "Even a little twenty-two is going to make a nice surface for a thumbprint, sweetheart. Small, I admit. But you're going to have, what, twenty-five of 'em? Twenty-five chances to piece together a print."

"If they didn't wear gloves."

"If they didn't. And kids are notoriously stupid. Wear gloves when they heist the truck, but *don't* wear 'em when they're loading the gun. Plus..." and he held up one finger.

"Plus?"

"Twenty-twos are slimy little suckers. It's hard as hell to manipulate them wearing gloves—unless you've got a pair of surgeon's mitts."

"Could be. I'll be meeting with Mears this evening or tomorrow to see the sum total of what he's got. So far, it's not much."

She reached out to accept the glass of tea, and Francisco set the coffee cup on Gastner's table.

"Angie will be out in a bit," he said, settling into the second lawn chair. "She's working. Can you imagine that? *Working.*"

"On what?"

"She's got this one sonata by Lukie Maoma. He's one of the current stud ducks in Hawaiian music? Anyway, it's a great piece of music, with all kinds of traditional island motifs. And it's one of those pieces that just suits the voice of the cello beautifully... especially the way Angie plays." He leaned forward eagerly. "But the second movement is so *pianissimo* double, sometimes even triple *p*, that it's a challenge to encourage the cello to wake up, but never to stray into sounding scratchy or incomplete." He made a fist for emphasis. "I mean good, full, round notes, but still *triple-p*. *Mucho pianissimo-issimo.* Notes that are just rich whispers, 'like the sea on a calm evening,' Maoma says."

"But still reaching the audience somehow?" Estelle said.

"Exactly, Ma. That's exactly right. William Thomas sleeps

right through it." He changed tracks effortlessly. "Oh, and remember that dinner is over here tonight. Will six still work for you?"

"I think so. I can *make* it work." She looked at Bill Gastner, who was grinning like the Cheshire Cat. "What's up your sleeve, *Padrino*?"

"Are you ready for this?"

"Oh, yeah, huh," Francisco said, obviously knowing what was coming. "Freshen that?"

"Absolutely." Gastner handed his coffee mug to his godson, and then turned to face Estelle, eyes twinkling.

"I found the books." He clapped his hands in delight. "How about that?"

"The mercantile records?"

"Yep. Three volumes." He held up three fingers, and bent each in turn. "Volume one from 1878 through 1884, volume two from 1885 through 1888, and volume three from '89 until the store closed in '91." He grinned. "I was so damned excited that I drove my new power chair around the block, and then through that jungle in the back yard. Damn near killed myself."

Estelle relaxed back. "So," and she beckoned for more.

"Well, I lucked out. See, one of Mary's sons—remember that she married Jules, the founder's son who took over the store and then promptly died of an infected tooth? Well, she then married Frank Silverman, a savvy businessman who tried his best. And then had the four kids." He grinned at Estelle, whose eyebrow was raised in mild confusion. "Don't get lost in the unimportant family saga. That's just obituary stuff. What's important is that Mary's son Irving—Irving Silverman—is now eighty-one, that young sprout, and lives up in Ratón when he's not wintering in one of those awful Florida places." He reached up and accepted the coffee mug from Francisco. "Thank you, Jeeves."

"And he has the journals?"

"He does."

"¡*Ay, caramba!* That's amazing, *Padrino.* Did you tell him about the gun you found?"

"After a while. First I had to listen to his litany about how goddamn old he was. He's one of those geezers who's goddamned impressed because he's survived this long. I had to hear all about his having two knee replacements, shoulder work, two strokes, and a heart bypass."

"You've got him beat, *Padrino,*" Francisco offered. Gastner grimaced.

"You could have gone all day without reminding me of that, sprout. So, anyway." He took a thoughtful sip of the coffee. "Irving says that I can look through the books in person if I'll come to his place in Ratón."

"At least he has the year that the gun was shipped to his grandfather's store."

"That narrows it down, for sure," Gastner said. "And even though there was no such thing as gun registration back then, the buyer's name should appear in the journal, I'd think. That's just common sense."

"That's a long drive up there. To Ratón."

"Seven, eight hours. I figure if I bother to go I'll spend the night in Santa Fe and then go on up the rest of the way." He shrugged. "Not to mention that there's an offer on the table to fly me up there, door-to-damn-door. Can you imagine the look on old Silverman's face if that happened?"

"Just say the word," Francisco said. "We'll be back from Hawaii on Sunday, so a little jog to Ratón and back on Monday is as convenient as it gets…while we still have the jet in the neighborhood."

"A little jog," Gastner laughed. "Anyway, we'll see what old Silverman has to say after he takes a look through the journals. It may just be a wild goose chase."

Estelle shifted so she could reach the chirping, vibrating

gadget in her jacket pocket. "Speaking of wild goose chases." She stroked the iPad's face and then settled it to her ear.

"Yo," Sheriff Robert Torrez greeted. "Where you at?"

"I'm sitting in the shade with *Padrino* and my son at the new house."

"I'll meet you on 14, first turnoff north of Waddell's. You'll see the traffic."

Estelle's heart sank, but she worked to keep her tone neutral. "What have you got?"

"Miller says it looks like a single fatality. Back off the road a ways. We don't want to do the initial after dark."

"Does Luke recognize the victim?"

"Nope. I'm about ten out. We'll see then."

Estelle glanced at her watch. "I'm on my way. ETA about thirty."

"Or less," Torrez said, and disconnected. His description— the first turnoff after Waddell's development—matched property owned by the Thompsons. Had Kyle stumbled again? Or Lydia? Or any one of the many locals who still hunted that ground? An unsuspecting birder too far afield? The unknown surveyor stake vandal?

Estelle looked up and met her son's eyes. "Sorry, Francisco. I need to roll on this. Give my love to Angie and William Thomas."

"A bad one?"

"It looks that way."

"You're going to miss dinner?"

She offered a game smile. "Unless you all eat around midnight or so."

"That can happen."

She pushed herself up and hugged her son. "You're a sweetheart, *hijo*." She stepped across to Gastner. "I'll keep you posted. And you can let me know what you decide about a visit to Ratón." As she settled into the car, she reflected that former

Sheriff Bill Gastner had returned her hug, but he hadn't offered to ride along. Then she wondered what Sheriff Robert Torrez's reaction would have been if she'd just said "no."

Chapter Seventeen

The Charger's air conditioning almost kept up with the harsh late afternoon sun that baked through the windshield. Before long, the sun would hide behind the bulk of the San Cristóbal range that separated Posadas County from Mexico, and the evening cooldown would be abrupt.

The snarl of the engine and the roar of tires on hot macadam drowned out the radio, and Estelle turned up the volume so she could keep track of the dispatcher's traffic.

Happy Hour had started at the Broken Spur Saloon, and as she flashed by, Estelle caught sight of a gaggle of tourists disgorging from their bus. In another mile, she braked hard for the intersection with County Road 14, and the drop from the state highway's macadam to the graveled county surface was jarring. Six miles of dusty switchbacks farther on, a discreet black-on-white sign with an arrow announced *NightZone Parking*. The generous paved parking lot welcomed half a dozen cars, but a large group of tourists was gathered at the east end of the parking lot where the portico protected rail passengers while they waited for the train.

In another mile, a yellow crime-scene tape stretched across the county road.

Deputy Luke Miller's Tahoe was parked diagonally so that it blocked both lanes of the narrow thoroughfare, and he walked quickly toward Estelle's vehicle. A bony, almost gawky man with hair more white than blond, he bent down as if he wore a back brace, hands on his knees.

"Sheriff wants foot traffic only, ma'am," he said. "Might be good to leave your vehicle right where it's at. Obregon is up the road half a mile blockin' the other way."

"Tell me what we have, Luke."

"Well"—he pivoted without straightening up and pointed off to the east—"see where this first mesa's edge runs right along that line of juniper? About a hundred yards out?"

"All right."

"Just below that. It looks like we got us a hiker who took a header."

"Dead?"

"As dead can be." He touched his forehead under the bill of his cap. "A hard look through the binocs shows his whole frontal crushed in. ME will tell you more, but looks to me like he went off headfirst somehow, and landed smack on his skull. It's nothing but a jumble of rocks off that ledge."

"So it's a male."

"Yes, ma'am. Appears to be."

In the distance, Estelle could hear sirens, and as she got out of her car she saw Robert Torrez walking cross-country toward her, avoiding the two-track that broke off from the county road.

"Sheriff wants people to stay off the two-track," Miller reminded her.

"I can do that." Estelle waited a moment as the sheriff approached.

"Nobody drives on that lane," Torrez said by way of greeting, and he nodded at the deputy. "Have the ambulance wait out here until we give an all clear. ME's going to have to walk in like everybody else. We got a few tracks, and I don't want 'em obliterated." He looked off into the distance and closed his eyes, as if trying to sift through all the aromas that the prairie had to offer. After a few seconds, he turned to Estelle. "You might want to bring your camera, too. Calls out to Linda, but I don't know what she's doin'." He glanced at his watch. "Let's take a hike."

They'd covered no more than fifty yards of humpy, bunchgrass-strewn prairie, dodging clumps of contorted cholla and wasted beavertail cacti when Torrez stopped abruptly and drew in a huge breath. "He's not goin' anywhere. No need for us to break a leg tryin' to hurry."

"You recognize the victim?"

"Yep."

One painful factoid at a time, Estelle thought, not without a little irritation. "So who have we got?"

"His license says S. Kyle Thompson." The sheriff glanced sideways at Estelle.

She stopped short. "Where's Lydia?"

"Don't know. Not here."

"Have you actually ever met Kyle Thompson? I mean, you'd recognize him?"

"Can't see this guy carryin' Thompson's papers in his wallet if it's not him."

After a spread of creosote bush and acacia, they reached a sparse grove of stunted junipers, and Estelle could hear the breeze just beyond playing among the rocks of the mesa-face. On ahead twenty-five yards, a forest green Subaru Outback was parked, the only set of vehicle tracks that was obvious on the two-track leading directly to the little station wagon.

"Stay over this way," the sheriff instructed. He led her around a copse of runty junipers competing with an enormous cholla cactus, and an assortment of cow plops. In a moment, she was standing on top of a house-sized boulder with a grand view to the north and east.

The view downward wasn't so grand. The victim lay on his

face, arms and legs spread-eagled as if he'd been determined to fly. Instead he'd plunged face-first the forty feet to the rocks below. The artfully eroded sandstone under his head was blood-soaked.

"Was Luke down there?" Estelle asked. The deputy had been with the Sheriff's Department for less than a year, and Estelle was not yet confident that Deputy Luke Miller could resist galumphing his size thirteens through a potential crime scene before calling for assistance.

"Nope. He stopped right where we're standin' and called it in." He pointed south with his chin. "I took one climb down over there, stayin' on the hard rocks, and checked his wallet. It's in his left back pocket."

"And that's Kyle Thompson."

"Says so."

Estelle set her camera bag down and unzipped the main compartment, selecting a wide-angle lens. "*Ay,* this is going to be so bad." She took a deep breath and held it, then let it out as if she were exhaling a jet of smoke. "You ran the plate on the Subaru?"

"Yep."

"Thompson's?"

"Yep."

She moved to the edge of the rock, the sandstone curving down and away from the souls of her boots. "I want some overalls before everyone shows up."

"I'll keep trying to locate Linda."

"That would be good." Estelle had confidence in her own photographic abilities, but no one produced photographic results like Linda Pasquale. Seemingly impossible shots were commonplace for her. "Show me where you climbed down."

By the time the undersheriff had reached the body, she'd fired off fifty or more images covering the arc of land that included the boulders making up the cliffside. Then, she concentrated on the undisturbed area immediately around the corpse. Finally, she knelt beside the man.

Damage to the victim's upper face and skull was massive. The curdle of brain tissue oozed out where the skull had cracked open. Bending low, Estelle saw the damage epicentered above Thompson's right eye. It appeared that he had dived straight into the rocks, with no last-second squirming in midair to avoid the face-first contact. If the cap that was lying amid the rocks yards to the victim's left had been on his head, it hadn't offered any protection.

Even so, the victim's heart hadn't been convinced. It had continued to pump a gusher of blood until the lack of command signals from the brain switched it off.

Estelle knelt on the sun-warmed rock beside Thompson's broken head. He was a large man, probably weighing two-twenty or better. The skull's frontal bone was stout, taking lots of abuse during a lifetime. But forty feet down onto solid, unforgiving rock? The crashing impact had popped his skull like smacking a coconut with a large hammer.

One pant leg had hiked up enough to reveal the black ankle boot, a heavily braced affair that included the entire foot and ankle, leaving only the socked toes exposed. Even if the damaged joint wasn't sore, the contraption would have forced Thompson to limp, throwing him off balance.

"You want to do some measurin'?" Torrez's voice was gentle, even patient, floating down from above.

"Who do you have coming?"

"Taber will be here in about three minutes. Mears in about five. Camera girl is parked out at the road and is loadin' up. Guzman is attending. He'll be here in a bit."

"Let's wait on Taber for the tape." Estelle continued to stare at the boot, her eyebrows practically knit together in a frown line over her nose. "What were you doing, Kyle?" she whispered. Twisting in place, she looked up at the rock from which the man had plunged. A commercial wooden cane lay at the base of the rocks.

"What?" Torrez asked.

She held up a hand palm out, and continued to stare toward the cane without crossing the intervening ground between her and it. Eventually, Torrez became impatient.

"What?" he asked again.

"Bobby, the geometry of this doesn't make sense to me."

The sheriff palmed a small tape measure and tossed it down to her. She caught it and deftly extended the tape until it reached back and bumped against the rocks. She knelt and touched the measure to the victim's right foot. "Nine foot four inches." She looked up at the sheriff. "That's what bothers me. And you can see it from up there. That cane, assuming it's his, is actually leaning against the base of the boulder."

"Yep."

"If he was just standing on the edge and lost his balance, why would he hit the ground way out here? I mean, his feet are almost ten feet from the base of the rocks. "

"Takin' up high diving," Torrez said.

"Maybe so. He had a sprained ankle—might have been an actual fracture somehow. He's going to jump with that? He's going to have to take a running leap."

"Somethin' to ask your husband when he gets here. With that thing on his ankle, he's gonna be kinda careful how he walks."

She extended the tape once again, this time until it reached the white baseball cap lying crown-down in the rocks.

"Nine feet," she said. "Both he and his cap landed out here. His cane didn't."

"A lot of ways that could happen—and that's sayin' that the cap and the cane are even his."

"Wow, look at this!" Linda Pasquale announced from on high, stepping carefully up behind the sheriff. She reached out a hand and gripped Torrez's belt, then squatted, keeping her center of gravity low, one hand clutching her weighty camera case. "Some latent desire to be Icarus, or what?"

Sheriff Torrez glanced down at the young woman, who didn't appear to be the least bit intimidated by his glower.

"The ambulance ETA is about five minutes. We passed 'em on the way down. Lydia Thompson just arrived. Jackie's keepin' her back at the car until you give the word."

Estelle gazed up at the young photographer thoughtfully. "And who informed Lydia?"

Linda shook her head. "Information like that is above my pay grade." She twisted gently, surveying the rocks. "You want the whole schmeer on this?"

"Everything. Right now, a side view of the whole scene. Make the relationship between the body's position and the base of the rock wall clear, so we can draw a schematic from it. And the cane. And the cap."

Estelle turned her attention back to the corpse. Kyle Thompson was dressed in blue jeans that showed little wear—the view from the backside showed no gouges, rents, or tears. He wore a light summer-weight cream-colored shirt that also showed no sign of the victim's injuries. The ball cap showed no blood or other signs of impact to the portion that she could see.

Still kneeling, she settled back on her haunches as she manipulated her phone, tapping her husband's number.

"I'm on the road," Dr. Francis Guzman responded. "Just coming up on the Spur." Almost a decade before, he had accepted the position of deputy medical examiner. Dr. Alan Perrone, the ME, had pointed out that there was no one else to take the position, and most of the time over the years before his appointment, Francis had unofficially filled in when needed anyway. His excuse—that he wasn't good at interrupting what he might be doing to charge off into the hinterlands—hadn't won his case. "Nobody is prepared for these deals," Perrone had reportedly told him.

"One of the deputies will walk you in," Estelle said. "And the victim is Kyle Thompson...Lydia is on-site but won't be identifying the victim until you're finished."

"Fine. Somebody's staying with her, I hope."

"Of course. And one thing, *Oso*," she said, switching to her pet name for her husband. "Did you treat Kyle for a *fracture* or a sprain? He's wearing one of those ortho-support boots."

"Both. He told me that he used to sprain his ankle all the time—enough that it kept him out of sports. And this time he not only sprained it, it looked as if he cracked the navicular bone somehow...and that might be attributed to previous injury, too. Anyway, he shouldn't have been hiking and rock-climbing on it. Was he using crutches?"

"A cane, no crutches. Maybe they're in his car. We'll see you shortly."

"Yep. I see a deputy standing in the middle of the road, so I'll talk with you in a few minutes."

Estelle closed her phone and waited while the sheriff turned away from the edge, putting some distance between himself and the drop. When he paused and looked back, she said, "We need to know if he had crutches. Maybe still in the car."

"I'm about to find out," Torrez said. "And I want to make sure we got some control over this mess."

The undersheriff stood with hands on her hips and motioned to Linda, who was making her way, one digital image after another, toward the victim. "What we *do* know is that if he just tripped somehow—easy to do with walking made awkward by that boot—he would have tumbled down the face of the rocks."

Estelle made her way over the rough and uneven ground, uphill to the face of the boulder. She inspected it closely, running her hand gently up its surface. She reached up as high as she could, and her fingertips were still thirty feet or more from the upper edge. Swinging her arm in an extended arc, she stopped with her hand pointing at the body—more than a body length from where she stood.

"That's where the blood is," she said, more to herself than to Linda. "He didn't land up here close to the boulder, didn't lose his balance and tumble down, clawing at the rock face, and then after he hit bottom, didn't crawl or struggle farther downhill until he bled out. There are no gouges where he might have struggled, no blood trail where he might have crawled, no marks that suggest he was dragged."

"Just *whump*," Linda observed.

"That's right. Just whump. The only thing that makes sense to me is that he *hit* the ground over there." She pointed at the corpse. "He *landed* right where he's lying now, not over here. The blood pattern says he landed, cracked his skull, and then stayed put."

"That's his ball cap?"

"Most likely. And that's another thing. If he just lost his balance and tumbled, why would his cap be flung so far? There was no wind. If he simply lost his balance and fell, and if during that fall his cap tumbled off, it would tumble straight down to the base of the rocks, no?"

Not pausing a moment to consider all these questions, Linda Pasquale framed every conceivable angle or corner of the scene, shooting dozens of exposures. Estelle watched as the photographer moved in close and took as many detailed photos of the body as possible without disturbing its position. After a moment Linda straightened up and shook her head sadly.

"I know that Frank Dayan wanted to talk with this gentleman in the worst way." It had been more than a decade since Linda had worked for Frank Dayan and the *Posadas Register,* but her photos of non-law-enforcement-related events still appeared on its pages on a regular basis.

"You have it pretty much covered?" Estelle could hear quiet voices approaching.

"I'm set." Linda stepped back.

Captain Jackie Taber appeared to one side of the boulder above them, one hand firmly on Lydia Thompson's elbow. The sheriff moved so that he was within easy reach of Lydia's other arm. Sandwiched between Taber's stout, almost brawny frame and Robert Torrez's six-foot-four hulk, Lydia looked frail and diminutive. The breeze played with her light jacket, just enough to reveal that she was wearing her heavy "snake" gun.

"Nuh." The young woman managed the single, strangled groan and sank to the rocks. Taber knelt with her, keeping a hand on each shoulder as Sheriff Torrez released his own grip. Estelle worked her way up through the rocks, following the narrow crevice between two boulders. Once on top, she knelt beside Lydia Thompson, who extended a hand to her.

"I'm so sorry," Estelle whispered, and Lydia covered the undersheriff's hand with both of hers, as if she were the one to offer sympathy.

"He said he was coming out here to take some photos. This was his favorite site on the property, and he wanted photos taken right at high noon." She drew in a shuddering breath. "I should have been with him, but he insisted he could manage. We were going to meet up on top for dinner." She bit her lip, moaning out a little squeak of distress. "I saw all the traffic over here, and knew something was wrong." She bit her lip, stifling back a cry. "He's been out here all that time? Just lying here, all by himself?"

"We think so, Lydia. There's no sign of a struggle, no sign that even immediate first aid would have helped him."

"The blood..."

"From a massive skull fracture. The ME will confirm that when he gets here in a few minutes."

"How..."

"We don't know yet, Lydia. I'm sorry. The ME will be here in just a few minutes."

"Who found him? Did he manage to call for help?"

"No. Deputy Miller discovered him."

"But how? Somebody must have told him Kyle was here."

"We haven't had the chance to talk with the deputy yet." Their hands still locked, Estelle's gaze searched Lydia Thompson's face. A tear had broken loose from her welling right eye and now tracked down flawless skin to the corner of her mouth, followed in seconds by a tear from her left. The woman was perhaps a little older than she had first appeared when Estelle had met her at *NightZone,* but was toned and fit.

"I want to go down." She rose abruptly, and both Taber and Estelle stood with her. "Please. I need to do that. I won't touch anything." She wiped her eyes and closed them, turning to let the late afternoon sun beat on her face. When she opened her eyes, she looked at Estelle. "I won't touch anything. I know the procedure."

"When the medical examiner arrives, he needs to work without members of the immediate family present," the undersheriff said. "If you know the procedure, then you know some of it is unpleasant. You don't need to be there."

"But I do." She frowned hard, looking at her husband's corpse down below. "I need to be."

"I'll take you down now, but when the ME arrives, I'm going to have to ask you to leave the scene." Lydia Thompson almost nodded, and Estelle accepted that as assent. She took her time returning downhill to the body, blocking Lydia's path and forcing the younger woman to keep to a slow, careful pace, staying well out of the immediate site.

"Do you recognize the cap?"

Lydia glanced at it, and nodded.

"And over by the rocks...the cane?"

"He was using that just temporarily. He bought it at the drug store. He has crutches, too, but they're back at the hotel. He couldn't stand to use them." Without warning, she fell to her knees beside the victim, hands clamped into tight fists in her lap. Estelle stayed close, one arm around the young woman's shoulders.

A little whimper, and then Lydia breathed out a heartfelt, "Oh, my." She pressed both hands to the top of her skull, as if a pounding headache had brewed. After a moment, she relaxed, let one more whimper escape, and extended one shaky hand. Without touching it, she pointed at the spine of rock directly under her husband's head, a sharp little blade of sandstone.

"He…he landed on that, didn't he?" She twisted and looked back up the rock face from which her husband had fallen. "If he'd landed in, like that sand over there," and she pointed with a wrinkle of her nose at a flat area between boulders where blow sand had collected. "If he'd landed there, it might have been all right."

She stared at the spot of sand, her expression more incredulous than anything else. "Why out here?" She reached out a hand as if to touch the corpse, then checked herself. "So far out. I mean, how could he?"

With a hand on her elbow, Estelle helped Lydia to her feet.

"I want to hear what the medical examiner has to say," Lydia said.

"We can give you a full report when he's finished and has time to document his findings."

Lydia turned on Estelle, red blushing her cheeks. "Oh, don't give me that bullshit, Sheriff Guzman." She thumped her fist against her chest. "Here I am, right now. I want you all to talk to me. As you investigate…*this*," and she waved her hand to include the scene, "I want to *know*. My husband would want me to know."

When Estelle didn't respond, Lydia said, "Look, let me tell you something." She yanked the tail of her shirt out of her pants and pulled it up, exposing her belly up to the bottom margin of her bra. The surgical scars across her tawny midriff looked all too fresh, not something done when she was a child. "Kyle held me that night, held my guts together, kept talking to me, rode with me in the ambulance, stayed with me through the worst five weeks in the hospital that I've ever experienced, the worst five weeks of my life. And now this. Here *he* is, lying out here all by himself, and I didn't even get to hold his hand?"

A distant clearing of a throat broke the tension, and Estelle turned in place to see Linda Pasquale trying to blend in with the scenery. "The ME is here, Estelle."

"Lydia, I know all of this is hard for you. But when the ME is working, I want you out of the immediate scene. If something comes up that you need to know, I'll make sure you're included. That's the way it's going to be. We're all concerned with certain unanswered questions." She nodded toward the boulder. "The best place for you to wait is back by your vehicle."

Lydia tucked in her shirt, her glare fixed on Estelle. The undersheriff could see the young woman's cheek muscles clenching.

"I'll want to talk with you in a few minutes," Estelle added. "We need to know about your husband's day. How he came to be out here. Who he might have been with. I need to know about *your* day. How it was that you weren't with your husband when he decided to hike out here."

"I can help you." Lydia's glare had softened, and her voice was a whisper.

"I'm sure you can. Just not this moment. Stay by your vehicle. That way, if the sheriff or I need to speak with you, we'll know where to find you."

Dr. Francis Guzman appeared up above, flanked by Bob Torrez and Captain Jackie Taber. He changed his hospital slippers for sturdy hiking shoes, but otherwise was dressed more for the operating room in hospital scrubs with the Posadas Emergency Services badge on the left breast.

"Over there?" he asked, pointing at the marked route down through the jumble of boulders.

"Yes. Let Lydia come up first." Estelle touched Lydia's elbow. "She's provided a positive ID for us. Captain, she'll be staying out where her vehicle is parked until we're finished here. She'll need some company."

"Understood," Jackie said, and moved to intercept Lydia Thompson as she made her way up through the rocks.

Chapter Eighteen

For a methodical fifteen minutes, Francis Guzman sorted through the scene of Kyle Thompson's death without saying a word, and Estelle didn't interrupt him. "Most likely four or five hours," he said finally. "What time did you arrive?"

"Five thirty seven. Miller called it in right at four thirty."

He glanced at his own watch, pushing in the little control button to light the dial. "And it's going on seven thirty now. So." He knelt once more while balancing carefully, then reached out to turn the victim's head a little. "Linda?"

"Sir?"

"You have all the original position photos you need? We want to turn him over."

"I have a plethora."

"That's always good." Dr. Guzman moved the corpse's left arm, now awkwardly stiff, so that it lay close to the torso. "Okay. *Querida,* you want to work his feet?" Together, they gently rolled Kyle Thompson onto his back. For a long moment, the physician stood silently, regarding the corpse, the evening shade of the rocks illuminated now in the twin arc lights whose cords ran down the boulders from the small generator on top. Then he knelt again, methodically examining the facial damage. He finally snapped the flashlight closed and stood up.

"He hit hard enough to cave in just about the most difficult part of the skull to damage," he said. "Really, really hard." His right hand went up to his own skull as if in sympathy. "No other wounds obvious. The lack of gravel or whatever crunched into the palms of his hands tells me that he led with his head, which is kinda strange. And no torn clothing, scuffed elbows or knees or broken skeletal bones that are obvious, so he didn't just tumble down the rocks." He turned and looked at Estelle. "Autopsy's going to be interesting."

An hour later, with the canyon's light sinking into darkness and the arc lights dazzling harshly among the rocks and boulders, Estelle followed the gurney bearing Kyle Thompson's body up the narrow trail to the ambulance parked immediately behind the Subaru. She spoke briefly to Deputy Luke Miller, then walked the hundred yards or so back to the county road.

Lydia Thompson sat on the tailgate sill of her Explorer, kept company by Captain Jackie Taber. The dome light of the vehicle haloed Lydia's tousled blond hair, now out of its ponytail and hanging down on either side of her face.

"Let me give you some time alone," Jackie said, and Estelle nodded her thanks.

"Lydia, your husband's body will be taken to the hospital now. There will be an autopsy tomorrow. I don't know exactly what time." The young woman nodded dully without looking up, her hands working to compress a wad of facial tissue into a tiny ball. "Dr. Guzman believes that your husband died sometime early this afternoon, perhaps as early as noon."

Lydia almost managed a weak laugh as she looked up at Estelle. "Is that what you call him at home? *Dr. Guzman?*"

"Only when I'm trying to get his attention."

"And then he responds by calling you *sheriff?*"

"Never. It's *undersheriff*, anyway. And yes, sometimes he calls me that." She sat down on the door sill beside Lydia. For a long moment, long enough to earn the woman's attention, Estelle regarded her silently.

"What?" Lydia Thompson asked.

"I'm curious about you, Mrs. Thompson."

"There's not a whole lot to know."

"How did you meet your husband?"

"I met Kyle when we were both working for the New York State Police."

"I see." Estelle nodded at Lydia's midriff. "And that?"

"That happened eight years ago near the little town of Avoca, New York." She paused as if trying to decide whether or not to continue. She closed her eyes and puffed out her cheeks, then said, "A stupid quarrel between two neighbors over the location of a flower bed. Another trooper had responded twice to the incident before I joined him for the third visit. I'm sure you've had experience with family disputes."

"Indeed."

"In this case, a reality-challenged sixteen-year-old decided to engage. With a twenty-gauge shotgun loaded with double-ought. He got off three shots before the other officer put his lights out." She put an index finger to her forehead between her eyes.

"And you with no vest?"

"Stupid, huh? A beautiful day in May...very much like this one. An argument over a bunch of begonias or whatever they were..." She shrugged deeply. "Anyway."

"And your partner—the other officer—was..."

"Kyle." She smiled painfully. "I had a crush on him already, and I guess it was mutual. And that day, he never let me go. Never left me for a minute. Not that afternoon, and not during the months of hell that *he* went through after the shooting."

"I'd think he'd be treated as a hero."

"Yeah, right. See, the thing was..." She blinked hard against tears. "The shotgun the kid was using was plugged for three rounds. So when Kyle fired, the kid was holding an empty gun." She looked at Estelle and shrugged. "Even if he'd known, which he didn't, what was he supposed to do, wait for the kid to reload? And he was a little shit, the kid was. About half Kyle's size. He could have just grabbed the kid, tore the gun out of his hands, and punched his lights out."

"But as you said, he wouldn't have *known* the gun held only three."

"Of course not. Anyway. Months of hell. By the time we left New York…" She held up both hands to form a bracket. "When we saw the 'Welcome to the Commonwealth of Pennsylvania' sign, with the Empire State sign in our rearview, we both cheered."

"Why New Mexico?"

"An army buddy of Kyle's lives in Albuquerque and got Kyle started. Turns out Kyle had a flare for real estate, for development. Utterly fearless." She gestured at the dark prairie with both hands. "Loved all this."

"Why did he come out here today?"

"Just to look. He wanted to prowl around some, play with ideas."

"But you didn't come with him."

"I wish to God that I had."

"Why didn't you?"

For a moment, Lydia didn't answer. Finally, she pushed herself off the tailgate sill and stood up. "You mean, where was I at 12:05 p.m., or whatever the time was when Kyle took his header?" Tears formed again, but she did nothing to wipe them away. "We took Mr. Waddell up on his offer, and I was taking a nap in that obscenely comfortable, dark room up at the *NightZone* hotel. My gut ached, but I think it was too much green chile for breakfast. I didn't feel so much like hiking. Even as slowly as peg-legged Kyle would go." She shook her head in misery. "So I wasn't with him."

"He had other family?"

Lydia nodded. "A beloved grandmother, for one. She's in Philadelphia now, in an assisted living home. This is going to kill her. His mom and dad are divorced, but they both live in Jamestown, New York. He has a younger brother in the Oswego County Sheriff's Department, and an older brother who's a prosecutor in Buffalo." She stifled a groan. "I'll call them in a few minutes, after I pull myself together. I don't know what they're going to want to do."

"What do *you* want to do, Lydia?"

She clasped her hands tightly and pumped her arms up and down like a little kid trying to ward off a tantrum.

"I just don't know. I just...don't...know." She slammed the truck's liftgate closed. "I'll be in my room if you need me."

Plunge from holding the world by the tail to not sure the sun was going to ever rise again, Estelle thought. She watched the dust trail of Lydia Thompson's Explorer as the woman drove away, just a faint ghost in the night.

"We're finished with the victim's car, ma'am," Deputy Luke Miller said.

Estelle turned away from her thoughts. "Good. We need to make arrangements to have it taken to the county yard. We may not be done with it just yet. Will you do that?"

"You bet."

She watched him turn and walk away, his every step driven by confidence. "*Ay.*" She breathed out a sigh and turned toward her own car. If everything else were as simple as towing away a parked car.

Chapter Nineteen

Her greeting at the *NightZone* gate was not as effusively welcoming this time. Rafael Gonzales had gone off shift, but Estelle was pleased to recognize Rolando Ortega manning the gate. As she pulled to a stop, he appeared in the guard house doorway, managing to appear like a large shadow in the glow of the single solar-charged light.

He looked like a guard—certainly not fat, but burly and powerful, well over six feet tall, wearing the same style of natty quasi-uniform that Rafael Gonzales had been sporting earlier. The dim light enhanced his guard-like appearance, since it was impossible to tell exactly how old he was—maybe sixteen, maybe forty.

Well aware of how anathema unnecessary lights were, Estelle had switched off the county car's lights as soon as she had swung into the park's entrance.

"I need to go topside to meet with Mr. Waddell," Estelle said. "Open the gate for me, and then if you want, call Mr. Waddell and let him know that I'm on my way up. I won't use my headlights." She smiled, all the time watching the young man's range of expressions.

He started to turn toward the guard's office—it was too

elegant to be a shack—and on impulse, and in no mood to wait for permission, Estelle said, "Hey?" He turned around and at the same time, she flicked all the switches on the console. The Charger lit up like a frantic Christmas tree, headlights oscillating back and forth from low to high beams, the grill wiggle-waggles dancing wildly, the row of lights in the back window shelf producing their own kaleidoscope above the blinding taillights. She immediately doused them all. "Or I can go up quietly." Estelle grinned at the flustered young man. "Quietly and dark."

He tapped the remote for the gate. "Yes, ma'am."

"Thanks, Rolando. I'll be quiet." The Charger muttered up the hill, the star and moonlight offering just enough bounce on the black asphalt's striping to make the drive pleasant. She brought the car to a full stop twice, once for two deer browsing half on the pavement and half off, and once for a skunk family, mother and five tiny stinkpups trailing behind.

By the time she stopped in front of the administration building, Miles Waddell was standing out front, hands thrust in his jeans' pockets. He reached out and took the Charger's driver's side door handle, offering a gallant hint of a bow as he opened it.

"Rolando said you were on your way up. Welcome back. By the way, I saw Lydia a few moments ago," he said.

"Miserable day for her. Thanks for offering them a room. She will be more comfortable here." *Then again,* Estelle thought, *how can she be comfortable anywhere?*

"I don't know. If they'd stayed at the motel in Posadas, this might never have happened."

"We have no crystal ball, Miles." It was hard to see his face in the dark. "Do you have a few minutes for me?"

"Of course I do. Glass of iced tea or something?" He started to turn toward the building.

"No, thanks. Actually, this is just fine out here." The night air was deeply silent, with no breeze to awaken the prairie fragrance.

"Well, sure."

"I have to admit that I played games with Rolando down at the gate." She smiled at Waddell. "I didn't want him to think that he had a choice about whether or not I was coming up."

"Oh, he should know that. He's just learning the ropes, though. He's rotating through all the various jobs we do, including something as dull as manning the gate. A couple weeks there, and he'll transfer somewhere else for a bit. And so it goes."

"I missed Rafael—he's a real jewel."

"Isn't he something? And right now, he's riding the rails, turning his charm on all the passengers." He grinned, clearly enjoying his role as mentor and director of personnel. "But don't worry. Rolando has his skills, too. He'll work out all right. Anyway, you're here, and I'm delighted."

"Where were the Thompsons staying? This place is so large, I'm lost." She pivoted at the waist. With no exterior lights, it was easy to be lost, she thought. The tiny solar buds barely outlined the black walkways.

"Ah. They're...I mean *she*, is in Sagittarius, one of our suites just beyond the dining room. Just go past the main dining room doorway, then in a little bit, bear right when the hallway forks. Sagittarius is the first room on the left."

"When did they actually move in here?"

She saw Waddell's shoulders shrug, and an expression that might have said, *what does it matter,* but instead he explained, "Well, let's see. I left a note with Divon at reception—that's just inside and to the left? I left a carte blanche note that said if the Thompsons arrived, just to go ahead and check them into Sagittarius."

"When did you actually do that?"

"It was right after our abortive meeting that morning...what seems like a week ago, now. I wanted to make sure that the desk had it on file...I guess so that the Thompsons didn't think that my invitation was just an empty promise."

"Did you actually see them check in?"

His dark form shifted, and one hand reached out to make contact with Estelle's right shoulder. In the darkness, she couldn't see his face, but his tone was concerned. "Estelle, are you on the track of something here? What's up? What does it matter whether or not *I* saw them?"

"I'm trying to put things in perspective, Miles. That's all. We've had an unattended death, and that always prompts questions. So…"

"Call me a little bit stupid, then. Now, did I see them check in? No, I did not. But I *did* happen to walk by the desk shortly after noon or so, and Maddy said that they'd checked in, and were having lunch. I told her to be sure that the waitstaff knew they were my guests, and she said she'd double-check about that. You've met Maddy, right?"

"Indeed. A delightful young lady, and a real treasure to have on your staff, Miles." *If she'd be a little more careful about picking her boyfriends, that would help,* she thought.

"Oh, she is. Anyway, then I ducked into the dining room for just a minute, saw the Thompsons at one of the two-tops over by the windows, and went over to chat with them for just a moment or two. They seemed content, happy with things, and so I left them to enjoy their lunch." He shrugged. "Because they obviously were, and I didn't want to intrude. I didn't want to appear to hover, you know. And that was it."

"You didn't see them after that?"

Waddell shook his head. "I had a long session over at SunDance…that's the solar telescope? My plan was to invite the Thompsons to have dinner with me. That obviously wasn't to be."

She reached out and squeezed his arm in sympathy. "During your brief talk with them, did either of them mention plans for the afternoon?"

"Nothing that I took seriously, Estelle. Mr. Thompson said that he'd probably try to take a walk to work off some of the calories, and the missus said she was going to take a nap. You know, the sort of things we say whether or not they're totally true."

"And you didn't see them after that."

"No, I did not. I don't know how far Mr. Thompson could have walked, with that bum ankle of his. He was wearing this gigunda boot thing." He shrugged. "Later on, a little bit ago this evening, I heard what had happened, and just before you drove up, I'm told that Mrs. Thompson rode the tram up and went straight to her room. The last thing I wanted to do was disturb her."

"So her vehicle is down in the parking lot?"

"I would assume so. You're impounding Mr. Thompson's vehicle? I was told it was towed away."

"We have."

"Oh, my." He shook his head sadly. "Such a mess for them. And all this on top of that shooting in the village? My God, what's next? I mean, are you making any progress on that at all?"

"Some long hours ahead, Miles."

He reached out and offered a half hug. "When things calm down, grab your hubby and whatever boys are home, and Bill, too, and come on up for a good dinner. My treat. How about that? A *great* planetarium show on black holes coming up next Saturday night. Show starts at eight. How about then? Come for dinner at six thirty, show after. Get our minds off all of this."

"I'd love that."

"Then let's plan on it." He held up a hand. "And I promise—I will not pester Francisco about playing."

"He'll make that easy. He and Angie are flying to Hawaii for the weekend. She has a concert out there."

"Oh, wow. I'm sorry to miss them. But the offer stands for you, Francis, and Bill." He pushed a button on his watch, illuminating the dial. "And Estelle, I'm ready and willing to help you folks in any way that I can. You know that. If something comes up, any appointments I might have, I can break. All right?"

"I appreciate that, Miles." He offered a warm, firm handshake that, busy or not, he seemed reluctant to break. She had time to reach her car and settle inside when her cell phone vibrated as if the great cell tower in the sky had been monitoring her activities and reported to the caller that she was now free. The phone identified the number as the sheriff's.

"Guzman."

"Hey. You inbound?"

"Yes. I just finished talking with Lydia and Miles."

"Got somethin' to show you. Stop at the office on your way."

"ETA about thirty."

"Yup. Then we'll have time to head on over to the hospital."

"The hospital?"

"Yup. See you in a bit," and he disconnected.

Estelle couldn't tell the sheriff's mood from the cryptic conversation, but he hadn't offered any options.

Chapter Twenty

Both the sheriff and Linda Pasquale met Estelle in the dark-room down in the basement, and Torrez couldn't keep the trace of smile off his face. He pointed at the binocular microscope, one objective of which had been replaced with a camera, a jerry-rigged affair that had given new life and purpose to the aging microscope that still showed the PPS decal on the side, acknowl-edging its Posadas Public Schools origin. Torrez reached across and took an eight-by-ten enlargement off the pile of photos.

"Look at that," he said. "You couldn't get any clearer'n that."

"I sense a well-deserved compliment," Linda Pasquale stage-whispered. The image was clear, but almost abstract, with only one limited plane in focus. A glance at the microscope stage showed two twenty-two caliber shell casings standing side by side, headstamps oriented upward. Every rill, scratch, and dent in the brass of the cartridge casings' base stood out clearly, as did the manufacturer's cartouche, or headstamp—in this case the single word "Super" framed in a small rectangular shield, overlaid on a large X.

"The one on the left is from the ammo that was in the maga-zine of Quentin's rifle," Torrez explained. "The one on the right was found in Glenn Archer's Navigator.."

"Winchester Super-X," Estelle said. "Quentin told us that the last time he went shooting, he was using Remington bulk ammo, no?"

"Yep."

"But that's not what interests us, is it?"

"Nope."

She reached out her hand, and Linda, always the mind-reader, handed her another photo, this one a comparison enlargement of the two casings, but only the area that had been struck by the rifle's firing pin. "*A* is Quentin's, the one on the left," Linda said. "*B* is the one from the vehicle."

The images had been enlarged as far as the margins of the paper allowed, and Estelle sat on one of the darkroom stools to study the photo.

"They ain't nothin' alike," Torrez said, growing impatient with the silence. "Not a match."

"You fired this one today?"

"Yep." He pulled a ballpoint pen from his pocket and used it as a pointer, touring around the firing pin strike area. "This little flat spot here, and that kinda like a little dig right there? You don't have that on the others."

"I've done five of the twenty-five found in the truck," Linda offered. "Same results." She tapped a short stack into order and handed them to Estelle. In each photo, the results were identical and obvious. The nose of the firing pin had left a clear, individual identifying mark in the soft brass of the shell casing.

"I'll do 'em all," Linda said, "but I don't think the story's going to change."

"It don't matter that we can't match the slugs," Torrez said. "That gun," and he nodded at the rifle that stood in the floor rack, the partially customized gun that they'd picked up from Quentin earlier, "didn't fire any of those slugs."

"Unless he got busy with a little file and did a quick touch-up job on the face of the firing pin," Estelle said.

"Yeah, well, he ain't that smart."

"But it's possible." Estelle knew that Quentin *was* smart, although whether or not he had the machinist's skills to hide altering file marks was a fair question. When Torrez remained silent, Estelle added, "Possible, but not probable."

"That's right."

"And just to cover our butts," Linda said, "the sheriff fired five rounds from Quentin's rifle." She found the comparison photo and pulled it from the pile. Five twenty-two casings, headstamps oriented identically, posed side by side. The firing pin's imprint was clear, the various scuff marks repeated from casing to casing…the differences between those and the casings recovered from Archer's Navigator clearly visible.

"Well done, Linda," Estelle said. She turned and regarded the sheriff. "You're feeling a little better about this?"

"That gun didn't shoot up the newspaper office," Torrez said. "But that don't mean he didn't use some other rifle…just not this one. It's a common make."

"And what do we have that leads us to think that your nephew might have done all this? We're back to square one, Bobby. Just that Quentin *might* have had a grudge against the newspaper for printing his DUI story?"

"That's enough, ain't it? I mean, that's a start."

"And we certainly need a place to start." Estelle paused. "I think you need to cut your nephew some slack, Bobby. Let's go with what's simple, and *likely*." She stood up and handed the stack of photos to Linda. "Excellent work. Just excellent." The young woman waved an "aw, shucks" hand. Estelle turned back to Torrez. As a master of not showing emotional expression, the sheriff still managed to look relieved.

"The hairs they collected? Mears sent 'em off along with samples collected from Quentin's truck seat. Long shot, and any lab work is gonna take forever. But we got a start." Torrez said.

"That's good. It seems likely to me that whoever did this

assault was pretty serious. Thought it through. And that puzzles me, because taking a joyride in Glenn Archer's SUV has *kid* written all over it. Unless that's what they want us to think." She glanced at the clock. Midnight was already twenty minutes old. "You mentioned the hospital, Bobby. Is Pam doing okay?"

"Ain't that. Perrone's here, and he's workin' with your husband. They want to talk with us."

Chapter Twenty-One

"Like this." Dr. Alan Perrone made a diving motion with his hand. "Francis tells me that the victim's feet ended up nearly ten feet from the rocks where he took his dive. That's what got us both thinking. No way he's going to do that without some help. And now I hear that you have reservations about how the fall happened as well."

He drew the sheet back, exposing the corpse down to the waist. "Not a scratch, right?" The body lay facedown. "And I agree, the head injury was massive, probably instantly fatal. No scuffle marks on the ground around him, so his legs didn't twitch. Exsanguination made a sizeable pool around his face but nowhere else. So I agree with Francis." He smiled at Estelle. "Who, by the way, had the good sense to head for home when he had the chance. I told him I'd shoo you that way if I could after we're done here, but I wanted to share this with you as soon as I could."

"We appreciate that, Alan. So tell us what you think."

"He took a hell of a header, and landed facedown on the rocks. That's what I think." Perrone turned and sorted through photos until he found the one he wanted, a portrait of the impact zone where Linda Pasquale had taken special pains to focus on the wedge of rock that had cleaved Kyle Thompson's skull. "Looks like a dull axe, doesn't it?"

"Ain't none of this is news to us," Sheriff Torrez muttered.

"I wouldn't think so," Perrone said. "But patience, Sheriff. This might be news." He reached up and swiveled the stainless steel examination light closer so that it flooded the corpse's upper back. "Eagle eye saw this before I did," Perrone said. "You can see it better at an angle." With a gloved finger, he traced the mark without touching the skin, just to the left of the spine's first and second thoracic vertebrae, high on the back between the shoulder blades.

"Well, shit," Torrez muttered. "That's startin' to be a bruise."

"Starting to be," Perrone agreed. "I asked Linda to stop by to do the documentation. This is so faint, we're going to need her expertise before the autopsy. But this is what's really interesting, folks. Hang on a minute." He turned away from the table and stepped to one of the tall, narrow cabinets, returning with a man's hiking shoe enclosed in a plastic evidence bag.

"This is one of Mr. Thompson's size thirteens, considerably larger than the outline of our bruise. Now, I'm sure he didn't kick himself, but the shoe will do to make my point." He held it above the bruise, the heel just a fraction of an inch above the skin. He waited while his audience absorbed what they were seeing. The outside arc of the bruise roughly suggested the outline of the shoe's heel.

"You're sayin' he was kicked?"

"That's my guess." He grimaced at his own choice of words. "Let me amend that. Not a *guess*. That's what I really believe happened. See, this area started to bruise…well, let me paint a scenario for you. It started to bruise the instant that someone's shoe crashed into the victim's back. Now," and Perrone held up an index finger as if he were lecturing a class, "Kyle Thompson measures out at 193 centimeters tall, give or take. That's about six feet four for you metrically challenged folk. That's the number to remember. Six-four."

He turned to the sheriff and took hold of one arm. "That's your height, more or less, right? So observe." He turned the sheriff in place and rested a hand on his back. "That means the tops of his shoulders are about five feet off the ground. Maybe five-two or five-three. More or less. This bruise is a little less than that, but close there to."

Perrone stopped and looked at each one of them. Torrez scowled impatiently.

The morgue door opened, and Linda Pasquale stepped in and beamed at the group. "Hi, guys. Séance time?"

"Ah, good. Mrs. Pasquale, impeccable timing," Perrone said. "So, as I was saying, picture this impact, this kick, five feet or more off the ground." His finger once more traced the portion of the bruise nearest the spine, and then he held the shoe in place. Then he turned and held the shoe in that same position against Torrez's back.

"That is some high kick, sports fans. And the toe points upward and to the victim's left, so in all likelihood, it was a *right* foot. And the bruising would have turned out to be considerable except for one thing."

"His heart stopped," Estelle said.

"Exactly. So we have a little bruising, enough to capture on film, but not enough to make a really livid mark. On top of which, blood sinks downward. The lividity patterns would appear on the front of the body as he lay there, the blood draining away from the surfaces of the back."

"All this says that you believe he was kicked off the rock?" Estelle asked.

"I do. We took our time and really looked, folks. There isn't a single bruise on the body *except* this one. He has an injured ankle that was obviously under treatment at the time of his death, and you can see substantial bruising there, for sure. But not a nick, not a cut, not a defensive wound or bruise that we can relate to his fall. Some gravel ground into his left palm as if it struck the ground at the same time as his skull did." He shook his head. "Just this shoe print, if I may be allowed to call it that, and of course, the massive head trauma. Well, that's *almost* it."

"Almost?"

"The victim has a fracture of the neck, right below the occipital." He pointed. "There's an X-ray on the monitor. But it's nothing unusual. In fact, we'd *expect* a fracture where the victim lands headfirst, jerking the head backward, so hard that there's compression fractures in the neck vertebrae."

"That would have been fatal as well?"

"Absolutely. But that's it. Perfectly predictable. Our victim wasn't picked up by a couple of thugs and tossed to his death. The results of those fingers clamping on him would have shown up. I picture him standing on the brink, admiring the scenery. He's a little awkward, maybe even a little off balance, and his assailant comes up behind him and *bam!*" Perrone clapped his hands. "An aggressive kick near top dead center, and..." He made an outward zooming motion. "Over he goes. Pitchin' headfirst."

Perrone stepped back to the locker and removed an evidence box containing various articles of clothing, each piece additionally wrapped in its own labeled evidence bag. "His polo shirt shows damage on the front, as we would expect from the crash landing. But also, there's scuffing, with dirt particles driven into the fabric, on the back." He drew out the shirt and spread it on one of the stainless steel tables. "See what you can do with that, Linda."

"The impossible is our possible," Linda quipped.

"No tox yet, though," Estelle said.

Perrone glanced at the undersheriff and raised an eyebrow. "Blood alcohol was negligible. About what we'd expect if he'd had a single drink for lunch. Nothing more. As you folks know, full tox will take a while, but I tell you, I don't expect anything."

"Linda, what do you think?" She watched Pasquale as the young woman examined the shirt fabric without actually touching it.

"With the mark on the back…" She shrugged. "I can filter it up to help, but what you're going to end up with is just a mark that contrasts a little with the surrounding skin. No obvious patterns or stuff like that. Now this shirt? The light-blue fabric might give us a little more, but not much."

"Do what you can."

"Of course. Always."

Estelle glanced at the sheriff, and caught the glower. "Bobby?"

"So we got a karate kick to the back? With enough power to send him headfirst over the edge in some wild dive?"

Estelle didn't respond, but knew what was coming. On more than one evening occasion, she'd seen the "Karate Kids" coming out of the basement of the First Baptist Church after a session of taekwondo. Quentin Torrez, already proudly sporting a first-degree black belt, was an avid coach for the younger participants.

"It *could* have happened that way, Sheriff. *Could* have. Or the circumstances might have been totally different, something none of us visualized. However it happened, if I'm right about this being a kick bruise, then the assailant somehow got directly behind Mr. Thompson, who at the time would have had to be standing on the edge."

He sighed. "It's the face full of rock, ten feet out from the edge, that's signature. This man stood six-four, so the arc of his fall isn't extraordinary. In fact, a healthy athlete could manage the same trajectory without an Olympic-class leap. But I gotta tell ya, he *didn't* just slip or lose his balance and tumble down the rock face, frantically trying to catch himself as he went. He didn't end up at the bottom of those rocks in a heap, with scrapes and cuts and broken bones. And he didn't hit the ground close in and then crawl out to expire on the rocks. All of that much is pretty obvious, for whatever it means."

Perrone crossed over to one of the sinks, stripped off his latex gloves, and began the process of washing his hands. As he did so, he said over his shoulder, "Full autopsy tomorrow…later this morning, I mean." He glanced at the wall clock. "He'll keep 'til then. But both Francis and I thought you should know about the bruise on the back."

He took a deep breath as he dried his hands. "Somebody else was out there, folks. Bet on it. This is not just some simple hiker's injury. The laws of physics say otherwise. The only *other* explanation is that the victim took a running jump, flinging himself out—a really creative, difficult suicide, considering the sore ankle, and given the uncertainty of success."

"Come first light," Torrez said, "we need to get back out there and take another look—all the way out to the county road. You, me, and pick up Taber on the way."

Estelle nodded at Linda. "And the magician with the camera too."

"Of course," Torrez said, more affably than usual. He reached out and punched Linda Pasquale lightly on the left shoulder, a display of emotion adequate to last him for the rest of the month.

Chapter Twenty-Two

By ten o'clock the next Monday morning, the sunshine of that first June day had baked the prairie to a fragrant potpourri of creosote bush, black sage, and the myriad species of composites in full yellow bloom. Estelle Reyes-Guzman still felt logy despite four hours sleep, and on top of that, frustrated that the new day had brought no positive results at the Kyle Thompson death scene.

The prairie itself was a welter of old tracks, both two- and four-wheeled, cut after the last rain that the sky had managed. The gravel was hard, baked stove-top dry, with small patches of blow sand here and there. Even knowing exactly where Thompson's Subaru had been parked, it was impossible to follow any kind of trail where he might have walked to the cliff edge.

The Subaru's tire tracks marked clearly where he had parked, however. The left front tire had crunched over a patch of bunchgrass, and the right front had forced its pattern in a small patch of sand. One of Linda Pasquale's photos showed the Subaru being hooked up to the car carrier that had removed it from the site, and it was simple enough to find the exact spot where the little car's tires had rested. Which told them nothing.

Had Kyle Thompson followed a direct line from Subaru to the jutting top of the rim rock from which he'd then fallen, he would have limped just under two hundred feet. He had left no discernable footprints during his hike, not even scuff or drag marks from his therapeutic but awkward boot. With her hands in her back pockets, Estelle strolled back out toward the county road, then turned and headed north, concentrating on keeping her eyes open and probing every shadow, every dip and hummock.

The urge to doze off was strong, reminding her of an old, worn-out horse she had ridden as a child, growing up in Tres Santos, Mexico. The animal would plod along the dirt road, his old bones soaking up the warmth, and after a little while his ears would flop akimbo, his eyes would sag shut, and his lower lip would hang loose. He could walk for miles, sound asleep on his feet. Only when tripping over the occasional pebble did he jar awake for a moment.

Two hundred yards up the road, a deeper two-track cut angled off to the right. It bore a collection of tracks, perhaps where the surveyors had turned in, perhaps where the vandals of the surveyors' stakes had driven onto the private property. Some of the tracks were cut by wide, aggressively lugged tires, like those of an ATV. Several of the tracks were singles, like those of motorbikes. Those, Estelle reckoned, would have become a major challenge for the Thompsons. Their land covered a large area frequented by recreational riders and hunters. To expect them all to suddenly stop and find new ground to explore was unrealistic.

Years before, when the department was looking for a lost child, Estelle had driven down this two-track, and she knew that it angled south after a while, cutting across the prairie below the rim rock on which Thompson had been standing.

As if she had all the time in the world, she strolled down the path, examining each set of tracks as they cut this way and that.

The morning sun pounded her shoulders, and she made it a point to amble, looking at every bush, flower, and dimple in the prairie. The two-track meandered, cutting around boulders that lay on the prairie as if tossed aside by some giant playing ball, then angled sharply to the north as it plunged down into one of the side spurs of the arroyo that cut the land like rumpled corduroy. The surveyors had come this way, no doubt—so had the vandals who had pulled up marker stakes. Here and there, she saw motorcycle tracks, marking a wild ride for some brave cyclist.

Her radio burst alive with a bark of squelch. "Lemme know when you're directly below where Thompson fell," Torrez said. She looked up and could see the sheriff, his large figure standing well back from the edge of the boulders. Ever the hunter, he'd had no trouble seeing her moving through the shadows of the vegetation, now and then obscured by the rock formations.

"It's about fifty yards ahead of me."

"Anything interesting?"

"Not yet. Lots of vehicular traffic, but there's no way to tell how old the tracks are."

He clicked the transmit button twice in acknowledgment, then came back on the air. "That old road winds all the way around, then takes off to the east. Ends up down at Prescott's ranch."

Of course he would know, Estelle thought. The sheriff had spent hundreds of hunting hours in this country, almost all of it on foot. She pressed her own transmit bar to acknowledge. Another few yards and she stopped. The motorcycle tracks swung a little to the right, and a single footprint marked the blow sand of the two-track—a single footprint, this time on the right side of the motorcycle's track.

And then, that was followed by an odd collection of tracks. Another print on the right side, and then another, and then a scuff and dig on the left, along with a deep shoe print, only a partial where the sand had blown off a smooth jut of sandstone.

Estelle crouched for a closer look. "So what's this?" she said aloud. Without shifting position, she looked up the near-vertical, rock-jumbled slope toward the shelf where Kyle Thompson's body had crash landed.

"What?"

The single word from Bob Torrez amused Estelle. Without a doubt, he'd seen her stop and kneel. He had to know why.

"I'm considering coincidences," she radioed back. "Someone was down here recently. Unfortunately, I have no idea *how* recent."

"You need Linda down there?"

"Yes." *And that's not all I need,* she thought. She knelt and positioned herself as close as she could without disturbing any of the tracks. The edges of the boot print included only from the toe back to the arch area in front of the heel before the underlying stone made impression impossible. None of the sand grains, nor the bits of gravel, had tumbled down from the edge of the print. It had not been cast long enough ago to be even a little weather worn. The same was true of the motorcycle's tire track. In the few spots where it had been able to print, the impression was sharp and unworn.

"The sheriff sent me this way," Linda Pasquale said between deep breaths when she joined Estelle a few minutes later. Nodding back the way she'd come, she added, "I came around the long way, following what few tracks you left." She shrugged the strap of her camera bag up on her shoulder.

"This is one of those things," Estelle said. "Fresh tracks here, and what looks like a motorcycle dismount…and absolutely nothing to suggest that it's in any way related to Thompson's death." She watched Linda bend down to examine the tracks. "The only thing we know for sure—well, reasonably for sure—is that the prints didn't come *after* the incident. Too many of us hanging around at all hours. It's likely we would have seen something."

"Uh huh," Linda said, and lowered the camera bag to the ground. "Unless they watched us and waited for a moment when the place was deserted. I'd wonder why, is what I'd wonder. You're thinking that someone rode around on the old two-track, then parked it here, and then what? Scrambled up through the rocks, maybe all the way up to where Thompson was standing on the very top?"

"That's one scenario. For someone fit, it wouldn't take long."

"Now why would he do that, though?"

"To talk to him? To Thompson?"

"And things then degenerate, and while Thompson is gazing out at the scenery, pow! The kick and over he goes."

When Estelle said nothing, Linda turned her attention to the motorcycle track and the mark that the kickstand had made. "Or was he lying in wait all that time."

"That would mean that he—or she—knew in advance that Thompson was headed over here. And lying in wait, down here when Thompson is up there, makes no sense either. Thompson would certainly have seen him climbing toward him."

She hefted her camera and double-checked its settings. "I think this is a chance thing, Estelle. Nothing else makes sense to me." Her camera clicked and she added, "Of course, in all fairness, there is a whole universe of things that don't make sense to me."

Estelle looked up past the rocks to the vista shelf where Kyle Thompson had taken flight. Once again, Sheriff Torrez appeared and was gazing down at them. She saw him lift the small handheld radio.

"Anything?"

"Someone parked a motorcycle here."

"That's it?"

"That's it."

"You got any tracks comin' up the hill?"

"It's impossible to tell, Robert. It's nothing but a rock jumble."

"Is the tire print good enough to make a casting?"

"Maybe."

"Pasquale is here now. I'll send him down with the cast kit."

"Ten four."

"This is one of those things," Linda said cheerfully. "If you cast it, you won't need it. If you *don't* cast it, you'll wish you had."

"Courts don't think much of tire casts in this day and age," Estelle said. "Too many tires out there, and with an example like this one, not enough detail for any kind of real match. There would have to be a clearly identifying mark that could be compared."

"Remember Davy Schofield?"

Estelle grinned. "Oh, yes. I remember Davy. We show him an eight-by-ten glossy of a smudged shoe print left on a wet cement floor. Any attorney worth his salt would take one look and just laugh. But Davy takes one look, and figures he's had it. He confesses to what, sixteen residential and a handful of commercial burglaries?"

"Spooked by a photo that no court in the world would accept," Linda added. "You never know."

"True enough."

"Hey?" Torrez's disembodied voice said. "Lydia Thompson is parked out at the county road. You need to talk with her?"

For a moment, Estelle pondered that. "Is there something specific that she wants?"

"Other than results, you mean?"

"Of course."

There was a pause. Her view up the steep slope was partially obscured, but she could see Torrez, still standing on the rock promontory, but this time twisted around as he looked back toward the county road.

"She wants to talk with you," Torrez said after a moment.

"I'll be up in a little bit. And no, I don't want her coming down here."

"Ten four. Pasquale's on his way."

Family first, Estelle thought. In moments of emotional crisis, family members were the first to strike out against their own. Wives stabbed husbands, husbands beat wives, parents roasted or boiled their own children. Look first to family. That's what the statistics about perpetrators claimed. Still, she found it hard to believe that Lydia Thompson would have lashed out at the same man who had literally held her together years before, after the three crippling shotgun blasts…and then stayed by her side during the long months of surgery, recuperation, and therapy.

"I'll show Sergeant Pasquale what you need," Linda said helpfully.

Estelle smiled at Linda's formal reference to her husband. "Just a standard tread cast," she said. "We both know how much he loves to make those." She nodded at the rock rubble hillside above them. "I need to know how long it takes to climb from here all the way to the top, where Bobby is standing."

Linda Pasquale didn't ask *why* she needed to know that, and had she done so, Estelle would have been hard-pressed to explain herself. But there had been at least two people on this hillside—Kyle Thompson and the owner of the foot that had kicked him over the edge. Had there been others? Who knew?

Had the motorcyclist ridden through here on the same day? A week before? And if he had ridden through on the day Thompson took his plunge, what had he witnessed? Had the motorcyclist only paused to innocently adjust his helmet? To light a cigarette? Had he glimpsed Kyle Thompson high above him? Had they conversed, shouting back and forth across the yawning space? Had the motorcyclist then clambered up through the rocks to talk face-to-face with Thompson, or had he witnessed the fatal kick from down here?

The scrape that one could imagine had been made by the bike's kickstand told an interesting story, Estelle mused. For a brief pause, why lower the stand? The rider clearly dismounted. And then what?

"Remember the slithering critters," Linda reminded helpfully.

"Oh, *sí*," Estelle stood for another minute, gazing uphill, plotting a likely route. She glanced at her watch, and set off, taking what appeared to be the easiest and most direct route. At one point thirty yards from where the motorcycle might have been parked, she stopped abruptly. Resting her left hand lightly on the massive hip of a pickup truck-sized boulder, she stood absolutely still, letting her gaze cover the ground in front of her a few inches at a time.

When she was sure of what she was seeing, she knelt and examined the single shoe print that marked a smooth river of sand, narrow enough that only the heel had been captured. The tread pattern was anything but clear and sharp, but she could see the hint of a waffle pattern.

The print prompted another flood of questions with no answers, other than the realization that a human being had walked this same route...sometime.

She turned and held up a hand, catching Linda Pasquale's attention. "I need a photo up here," she called. "One fair boot print."

In a moment, Linda reached her position, and stabbed a short-stemmed blue flag beside the print. "You want to take some of these with you?" she asked, and Estelle accepted a small bouquet of the flags and slid them into her back pocket. "I always have them in my kit." She shot a dozen or so photos, including both background and close-ups. "You're thinking the killer went up this way?"

"I don't know what I'm thinking," Estelle said. "We have no sense of time that ties any of this together. The photos you took of the bruising on Kyle Thompson's back..." She waited while Linda scrolled through the library of photos stored in the camera's memory card, then brought the one she wanted to the viewing screen. She offered it to Estelle.

"Any chance of enough detail for a match?"

Linda scoffed good-naturedly. "Don't we wish. But, no, not unless we let our imaginations mingle with wishful thinking. Another Davy Schofield moment."

"That can be useful," Estelle said. "If that's all we have."

"As long as he's got the plaster mixed, you want Tommy to cast this too?"

"Sure. Why not." Several months ago, she'd watched Sergeant Pasquale work through the sloppy process during a show-and-tell day at the elementary school. The thirty-five fifth graders had been impressed—maybe if they were impressed enough, watching a plaster cast being poured might deter them from a life of crime. At the least, they might learn to stick to high, hard ground. "Okay, onward."

Total scrambling time to reach the spot where Kyle Thompson crashed into the rocks took a little more than two minutes. She ducked under the yellow tape and continued on up the hill, finding that the forty-foot rise required almost five minutes, ducking around boulders and slipping through the narrow passageways in the boulder jumble—and finding her way blocked by an ancient juniper that had somehow survived centuries without being crushed by tumbling rocks.

The victim's trip down was faster. He would have had time during his free-flight for one heartfelt scream.

"She's waiting over in her vehicle." Sheriff Torrez nodded over toward the county road as Estelle approached within earshot. "You might ask her why she and her husband drove separate cars."

Habit, Estelle thought, but didn't voice the opinion. A busy couple like the Thompsons would want their individual wheels so they were never marooned should one of them go off gallivanting.

Lydia Thompson, sitting on the passenger side of the older model Explorer with the door open and her feet on the ground, rose as Estelle approached.

"Am I a person of interest in this?" The sober set of her face verified that she was not kidding.

"Should you be?"

"What I mean is, I've tried to talk with the sheriff a couple of times. It's like having a conversation with a tree stump."

Estelle laughed gently. "I sympathize, Lydia." She rubbed her hand across the top of the SUV's doorframe. "As you must know, an investigation like this is a maze of little strands, some connected, some just drifting off into nowhere. I'm convinced that your husband didn't stumble, lose his balance, and take a header down the rocks. Everything tells us that after the fall, he remained, unmoving, in exactly the spot where he was found by the deputy."

"And he would have had to fly out that far," Lydia said.

"Exactly so. Preliminary autopsy findings indicate that he received a significant blow to the upper back."

"A blow. Like a strike of some kind?"

"Apparently."

"I mean with a weapon of some kind? A stick? Club? What?"

Estelle hesitated, giving her intuitions time to voice their concerns. "At this point, it appears that he was kicked."

Lydia's eyes narrowed as she looked askance at Estelle. "*Kicked* in the *upper* back? My husband is six four. How would that work?"

"That's one avenue we're pursuing," Estelle replied.

"But you've found no sign of a confrontation. No sign of a fight."

"True. Sergeant Pasquale is casting both a partial boot print, along with some evidence that points to a motorcycle, down below the drop off. Whether or not there is a relationship is anyone's guess at this point."

"I..." Lydia started to say, then shook her head in frustration as she bit off the comment. Her otherwise lovely, glacial blue eyes were red-rimmed. The unrelenting sun had chapped her tear-stained cheeks.

"At this point, is there anyone with whom Kyle was talking about this project? Had he met with anyone? He and Miles Waddell hadn't had the chance to sit down together and discuss any of the plans, am I correct in that?"

"No, they hadn't." She frowned into the distance. "A one-point-six-million-dollar whim, Estelle. That's what we have here. Kyle bought this acreage based on the development Waddell has already done, and based on BLM plans for across the road. Never, in all the earlier pie-in-the-sky discussions did the notion of a dark zone come up. Neither one of us had any idea that light pollution would be such a big deal to Waddell."

"You think Miles would have reason to try to stop any development on this property?"

"I'm not saying that." She turned and looked south, toward the *NightZone* mesa development. "My God, the money he's poured into that place. And then *we* come along, and there's the threat of development right under his nose. How's he going to react to that?"

"You know how, Lydia. He wanted to talk with you both, to see what your plans were. And I suspect if he saw a possible conflict, he'd do his best to compromise the impact."

"Kicking someone over a cliff is a hell of a compromise." She smiled bitterly. "You know, one thing is for sure. Kyle was a big guy, but he was fit…with the exception of that wrecked ankle. That explains to me why, if he *was* kicked, or punched, or slugged, or whatever, that the blow had to come from the back. From behind him. He never saw it coming."

Lydia vised her head between both hands. "He would have heard whoever it was. That's what I don't understand. Somebody walks in, or motorcycles in, or drives in with a car or truck… Kyle would have heard that, he would have turned around to greet whoever it was." She shrugged helplessly.

"I have to do something to help, Estelle. I don't know what, but I can't just sit in the motel, or up at Waddell's Shangri La, and twiddle my thumbs. I talked to Kyle's parents, and they're going to fly out to Albuquerque for some sort of memorial service. I have to think about that."

"Anything I can do..."

Lydia laughed hopelessly and held up both hands. "I don't know. I don't know what I'm going to do. Not a clue. If my gut could stand alcohol, I think I'd go back to my room and drink myself into a coma."

"Think hard, Lydia. Think instead. Who did Kyle talk with during the past couple of days? Since the two of you came down to Posadas. On top of that, who knew about your trip? Who knew that you two were here?"

The young woman straightened her spine with a grimace, and rubbed her belly. "I wish I could answer that. I mean, it was no big secret or anything. A friend or two or three up in Albuquerque knew. And of course, all the *NightZone* folks knew that we were here. A few over in the county offices." She grunted and stretched her spine again. "I'm in knots. I feel like this whole mess is going to split me wide open."

"You drove down separately. Why did you do that?"

Lydia cocked one eyebrow. "Kyle was going to drive on down to Tucson. He's got a couple of buddies who are interested in this as investment property. I did *not* want to go to Tucson. I wanted to do some camping here, trying to get a sense of the place." She smiled. "Get it to talk to me about what it wants." She drew a spiral in the air next to her ear. "How's that for spiritual stuff?" She patted the Explorer's flank. "Sleeping bag, tent, all the goodies in the truck." Her frown was heavy. "Don't think so now. The room up at Waddell's place suits." She smiled again. "So you see, no alibi."

"If you do go camping, especially if you do that before we have the perp in custody, will you let us know?"

"Of course."

"Call if you think there's something I can do for you. Or if you need to talk with Dr. Guzman."

Lydia shook her head, and this time patted her gut gently. "In the weeks and months after this happened, I came that close," and she held thumb and index finger an eighth of an inch apart, "to developing a lifelong love affair with opiates. That close."

"It wouldn't have been a very long life."

"No, it wouldn't. Kyle helped me out of that, too." Her face crumpled. "And here I am. And there *he* is. It doesn't take long for a life to turn around, does it?"

"No, it doesn't."

Lydia sighed heavily. "So what now?"

"We work with what we have. And with what you can remember. So take a deep breath, and give it your best shot. Every person, every phone call, everything you can remember. Think about the Realtors you dealt with, or the bank personnel. Just every single person. At this point, we need connections."

Lydia carefully pushed the door of the Explorer closed. "Okay." She grinned wistfully. "You know, back when all this happened," and she stroked her gut again, "I cried so much, for so long, that I just cried myself out. Kyle used to say that my tear ducts had been drained from over-work. And then he'd keep giving me these ridiculous get well cards that would make me blubber some more. After a while, like a good addict hitting rock bottom, I decided that all that crying was going to accomplish was to give me sore eyes. It wasn't going to help me heal, and it wasn't going to fix up my insides so that someday I might have a family." She shrugged helplessly. "So I quit. But that's what I think I need to do now. Go lock myself in Mr. Waddell's wonderful hotel suite and let it all go. I don't think that's going to work, but it's a nice thought, eh?"

"You have my number."

"Yeah, I do. Thanks." She nodded at the approaching figure of Sheriff Torrez. "And please tell the stump there that I'll be okay. I think I make him nervous."

"He'll get over it."

Chapter Twenty-Three

Estelle drove south on County 14 for a few hundred yards and turned into the *NightZone* entrance. She idled the county car across the ample parking lot to the colorful sun shades under which two dozen vehicles were parked. The collection of New Mexico license tags was mixed with the characteristically dull rentals with California, Arizona, and Texas plates. Two-thirds of the way down the row, Lydia Thompson's Explorer was sandwiched between a Range Rover with Louisiana plates and a Jeep Grand Wagoneer from New York.

The two tram cars were passing each other near the mesa rise's midpoint, and for a moment Estelle considered taking that approach to the mesa top, but, loath to leave her mobile "office" untended, she drove across the parking area to the mesa access road's gate.

This time, her greeter was a young woman. She appeared from the gatehouse even before Estelle had pulled the Charger to a stop. Her name tag announced Cecily Montaño, and the young woman's smile was radiant—enough so that Estelle had a fleeting image of Miles Waddell conducting "This is how to smile at visitors" workshops for all staff.

"Hi," Cecily greeted. "I'm Cecily, and does Mr. Waddell have you sign in, or do you just drive on up?"

"How's your day going, Cecily?"

"Oh, just amazing." Her smile faded. "So sad about our neighbor's accident, though."

Our neighbor. Estelle regarded the girl with interest. Rich, smooth coffee skin, raven hair secured in a pert ponytail with a turquoise clip, and unfathomable brown eyes, in concert with a body that could belong to a New York model. But like so many of Miles Waddell's employees, Cecily Montaño was no high-fashion import. Posadas born and raised, Cecily's list of accomplishments at Posadas High School had been impressive. Estelle knew that the girl had worked part-time at the Don Juan de Oñate restaurant, and then, when she graduated high school with honors, had taken an office job with the Bureau of Land Management's field office in Deming.

"Did you have a chance to meet the Thompsons when they were topside?"

Cecily scrunched up her face. "You know, never actually like *met,* you know. Lots of talk going around that they were visiting. Maddy Lucero said that they were in the restaurant a time or two. Such nice folks." She shook her head in sympathy.

"If you'll open the gate, I'll buzz Mr. Waddell and tell him I'm on my way."

"Will do. Oh, and someone said that your son was home for a while?"

"I hope I get to see him," Estelle said with a grin.

"Oh, I know how that goes. Well, tell him 'hi' for me. I mean, he won't remember who I am, but you know." She shrugged fetchingly and pushed the remote for the gate.

Halfway up the mesa road, Estelle slowed at one of the tight left-hand curves, bringing the car to a full stop. By straining hard against her seat belt/shoulder harness, she could see the county road down below, and the billowing dust cloud behind Sheriff Robert Torrez's unit. His speed wasn't surprising. Torrez possessed a habitual lead foot during the most peaceful of times.

Estelle settled back and continued on up the grade. When she crested the top and was well away from the torturous curves and the sheer drops, she nudged the auto-dial of her cell phone.

"This is Miles Waddell. Hey, two visits in one day makes it special, Estelle."

"I hope you have a few minutes for me."

"You betcha. I'm over at the solar unit, but I'll run over and pick you up. I'll meet you by the front door."

"Actually, let me walk over there. I need a little leg stretch."

"Well, suit yourself. I'll watch for you."

The geometry of the mesa was such that, by walking west a few steps from where she parked in front of the main building, Estelle could see far to the north. The mesa top sloped gently toward its north rim, and by stepping west so that she could see around one wing of the hotel, she could view the spot where Kyle Thompson had parked his Subaru.

After a moment, she turned and walked along the macadam ribbon, a track wide enough for one of the *NightZone* maintenance pickups, or one of the side-by-side ATVs, if the operators were cautious. With its artistic twists and turns, the path was designed for foot traffic, with occasional brass interpretive trail markers pointing out interesting flora along the way.

By the time she had passed the planetarium, the last building in the main group, she was halfway to the solar observatory on the south rim. The heavily tinted front door slid open, and Miles Waddell appeared. Dressed as usual like a ranch hand paying an impromptu visit for an over-the-fence chat, he paused at the edge of the portico, his foot up on one of the large sandstone boulders that marked the patio. He didn't step out into the sun until Estelle was a pace or two away.

"You gotta see this," he said, and beckoned her inside. "Just incredible."

The interior of the observatory was chilly, looking more like a business office complex. The telescopes themselves were above them on the second story, not the sort of hobbyist's units where one would peer into an eyepiece. All of the imagery was fed through complex fiber optics to the computers downstairs, with half a dozen monitors showing the telescopes' focus.

"Kurt, can you roll a replay of what you just showed me? On the big monitor?"

A stubby young fellow held up a single finger, without taking his eyes off the monitor directly in front of him, tapped several command keys, and then relaxed back. "You bet I can do that."

"This is Dr. Kurt Morehouse," Waddell said. "I stole him away from New Mexico State University. Kurt, this is Undersheriff Estelle Reyes-Guzman."

The young man's grip was limp, just the fingers making contact rather than a good thumb-to-thumb clasp, but his bland face was illuminated by electric blue eyes and an affable smile. "Welcome aboard." He immediately turned his attention back to the computer terminal below the monitor. "I've named this one MW-18, but that's just for our own files. Just for fun. And as you'll see, it's not so huge as it's just plain artistic." He grinned wider.

On the sixty-inch monitor above, an image of a small portion of the sun's left flank appeared, and Estelle watched in fascination as the long tongue of the flare lashed out from the roiling solar surface.

"This coronal ejection of plasma is kind of puny." Morehouse put one index finger on the sun's surface, and another where the flare appeared to vanish into space. "About a million miles or so, give or take. Not enough to disrupt things here on Earth very much. But we like it."

The ejection subsided, almost immediately joined by another eruption, one that snaked and curled like a living thing.

"It's a busy neighborhood out there," Morehouse said.

"Amazing," Estelle said. "You work here solo?"

"Oh, gosh, no. We've got a total of five techs on board. Three of them are upstairs doing some grunt work with the second unit's mounts. Marie is in the office arguing with someone from CalTech, and that shadow over there?" He nodded toward a dark corner where the form of a young woman was hunched over a keyboard. "Evi is working on logistics for one of our upcoming projects."

He straightened up and indicated the framed, full-color prints that filled the empty wall spaces. "And she's our photographic artist as well." He grinned at Estelle. "Prints available in the gift shop, perfect for birthdays, anniversaries, or Christmas."

Morehouse lowered his voice and looked sideways at Estelle. "I've heard a lot about you," he said. "Marie Waters is in the office because it's the only place here that's quiet enough to listen to her beloved CDs." He waved a hand at the ceiling. "All the ventilator and cooling fan noise."

"I can imagine."

"She has a crush on your son, the young Maestro Guzman." Estelle laughed. "Ah. I hear that a lot."

"I bet you do."

His handshake was a bit firmer this time. "Nice to meet you, but I'm sure you have more important things to do than yakking with me."

"I appreciate the flare show, Dr. Morehouse. But I do need to spirit the boss man away for a few minutes."

"Oh, oh," Waddell said.

The light outside was harsh, the air hot after the air conditioned interior.

"How about over here?" Waddell followed a narrow walkway to an elegant gazebo just west of the observatory, its foundation skirting hosting a spectacular collection of cacti and succulents, all chosen as species that could tolerate the rugged Posadas County climate. He motioned to the picnic table and its benches. "How's this?"

"Perfect."

"Let me get some water. One minute." He disappeared back into the building and shortly returned with two bottles of ice water and a handful of nut bars. He slid a water and two bars across to Estelle. "It occurred to me that I could likely be your number one suspect."

"What makes you think that?" She had not discussed the kick print on Thompson's back with Miles Waddell, but she wasn't surprised that the former rancher was quick to reach his own conclusions.

"Well, everyone thinks—okay, folks seem *surprised* that I let someone from out of town walk in and buy that chunk of New Mexico to the north of us." He held up a hand and ducked his head. "I mean, another bunch of acreage would be nice, insuring my project's privacy and dark skies. But I guess I wasn't quick enough on the draw this time. And who knows what Kyle Thompson was actually planning for that acreage?" He nodded at Estelle as he unwrapped one of the nut bars. "So. I'm all ears. What's driving your day?"

"We're seeing some coincidences, Miles."

"Coincidences? In what regard?"

Estelle hesitated, and then held up both index fingers, side by side. "First we have the drive-by shooting at the newspaper office. We don't think that the two victims there were specifically targeted. At that hour of the night, it's hard to imagine that they were *expected* to be there. A chance thing."

Waddell said nothing, his hands folded quietly on the table, his eyes locked on Estelle's.

"Then, Kyle Thompson dies in what looks at first like a freak accident." She paused. "As you've already figured out, it was no accident, Miles. We think Mr. Thompson was standing on the rocks, taking in the view, maybe even talking with someone. We believe that he was kicked in the back, hard and high, launching him forward."

"You really do think that he was murdered."

"I do. And right now, it's hard for me to believe that the two attacks—the one at the newspaper office, and the attack not long afterward on Kyle Thompson—aren't somehow related." She rubbed her two fingers together. "Too close in time, too close to other interesting coincidences."

Waddell tipped his chair back, one boot braced against the table crosspiece.

"We seem to be a magnet," he said finally. "And I'm not sure I'm liking much about that."

"*NightZone* is a huge facility, Miles. A huge facility in rugged country where a lot can be hidden. Lots of people, lots going on, lots of opportunity."

He looked at her, amused and concerned all at once. He started to say one thing, stopped, and rethought. "You're suggesting that I'm sort of the epicenter for some of this stuff. That's what I find hard to fathom."

"Not you personally, Miles." She shifted position. "Let me pose something to you. If we could wave a magic wand and make all of Thompson enterprises disappear, how might that impact your development?"

He looked puzzled. "I don't know. If Thompson's land comes back on the market, I suppose somebody would buy it." He shrugged. "Eventually. Like I said, I might even go after it, just as another way to protect my investment here. But thinking about that is premature. I assume that Lydia Thompson has her own ideas about the property. Give her a while to settle down, to come to terms with her loss."

"She seems sympathetic to your venture here."

"So far, she does. But who knows? And if worse comes to worse, remember years ago, when I first started out? Some jerks tried to stop my development by cutting down some of my power poles with a chain saw. That didn't work out so well for them, did it?" With some fussing, he tore open the second nut bar. "But you mentioned other coincidences?"

"Not long ago, a young man applied for a job with your rail boss."

"With Hank Quintana, you mean?"

Estelle nodded. "Things looked good for a job, until the *Register* published the weekly 'Sheriff's Report.'"

"Your young man was listed there. And I think we're talking about the sheriff's nephew, am I right?"

"Yes. Quentin Torrez."

"Ah. There's a young fellow with a lot of potential. His drunk driving arrest was unfortunate, but I hope he understands that our locomotive operation is a very special animal. Unique, I might say. Hank and I agreed from day one that the rail transportation operation is absolutely zero tolerance. It has to be. So while I might hire someone like young Torrez for any number of available positions at the gate, or even here topside, he will never work with the train crew.

"That's what Clay Simmons does for me, among many other things—background checks and hiring recommendations. I gotta tell you, this current mess of all the gutless politicians making marijuana legal is a real nightmare for us. It was bad enough before, worrying about bottle to throttle. But my view is that no matter what the state decides, no matter how they kowtow to special interests, the use of substance like that, or stronger, is *verboten* up here. Let 'em sue me if they feel discriminated against."

He munched reflectively on the nut bar for a moment. "Having said all that, and climbing down off my soapbox for a minute, let me be the first to say that I'd like to add Quentin Torrez to the staff."

He nodded at Estelle's surprised expression. "And you know, I probably will. I was thinking of calling him in for an interview later this week. One on one, you know? See where his head is. He's got friends here, and that can be both a plus and a minus. I mean, let's face it. They're all kids, right?" He grinned. "Anyone under thirty is still a kid to me. But Quentin Torrez has talents, I think. He could grow into a job here topside. Just not on the train or the tram. That's what I want to see. Grow a team that takes pride in this place."

"You've heard talk about what the Thompsons were planning?"

"Sure. Everyone has his own theory. Or did. And now what? I haven't gotten beyond the 'sorry for your loss' stage with his widow, and I don't want to push her. But what a mess she has landed in her lap."

"Do you have reason to believe anyone on your staff—anyone at all—held a grudge against Kyle Thompson? However petty?"

Waddell puffed out his cheeks. "No. I told a couple of the kids that they should curtail their trespassing on that property until things get straightened out. I mean, all their hunting and stuff." He smiled broadly. "Bob Torrez—the biggest kid of all. I don't think there's a square inch of this county that he hasn't hunted until he could walk the whole thing in his sleep." His eyebrows shot up. "And let's not forget our old friend, Bill Gastner. He knows that country. Hell, one of the truckers alerted me once that Gastner was hobbling along the county road using his walker, for God's sakes."

"I remember that. Who are the other hunters? These kids you're talking about."

"Of my staff?" He hesitated. "Am I going to get someone in trouble?"

She held up both hands, palms up, and Waddell nodded in resignation. "I guess it's their own fault if they get crosswise with you folks."

"They?"

"You know what I mean. Whoever it is. Or not." He looked down and brushed crumbs off his jeans thoughtfully. "Because every inch of *NightZone* has been posted, naturally hunters tend to use what became the Thompsons' land. That and the BLM acreage across the county road. And east of us, on the Prescott ranch. No prairie dog is safe."

"Who's your top dog hunter?"

Waddell grinned. "Our resident assassin would have to be Charlie Pogue. I think you know him. Certainly no kid anymore. I hired him away from the electric company." He held up his hands to mimic a small box. "He carries his little black tally book when he hunts. I don't know for sure what his daily record is, but it's thousands of dogs over the years. Bob Torrez knows him pretty well."

"As do I," Estelle said. Charlie Pogue's image came to mind, a short, dumpy fellow with hair buzzed to a burr on his big, round head, in his off-hours volunteering as assistant defensive coach for the Posadas High School Jaguars.

"He's got quite the setup," Waddell added. "Table with attached stool in the back of his pickup, uses a bipod. He's got some older model Remington with a suppressor. I would hope the whole rig is legal."

"It is."

"Well, you'd know, right? Every once in a while, he takes one or two of the kids hunting, usually in that flat country north of Prescott's ranch, or over on the BLM property across the road. He's a good influence."

"Who goes with him?"

Waddell frowned in thought. "Actually in the aficionado category? I'd say that Rafael Gonzales hunts as much as anybody. Maybe he practices his Japanese with them, I don't know. But he goes, both by himself and with Charlie. And some of his buds. I've seen a handful of 'em in the back of Charlie's truck. Looks like one of those pictures you see of those Taliban guys in their Toyota pickups."

"That's a sobering image."

"Yeah, well. Let's see. Rolando goes with 'em. He and Rafael are pretty close." He frowned at the western horizon. "I've even seen Maddy Quintana and Cicily Montaño along for the ride. And the Torrez boy, too. Young Quentin."

He looked hard at Estelle. "I don't fancy myself as a career center for young thugs, Estelle. I'll tell you right now that I think highly of my crew. I wouldn't keep them on if I didn't. I don't think I'm speaking out of turn to say that Clay Simmons thinks the same thing."

"I'd like to talk with him. With Charlie Pogue."

"That's easy enough. Right now he's working over in the auditorium with the new projector project." He flashed a smile. "Never stops. Bigger, faster, better, higher-res…it goes on and on." He leaned forward, lowered his voice, and clamped a hand on each side of his head. "I've created a monster, my friend."

"More like an amazing artistic creation, Miles."

"Thanks for that. I think most people think so. There are always a few who wonder why, you know. But what am I supposed to do, spend all my time playing golf and going on cruises? Give the funds to some charity so the administrators get rich?" He sat back. "I think not. And by the way, the latest from Chicago—the Sheridan-Waddell Heritage block sale is going through."

"You had mentioned that you were thinking of liquidating some of the remaining Chicago properties. This is one of them, I assume?"

"Yep. One less worry, and another three hundred million to invest out here."

"Congratulations." She sipped her water. "Is now a good time to meet with Mr. Pogue?"

"Hell, why not. Let's find him."

Chapter Twenty-Four

"That's his foot."

The foot belonged to a body far up inside the mammoth projector's innards. Waddell knelt down and crooked his neck. "Charlie, can you spare me a minute or two?"

The foot shifted and a gruff voice drifted out. "Give me a little bit."

"It's Miles," Waddell added, and they heard Charlie Pogue chuckle.

"In that case, check with me sometime next week."

"The long arm of the law would like to talk with you, Charlie."

"Use the little blue clip for that," Pogue said to someone else, and for the first time, Estelle realized that the electrician wasn't alone in the crawl space under the projector. "Tell the sheriff I don't have time to go hunting today."

"It's not Torrez, Charlie. It's Undersheriff Reyes-Guzman."

"Oh, my God." Pogue said something *sotto voce* to his assistant. "Do I have time to go take a shower?"

"Nope."

"Well, hang in there just a minute."

Waddell touched Estelle's elbow. "I'll leave you to him. If you need to see me again, I'll be back over at the solar center."

"Thanks for your help, Miles. I'll keep you posted."

"I'd appreciate that."

In another minute, Charlie Pogue heaved himself out, moving through the maze of struts and wiring harnesses like a fat inchworm. When his head cleared the access hatch, he paused, curled half on his back, and sucked several deep breaths. He looked up, regarding Estelle.

"Good afternoon, sir," she said.

"Is it? Hell, I don't even know what time it is. *That's* the kind of day it's been." With a grunt, he heaved himself first to his knees and then upright. He rubbed his ample belly. "Gotta do something about this gut." He extended a hand, and his grip was polite. He held up a finger and turned back. "Just wire all the blues, Efrin. I'll be back in a little bit."

"Efrin Garcia?" Estelle asked.

"Himself. Only help I got who knows one color from another."

"His mural in the auditorium proves that."

"Oh, isn't that something? So..." He bent down and swept some imaginary dust from his knees.

"Is there somewhere we can talk for a few minutes?"

"Sure." He looked around and pointed toward a door in the rear of the planetarium. "Let's use Bunny's office. I don't think she's here until later today."

They padded back across the thick indigo carpeting of the planetarium and entered a small, heavily insulated office crowded with six computer monitors and a bank of blinking hard drives under the bench-like desk along one wall. Pogue gestured toward the chair behind the desk, and took one of the padded straight chairs for himself. He folded his arms across his chest and leaned back.

"So."

"Mr. Pogue, thanks for taking the time to talk with me."

"It's Charlie. And given the way things have been going, I'm not sure this meeting is voluntary, is it?" He smiled, but the expression was from the nose down. His slate gray eyes remained sober and watchful.

"Mr. and Mrs. Thompson apparently hadn't had the opportunity to discuss with any of you folks their plans for the property next door. For the Boyd ranch."

"That's fair to say. At least they didn't talk to *me*. Not that I would be high on their list."

"Had you met with either of them?"

"No." A trace of crow's-feet deepened at the corner of Pogue's eyes. "As I said, I wouldn't be the one they'd meet with anyway. I'm not that high on the totem pole. Above my pay grade, as they say."

"I understand that on occasion you prairie-dog-hunt over there."

"As did a lot of people. But not so much anymore."

Estelle fell silent, her pen poised over the notebook page. "You hunt by yourself?"

"Most of the time." He grinned, but again without much humor. "Where are we headed with this? Don't tell me prairie dogs arc now an endangered species. Or worse yet, considered a game animal."

Estelle paused, letting her fingers leaf through the pages of the small notebook as if she might be searching for something. "At the moment, we're just in the process of discovery, Mr. Pogue. We need to find out who was where…and when. It appears that Mr. Thompson was not alone when he was killed in the fall. Some other issues involved with both incidents have drawn our attention as well."

"Both?"

"The vandalism and assault at the newspaper office, as well as the Thompson fatality."

He nodded slowly, eyes narrowed. "I heard about that drive-by thing. Are we going to have to put up with gang activity now?"

"We hope not—not that it makes any difference to the two victims."

"They're doin' all right? I didn't know that young reporter, but I'm sure everybody in town knows Pam Gardiner."

"Sure enough, in a community this tightly knit."

"I see what you're gettin' at now. Everybody talks, sure. And what I've heard is all in the 'what the hell's goin' on' category. This is the first time that I've heard that Thompson's accident was anything other than that…a slip and a fall. You're saying that you think that somebody might have been with him at the time." He glanced at his watch, a clear hint that he was eager to return to his project.

"When was the last time you were hunting in the area?"

"I don't hunt on the Thompsons' land anymore. I haven't since the posted signs went up last month. I favor that big playa over north of the BLM's holdings. You're thinking it was a hunter involved?"

"We don't know. You were hunting on the playa recently?"

"Sure."

"When might the last time have been?"

Pogue remained silent for a few heartbeats, but his gaze was touched with amusement. "What, I need an alibi now?"

"I can't imagine that you do." The image of Charlie Pogue launching his pudgy, short body into the air for a flying tae-kwondo kick prompted her own smile. "Did any of the kids go with you? Efrin? Quentin? Rolando? Rafael? Any of the girls?"

"Efrin went with me."

"When was this?"

Charlie frowned and looked down at his feet. His head waggled as he counted days. "Could look in my doggy book, but right off the top of my head, I'd say it would have been early last Thursday."

"Both had the day off?"

"No. We just went. Got out there just after seven."

"Good tally?"

He snorted. "You know. Sometimes there's competition.

That morning we had a Swainson's hawk doing his thing, so the dogs were a bit leery. Got a few, though. Enough to make the ravens happy."

"What was Efrin shooting? Did he use your rifle?"

"No, he had one he borrowed from somebody. From Rolando, I think he said." Pogue looked off toward the northern horizon. "He made one shot that just impressed the hell out of me. Nearly two hundred yards, with a dang little twenty-two. That kid's got eyesight I'd still like to have, that's for sure. The hawk's got nothin' on him."

He glanced at his watch again. "I need to get back at it. Anything else you need from me? I can't imagine you're all that interested in prairie dogs, Sheriff."

"Charlie, thanks for taking the time. I appreciate it."

"Tell Bobby not to be such a stranger next time you see him," Pogue said. "I used to see him out and around, but not so much since he became the proud papa."

"Give him time. A couple more years and he'll be taking Gabe out hunting, showing him all the prime spots."

"I would think there's enough country for everybody, but things are changing." Pogue laughed ruefully. "It's a whole different country than it was a few years ago, my friend. Lots of people, lots of laws, lots of posting...we aren't New Jersey yet, but we're sure workin' at it. I've heard the rumors, of course, but I don't know for sure what the developers were planning for that country north of here. But one thing's for sure. If not them, then it'll be someone else.

"If Miles Waddell was smart, he'd latch on to that property, just to protect all this." His hand swept an arc across the *NightZone* mesa top. "I mean, that useless range land is nickel-dime compared to what he's got invested in this place."

"And Miles Waddell is smart, Charlie."

"He is that." He nodded agreement. "Good show tonight, by the way. Come join us."

"Thank you. I might just do that." Estelle walked back through the planetarium auditorium with him, just in time to see Efrin Garcia emerge through the access door under the one of the projectors. He swept a hand up, pushed his curly black hair away from his eyes, and offered Estelle a wide smile, then said to Charlie, "Blue's done, Charlie."

"Then it's onward. Yellow's next, then white, orange, brown... the whole damn rainbow." He glanced at Estelle. "Damn good thing that the kid isn't color blind, eh?"

"A very good thing. Thanks again, sir."

"You bet. Visit anytime."

Miles Waddell is smart, Estelle thought as she walked back to her car. Of all the people with the most to gain by blocking Kyle Thompson's development plans, Miles Waddell headed the list. She reached her car, opened it, and let the door swing wide for a few minutes to exhaust the super-heated air trapped inside. But *Miles Waddell is smart,* she reminded herself. Even if he had designs on the acreage to the north, he wouldn't jeopardize his mesa-top development by striking out in a moment of thought-less impulse.

And Lydia Thompson? Estelle slid into the Charger, started it, and turned the air conditioning to its highest setting. Wives and husbands headed the list of perpetrators of domestic vio-lence. That's what the cold, hard statistics said. But there had been no hint that the familiar domestic pattern of violence or conflict fitted the Thompsons. On top of that, Lydia was no towering giant. Unless she could sprout wings, her husband would have had to have been bent over or even kneeling for her to place that kick.

Chapter Twenty-Five

Her phone played its classical chord, and Estelle waited until she had completed the left turn onto Twelfth Street before sliding the gadget from the center console pocket.

"Guzman."

"Hey. Where you at?"

"About to pull into my driveway, Bobby. I've got a convention." Bill Gastner's fancy red conversion van, complete with the oversized side door and hydraulic chair lift, was snugged close to the curb. Estelle's Honda Pilot, currently serving Francisco, Angie, and the baby, was parked in the garage, the garage door left gaping open. Estelle swung the Charger into the driveway.

"Did you get a chance to talk with Waddell?" Torrez asked.

"Yes. And Charlie Pogue."

"What'd Pogue tell you?"

"That he hunts prairie dogs just about as often as you do. And on occasion he's been known to take along a kid or two. Some of the kids who work up on the mesa with him."

Torrez greeted that news with silence.

"Most recently he and Efrin went out, over on the BLM land."

"Huh. Efrin?"

"Yes."

"Didn't know he hunted. "

"With a loaner gun, Charlie says. Efrin borrowed a twenty-two from Rolando Ortega. Made a spectacular two hundred-yard shot, Charlie says."

"Got lucky. Look, I spent some time with Marvin Petes."

"All right, good." Petes taught mathematics at the high school, and headed the taekwondo classes hosted in the basement of the Baptist Church twice a week—on Saturday morning for the peewees, and Saturday evening for the young adults.

"I ain't much on coincidence," Torrez said. "And now we got a quartet."

Estelle glanced toward the front door, where Francisco had appeared, William Thomas snuggled in his arms. Estelle held up a hand, begging for a few minutes.

"Who are we talking about?"

"Quentin assists Petes with the morning kiddy class, and most of the time works the night adult class too. Efrin Garcia just finished up earnin' his first yellow, Rolando Ortega is tryin' for his first blue belt, and Rafael Gonzales..." Estelle heard notebook pages rumpling. "Gonzales is a beginner. A white belt."

"Interesting."

"Our own little gang of four."

"There are certainly worse things for them to be spending their time doing." Estelle knew what the sheriff was thinking, and also knew how stubborn he was once he thought he had picked up a trail. "How many are in the class, total?"

"Nineteen."

"That's a lot for a village this size."

"Yup. I know most of 'em. You do too."

"That's another nineteen who are off the streets on a Saturday night, Bobby. That's a good thing."

"Yep. My numbnuts nephew is first-degree black, and he's proud as hell about that."

She recalled the thump of the flat of the sheriff's fist against his nephew's chest. "Quentin grows another inch and puts on a few pounds, you're going to have to be careful about smacking him around."

Torrez actually laughed. "You think?"

"Yes, I do. And by the way, Miles said that he's going to talk with Quentin about working up on the mesa. Just not on the locomotive or the tram. At least until he proves himself."

"He's got a ways to go to do that," Torrez said. "Maybe he'll start takin' some of that mystical learning that comes with the black belt to heart. You stuck at home tonight?"

Estelle chuckled at Torrez's sudden change of subject. "It's looking that way. I plan to spend an evening being a doting grandmother." She watched as her son ambled toward her, arms locked around the swaddled William Thomas.

"I'll try not to interrupt, but we know how that goes." Torrez's sudden flash of warmhearted concern amused Estelle even further.

"Yes, we do. Keep me posted."

She switched off and smiled as her son reached out and opened the Charger's heavy door.

"I hope you don't mind some noise," Francisco said. "We were going to do dinner here, since this is where the piano is." He took a step back. "Oh, and Pa says he'll be home in about thirty minutes." He regarded his mother with interest as she unwound from the tight confines of the sedan. "Long day?"

"So far, so long," she said. With the car door closed, she reached out and collected her grandson, fingering just enough of the blanket back so that she could see his tiny face, relaxed in deep slumber.

"Are you going back out?"

"I'm going to try hard not to," she laughed. "But as the sheriff just said, 'we know how that goes.' Right now we're facing something of a brick wall. It's going to take time to chip it away."

"Angie is the chef tonight, so you can relax over dinner. Then we'll play a couple of tunes for you, and if you're lucky, it'll put you right to sleep." He reached out and ever so gently stroked a thumb across the fatigue lines under Estelle's right eye. "A perfect pour today, by the way." Seeing the puzzled look, he added, "The cement. We have a footer now."

"Ah."

"The big news is that we're picking up Carlos and Tasha on the way back from Hawaii. By that time, the contractor will have the floor supports installed, and Carlos wants to look things over before construction goes any further."

Estelle felt the anxiety of the day slipping away, and she nuzzled the infant. "So many of life's surprises ahead for you," she whispered. "That's wonderful," she said to Francisco.

"And *Padrino* had some news, but I'll let him tell you all about it." He escorted Estelle toward the house, and even before they reached the front door, she smelled the fragrance. "Angie was in the mood for pot roast," her son explained. "I worked at the piano all day, and she cooked."

"But *she's* the one with the concert coming up."

"A little pre-concert break is a good thing. Keeps us sharp."

The aroma made Estelle's stomach growl. Perhaps his olfactory powers were still undeveloped, because William Thomas's little button nose didn't twitch.

"Wasn't sure you'd show up," Bill Gastner greeted. He ignored his walker and made his way across the living room free-style, stopping near the end of the piano to accept a hug.

"I wasn't sure either, *Padrino.*"

"Any closer?"

"I don't know." She shook her head, still fascinated by the tiny face so content to snooze. "It's worrisome."

"And there's no point in that," the old man said. "Come sit down, relax, enjoy, let the kids serve you."

She held William Thomas out toward Gastner. "I need to shed some hardware first."

He held out a stop-hand. "I don't do babies," he said. "*Maestro,* come fetch your son."

Infant safely transferred, Estelle stopped by the kitchen where Angie was making potatoes gorgeous, and Estelle was again struck how dramatically beautiful her daughter-in-law was, aproned and paring knife-wielding, her lustrous black hair tied back in a loose ponytail.

"I seem to spend most of my time out among the crazies," Estelle said as she hugged Angie. "It is so nice to come home to you guys."

"We appreciate the haven, believe me." Angie smiled and nodded at her handiwork. "Potato florets, the perfect stress relief."

"Give me a few minutes, and I'll join you." A "few minutes" turned into half an hour as she first shed her hardware and pants suit, then let the hot shower beat on her until the water heater couldn't keep up. A run of the fingers through her short hair sufficed, and she emerged from the bathroom swathed in a huge towel to find her husband in their bedroom, shedding his scrubs.

"Ah…you're going to have to wait a few minutes, *Oso.* I was piggy and used the hot water."

He held out a hand and she moved across to him. She reached up and ruffled his salt-and-pepper curly hair, sweeping it away from his ears. Then, with a hand lightly gripping each ear, she pulled his head down and stroked his lips with her own. His hands rested lightly on her hips.

"You smell as if your day has been less than pleasant." Her towel slipped, but she made no effort to retrieve it. Francis laughed as she wrinkled her nose.

"You, on the other hand," he said, "smell like rosemary and a bunch of other nice things. And we've got a feast coming up, by the aroma of things from that end of the house." Neither one of them showed any eagerness to change position.

"You and Alan finished with the Thompson autopsy?"

"Oh, *sí*. No surprises, but a confirmation of the bruise on his back. A really hard blow, enough to present some deep tissue hemorrhaging. COD was for sure the cracked skull, though."

"And Pam?"

"Safely in Presbyterian, and she elected to go ahead with the surgery. That's scheduled for first thing tomorrow morning."

"That's scary stuff."

"You bet. But she chose not to try to sidestep it. Doing nothing about it would be like living with a time bomb in her brain."

"I should have stopped by to see her earlier today."

"She knows that you're working on her behalf."

"Spinning our wheels on her behalf, maybe. An update on Rik?"

"He's sore but fine. Discharged and told to take it easy. "

"Good."

"Now let's enjoy dinner and other things, before the phone rings again."

In the utility room behind the bath, the hot water tank gurgled loud enough to be heard.

"I'll go get presentable. If I run out of hot water, the cold won't hurt me a bit."

Chapter Twenty-Six

Cell phones and other gadgets turned off, even the landline popped out of its wall connection, the Guzman home on Twelfth Street was as quiet as isolating technology could make it. Even the porch light was turned off. Estelle was curled on the sofa, her head and shoulder pillowed by her husband, with tiny William Thomas fed, changed, and snuggled between her right breast and her husband's left thigh.

Bill Gastner was trying hard to keep his eyes open, and he had found a position where he could gently rock the old chair forward without any squeaks as he sought his brimming mug of coffee with minimal effort.

Francisco sat at the piano, with the score of Lukie Maoma's *Sonata for Cello in E-flat* on the music stand. The cover was lowered over the keys, and he sat with his elbows planted, chin in hands.

The star of the show, Angie Trevino Guzman, had found a nick in the floor just beyond the piano that captured her cello's end peg securely, and the 300-year-old instrument had settled into flawless tune under the urgings of Angie's deft fingers. She closed her eyes as she ran the bow a final stroke along the rosin block, and smiled at her audience. "New bow," she announced.

"Organic horsehair from a genuine Lipizzaner stallion's tail, harvested in the dark of the moon. Or something like that." She used no music stand, and no sheet music was in sight.

The fat, lowest string of the cello growled as she stroked it once, twice, three times until it became apparent that she was playing every child's classic, "Row, Row, Row Your Boat," until the sound filled every nook and corner of the house. The second refrain of *"merrily..."* became a cascade of triple stops that then took off in a series of joyous arpeggios that ended with the fingers of Angie's left hand within a hair's breadth of the end of the fingerboard.

She adjusted one of the bridge tuners a tiny fraction, and said, "Okay."

Eyes closed, she waited for a few seconds, and then launched into a ferocious piece that Estelle guessed was Bach. The contest between the instrument's lowest register and the dancing treble continued for not quite two and a half minutes until Angie leaned forward a bit, opened her eyes, and let the last notes drift off.

She touched the same tuner again and frowned. "Some strings have a somewhat argumentative personality. Anyway, that was the "Prelude" from Bach's *Suite Number One in G*, and it's a great way to find out which fingers are cooperating and which are not." She grinned toward Gastner, who had taken the opportunity to retrieve his coffee mug. "And most audiences are very glad that it's only a little more than two minutes long."

"And we have company," Francisco interjected, craning his neck to look past the piano and the window curtains. "I think she's sitting on the top front step."

"You're joking," Estelle said.

"Never. I can see her feet." He had already risen, but his mother beat him to it, gently uncurling from her half-recumbent position.

"Let me get it." She made sure her husband's left hand had

corralled the slumbering infant. She paused as she reached Angie, and touched the young woman's right shoulder. "A two-minute intermission?"

"Estelle?" Her husband had already gathered up his grandson, and now transferred William Thomas to Francisco.

"No, it's all right. I'll get it." Estelle replied. "I think I know who it is."

She switched on the porch light and opened the door. Sure enough, a lone figure sat on the top step, her head cradled in her arms, arms resting on her knees.

"Lydia? Are you all right?" Estelle opened the storm door and slipped outside.

Lydia Thompson raised her head, wiped her eyes, and looked up at Estelle. "I shouldn't be here, I know that. I was going to ring the doorbell, or knock, or something, then I got to listening. That Bach piece was lovely. Your daughter-in-law?" She reached out a hand to the stair rail and pulled herself upright. She waited for Estelle to respond, and when Estelle didn't, added, "I shouldn't interrupt."

"What can I help you with, Lydia?"

"I saw you up at the astronomy park this afternoon. I saw you out on the solar facility patio, talking with Mr. Waddell, and I got to wondering."

"About what?"

"I wonder what he's going to do now."

"And he's probably wondering the same thing about you, Lydia. I suggest that you give the whole affair some time. Give yourself time to think. This whole tragedy hasn't given you time to do that yet."

"We don't even know what happened yet, do we? I mean, with Kyle. We don't know for sure."

"That's true."

She turned and gazed down the street, and Estelle reached in and closed the front door behind her, then waited patiently.

"I spent most of the late afternoon and through the dinner hour down at the newspaper office. Mr. Dayan was very helpful."

"I'm sure he was."

"Their morgue has copies back to 1913, when the paper was founded. He said they're making a concerted effort to digitize everything now so the old copies could be more useful." She rubbed her fingers together. "They've gotten so brittle now that the pages won't fold open without damage." She heaved a sigh. "Anyway..." She looked sideways at Estelle, assessing. "I read about the shooting."

"*The* shooting?"

"The deal with Manolo Tapia."

Estelle studied the young woman for a moment. "I spend a lot of time trying to forget about that."

"It's been a while."

"Seven years, four months, five days, nine hours and seventeen minutes." Estelle flashed a brief smile at the old joke. "But who's counting."

"It's hard, isn't it?"

"Yes. But I don't think I want to engage in a scar fest with you, Mrs. Thompson."

Lydia held up a hand. "No. You kept on, though. I mean, after you recovered, you kept on. That's what I'm getting at."

Estelle nodded but said nothing.

"I tried to do that. But I couldn't handle a couple important parts of the agility test." She made a face. "I probably could now. But Kyle had the itch to move. He missed out on the lieutenant's test by a couple of points, and that was a bummer."

A burst of laughter drifted out from the living room, followed by a series of wave-like chords from the piano.

"Wow," Lydia murmured, then shook her head. "I should go. It was impolite of me just to stop by." She stepped down to the sidewalk.

"You came by to ask me something."

Lydia turned, hands thrust in her back pockets. "I shouldn't be here."

Estelle nodded encouragement. "But you are, so…"

The young woman sucked in a deep breath. "Frank got to talking, and I mentioned that both Kyle and I had been in the State Police back in New York. We talked some more, and then he wanted to show me the police blotter from two weeks ago. The one where Sheriff Torrez's nephew was named for the DUI. Frank thinks…well, he thinks that Sheriff Torrez thinks…that the nephew might somehow be involved, upset because he didn't get a job with the *NightZone* train."

"Investigation is continuing." *And your skillful interrogation opened Frank Dayan's floodgates,* Estelle thought.

Lydia managed a full smile. "Haven't we all heard *that* before, eh? Anyway, Frank says that young Torrez might still apply to work up at *NightZone*. Just not on the train."

"He's free to do that."

"I can't help being a people-watcher, Estelle. I *know* that young Torrez would like to work up there…primarily because that's where his current flame works. The gal who is one of the waitresses at the restaurant. I think her name is something Lucero?" Lydia paused, giving Estelle the opportunity to provide the name—which the undersheriff did not do. "Anyway, she and young Torrez were trading some saliva when I happened to walk by. They took a step back behind one of the building buttresses for some privacy."

"There are a lot of young people up there," Estelle offered. "Lots of hormones."

"I guess. What I thought was interesting was seeing the Lucero girl similarly engaged with one of the other workers later in the day." She smiled and shook her head. "Get a few lovers' triangles going, and Miles Waddell is going to have a really interesting time of it."

"Lydia—"

"I know, I know." She didn't try to hide the tears that had started to course down her cheeks. "I need to just sit down and have a proper blubber, you know? But I can't sit still. I think about Kyle, and think about some creep sneaking up behind him, and…why? I mean, what did he ever do to anybody except buy some land and dream a little? And that's what I think about. Who would gain? Murder to protect self-interests? Waddell's a smooth dude. Do we really believe *NightZone* is all about the sun, moon, and stars? Is it possible that he has something else going on up there? And if he's guilty of nothing other than chasing his astronomy dreams, why would anyone want to hinder him?"

She shook her head, her face hard, touched with misery. "Or, murder springs from a lover's quarrel? Maybe. Murder for revenge of insult? Sure, maybe."

She finally wiped her eyes. "That's what I think about, Estelle. That's *all* I can think about. And my Kyle was caught right in the middle of it."

"I'll tell you this much, Lydia. I've known Miles Waddell for years, and yes…I think his development is exactly what it's touted to be."

"You're saying that I shouldn't talk to him?"

"No, I'm not saying that. You can talk to whomever agrees to speak with you."

"I have to do something. I can't just sit and…" She fumbled for the right word.

"Mourn?"

"Exactly." Her smile was tight, her eyes still glistening. "I'll try not to get in the way."

"We'd appreciate that. To put it another way, Lydia, we require that you do not get in the way, that you do not obstruct. And any tips that come your way—we'd appreciate those."

Lydia's gaze drifted over to the now-curtained living room window. They could hear voices, and an occasional piano note.

"I'd love to meet your son someday." She immediately raised her hands. "But not now. I'm sorry I interrupted your evening."

"You have my numbers, Lydia. Any time."

"Forgive me for intruding?"

"Of course."

Lydia Thompson extended a hand, and her grip was strong. "Thank you, Estelle."

"You're welcome." Estelle watched as Lydia walked back to her Explorer, parked half a block down the street—walked head down, absorbed in her thoughts.

"So what did you really want to talk about?" Estelle muttered aloud as the SUV pulled out and drove down Twelfth Street.

Back inside, she shook her head dismissively in response to the raised eyebrow from her husband. Then she extended both hands toward Angie, eager to put all the ugly thoughts of the past forty-eight hours behind her.

Chapter Twenty-Seven

Composer Lukie Maoma had chosen a truly pacific theme for the second movement of his cello sonata, and Estelle wondered how many of the Hawaiian audience members would nod off during the performance. She watched with amusement as Bill Gastner's head sagged toward his chest, his mouth going slack as his body relaxed to the music. At the other end of the aging scale, little William Thomas's thumb had almost made it to his mouth before he too slumbered.

The third movement seemed to pit ocean against shore, with currents racing into every cove, seeking passage. During those times when the music thundered, Estelle found herself wondering how Angie's centuries old cello managed to hold together as the notes burst forth. Then, as if admitting defeat, as if unable to wash the island paradise away, the ocean subsided, the storm clouds parted, and the music was carried away by a series of recurring swells that surged off to distant shores.

"Exquisite," Estelle said when the last note faded. Angie beamed and then turned to look across the piano to her husband, who had been following the score, note for note, his face furrowed in concentration.

"I'd like to hear measure sixteen of the andante again," he

said with a sober frown. "I wasn't sure of your passage from the *E* flat to the *A* flat." He allowed but a second to elapse before a wide smile lit his countenance. "I'm kidding, *mi corazon*." He closed the score and laid it on top of the piano, then held both hands out toward his wife. "It was perfect. Not just the notes. The heart, the soul… Maestro Maoma should be honored."

"Ah, so this guy is still alive?" Bill Gastner proved that he wasn't asleep. He opened his eyes and raised an eyebrow. "He'll be in the audience?"

"Maestro Maoma is ninety-one and very much alive," Angie replied. "And as far as I know, he'll be introducing this particular part of the program."

Gastner frowned and looked across at Estelle. "This guy is ninety-one? That settles it. I'm going to start running ten miles every day." He patted his belly.

"You could come with us, you know. You could meet Maestro Maoma."

"No thanks. I'd rather just imagine. Airports, hotels, restaurants…nah, I don't think so. I don't do them anymore."

"Only the Don Juan," Francisco added.

"That's right." Gastner pointed a pistol finger at the front door. "What did the young lady want?"

"I'm not sure," Estelle replied. "She's trying to find a way to grieve, I think, and not having much success."

"Tough road. One minute she has everything, the whole damn word by the tail, then the next minute her life's been trashed. I heard the name Manolo Tapia, just in case you were suffering under the illusion that you were having a private conversation. Why'd she bring him up?"

"She used to be with the New York State Police. She retired after a shooting incident about eight years ago that left her really torn up."

"Really." Gastner frowned. "And then she read about your episode with Tapia."

"Yes. Frank Dayan led her to it."

"So she figures you're a kindred spirit."

"I suppose."

"Yeah, well," Gastner said, "it's times like that when we find out some answers about basic character." He surged forward in his chair, both hands slapping the armrests. "And on *that* heavy note of philosophical twaddle, how about seconds on dessert? And then I need to take this old guy home."

"The only thing that's left is the cherry pie," Estelle said. "Maybe enough. And while it's being served…"

"You got any more of your wonderful coffee?"

"We will have," Francisco said.

"While we're waiting, maybe you'll tell me what's the latest news from your search," Estelle said. "I heard you made progress."

"To make a long story of brilliant detecting short, you recall that I mentioned that Irving Silverman, the eighty-one-year-old son of Mary Rosenblum Silverman, had the three volumes in his possession." Gastner steepled his fingers under his lower lip. "The *best* part is that he's excited to be part of the chase. That's what he called it. Part of the chase. He intends to scour through the books. I gave him a short list of what to look for, and he'll send me copies of the pages if he finds anything."

"So you're looking for…"

"The description of the lost Colt, maybe the serial number and purchase price, the name of the buyer, and in particular, any mention of the unfortunate Mr. Bennett, whom *I* think died with the gun in his hand."

"Wow," Estelle whispered.

"Wow is right," Gastner said happily. "What's amazing is that during those fifty years, old Irving has moved a number of times, and the old family books always went with him. He says that he almost threw them out any number of times, but never could bring himself to do it. Now he's excited that they may be of use to someone."

"You're going up to Ratón?"

"If there's mention in the books, probably so. I'll have to twist some arms, call in a few favors to do that, but if the information is there, Irving said that I could have the books if I'll promise to turn them over to the county historical society when I'm finished with them, along with a copy of my final report. Do I want to trust something like those treasures to the Post Office? I think not."

"That's quite a job you've taken on," Francis said.

"Hell, why not." He reached out and accepted the dessert plate and coffee mug that Francisco brought from the kitchen. "You gotta take the first step sometime."

Chapter Twenty-Eight

Estelle could have used a good night's sleep, but she didn't get it. Despite the best body massage in the world, and despite the delight of finishing unfinished business with her private physician and masseur, she spent the night in a toss-and-turn marathon.

At one point, she laughed loud enough, more in frustration than anything else, that Francis almost awoke. Grandparenthood had brought about more worries than when she had the two little ankle-biters racing about the house a quarter century before, or when she discovered in due course that neither son would ever fit any common mold.

Francisco, Angie, and tiny William Thomas would fly out to Hawaii, and she worried about that flimsy aluminum/titanium can jetting across the ocean—what did explorers used to call it? The *boundless* ocean—with no runway in sight for thousands of miles. Even on land, the hubbub was daunting...the noisy jet, airport, and city, and the crowds of well-meaning folks wanting to lean close and oh and ah in the infant's face.

When she chased those thoughts away, they were replaced by mixing and stirring the bits of data from the vicious vandalism of the newspaper office and the murder of Kyle Thompson...

and the obvious agony of Lydia Thompson, left with a gigantic hole in her life.

Her mind refused to be disciplined. For a while, Estelle forced herself to ignore the clock, which didn't help. The minutes were determined to drag. At one point she burrowed her head under the pillow, then groaned with pleasure as her husband's warm hand traced images on her back, ending up at the base of her skull where he worked the tight muscles.

"We could get up and enjoy a high calorie, high cholesterol, high salt, high pleasure breakfast," he whispered. He rumpled her pillow away from her ear. "Does that sound good?"

Eye now uncovered, she looked at the clock. 4:13. As she watched, the three changed to a four, about the fastest the clock read-out had moved all night.

"By the time you're out of the shower, it'll be ready." Before she could answer, her cell phone began its dance to music on the nightstand. He leaned heavily on her, his weight crushing her into the bedding as he craned to see the incoming number. "It's gotta be," he said, "the man with absolutely no sense of timing."

He slid partially off of her. "You want me to tell him you'll call back?"

"He doesn't call before the break of dawn to discuss the weather," Estelle said. Squirming enough to reach the phone, she picked it up.

"Good morning, Robert." *Feel free to call just anytime,* Estelle added silently.

The sheriff hesitated at the overly formal tone. "Got some bad news," he said, and Estelle came fully awake.

"What's going on?"

"It ain't his gun." He paused, as if that cryptic utterance would explain all.

Estelle relaxed back on the bed as Francis shifted a little to give her room. "Stop by my office. I got things to show you."

"And how are Gail and Gabe doing?"

Torrez hesitated, as if the question was outside his ken. Then he said, "Gabe sleeps through the night now. So that's pretty good."

"Something you should try sometime," Estelle said.

"Yeah, well. Not when we got things hangin'. I'll wait for you. Then we got some visits to make."

"Give me an hour. I'd actually like to have some breakfast this morning."

"I got the coffee on here."

Estelle laughed. "Oh, good, Bobby. I'm surprised you have any stomach left with that stuff you brew. Give me an hour." She switched off and let her right arm fall across her eyes.

"Any menu changes?" Francis asked. He'd slipped out of bed and donned underwear and a clean set of light-blue scrubs.

"What you promised before sounds just right, *Oso.*"

"Then *vamanos, muchacha.*"

"Groan." She sat up and swung her feet over the side of the bed, and then grinned at her husband's habit of turning on every light switch he passed on his way out to the kitchen. She got up and entered the shower, letting the high pressure spray beat on her neck and shoulders, standing with both hands braced on the tile wall. She stood that way, right on the verge of dozing off, until a waft of cooking bacon found her and jolted her into motion.

With minimal attention to her short, salt-touched black hair and with no makeup, she slipped into a freshly pressed tan pants suit, the generous leather ranger's belt far from high fashion, but offering secure support for gun, badge case, cuffs, spare magazines, and the Taser that had become a standard uniform accessory. Putting the suit's jacket on was something of a struggle, hampered as she was by the bulk of the ballistic vest.

At 5:05, she joined her husband in the kitchen.

"Scrambled a la Carlos," Francis announced, plating the eggs, bacon, and English muffin. "Moist, with a touch of gouda." He returned to the stove. "Coffee or green tea?"

"Tea, please."

"What did Bobby have that was so urgent?"

"He said, quote, 'It ain't his gun.' Unquote. End of message or explanation."

Francis brought his plate to the table. "The gun he confiscated from his nephew and did the ballistics on?"

"I assume so."

"In any case, that rifle didn't fire the bullets into the newspaper office."

"Probably not. Although we have nothing that positively tells us that the expended shell casings scattered throughout Glenn Archer's Navigator are from the same batch of ammo that strafed the *Register* office."

"But probably a safe assumption."

"Just too many 'probablies,' *Oso*." She held up a forkful of scrambled eggs curtained with melted gouda. "This is wonderful, by the way."

"Are we going to be home for dinner?" Francis grinned at his foolish question. "We don't know, do we?"

"No, we don't. But it's the last evening before the kids take off for Hawaii, so I'm hoping for a quiet dinner with the whole crew."

Francis reached across and tugged the visible edge of her vest. "It's going to be hot today, but keep that on."

"Of course."

"And don't send Alan and me any more autopsies."

"I'm optimistic."

She stayed that way until she walked into the sheriff's barren office. Torrez relaxed in his squeaky, army-surplus swivel chair, one boot up on the corner of his scarred army-surplus metal desk—furniture that the sheriff preferred, even though the county had offered an office makeover into the twenty-first century on several occasions. County Manager Leona Spears had once ducked into Bob Torrez's office, patted one of the gray, army-surplus filing cabinets, and sweetly announced that she was putting the sheriff's name in for the Luddite of the Year award.

Torrez's sole concession to the modern age was the new computer that dominated the corner of his desk. County IT guys hadn't asked if he wanted it, and he rarely used it. But it looked official. What he used more was the current map of Posadas County that dominated one wall…a copy of the same map in Estelle's office.

As Estelle entered, he turned slightly and reached for the twenty-two rifle that leaned against the wall beside the computer.

In his usual fashion, Torrez offered no greeting. "Here's the deal. This rifle is not the gun that I gave my nephew for his sixteenth birthday," he announced. His boot thumped off the desk to the floor and he sat up straight. An inch-thick, gray-colored ledger rested on his desk calendar. He laid the gun on the desk to his right, then flipped open the ledger. "I brought this in from the house," he said.

Estelle knew what the book contained—all his ammunition reloading notes over the years, all his gun purchases or sales, some sample targets clipped and fitted neatly to the pages, and miscellaneous other data. She waited patiently for Torrez to find the marker.

"I gave him a Ruger ten-twenty-two on September 6, 2017." He turned the journal so Estelle could see the entry, Torrez's block printing regular and heavy. "It's a rifle I bought from another guy about twenty years ago, so it's seen some use. Quentin told me he was going to make a new stock for it," and his hand drifted to the gun, almost caressing the fancy wood. "He's pretty talented that way. He wanted one of these thumbhole things. If he did, I never saw him workin' on it." One stubby index finger indicated the serial number in the book, a lengthy string of digits with a dash separating the first three from the rest. "That's the number of the gun I gave him."

"All right."

He picked up the short rifle, racked the bolt back and forth and handed the gun to Estelle. The serial number, stamped boldly on the left forward receiver flat, was not a match with Torrez's book.

"If I wasn't such a dumb ass, I woulda checked the number from the get-go. I just assumed, and we all know about that. I was too damn eager to test fire and look for results."

"It's an easy oversight, Bobby."

"Well, no, it ain't. Dumb rookie thing to do." He heaved a deep sigh. "Anyway, this ain't the gun I gave him. Same model, same caliber, same everything, except for that." He reached across and tapped the serial number. "It ain't the same gun. Period. End of story."

"When you asked him for the gun, he didn't say anything one way or another—just asked when he was going to get it back."

"Yep. And then he gives me this one." He examined the gun once more, easing the bolt back and then forward on the empty chamber. "So. He *knew* what gun I meant, and he knew that this one wasn't it. But he didn't say shit. He just let me take it, knowing I'd test it."

Estelle glanced up at the plain military-style wall clock. "He might have traded off the gun you gave him for his birthday. Maybe he saw this one, and liked it better."

"Maybe. We're sure as hell going to find out."

"He would be home still, I imagine."

"Yep." The sheriff didn't sound particularly eager. "Let's see what he's got to say." He pushed back from the desk and stood.

"Is there something that makes you think that Quentin swapped guns with somebody, and then that somebody might have used your nephew's gun in the newspaper shooting?"

"Don't know, do we?" Torrez said flatly. "All kinds of mighta. Mighta shot up the place with his gun, then got rid of it, knowin' I'd come lookin'." He almost smiled. "Mighta. 'Cause at the moment there's nothin' else. And on the other side of the county, we got a man dead because someone mighta kicked him over that cliff. And he mighta just took a swan dive 'cause his depression at a dumb real estate purchase drove him to it."

"There's not a single thing that says the two incidents are related, Bobby. Nothing."

"Except it's a small county. I don't know too many people that can come up with a flyin' kick so hard it sends a man into space. Could probably count 'em on one hand. And my nephew happens to be one of 'em, don't he?" He thumped the butt of the rifle on the desk. "You ready to rock and roll?"

"I am. You need your vest, Bobby."

"My nephew ain't going to shoot me," the sheriff said. Nevertheless, he gathered up the vest from where it had been hanging, protecting the back of a metal folding chair.

Chapter Twenty-Nine

Early morning sunshine glinted hard off the side of the small mobile home, and the chrome front fender of Quentin Torrez's motorcycle was like a flashbulb as the two officers walked through the unkempt weeds toward the front door.

The young man appeared in the doorway, almost ready for the day in clean jeans and a black polo shirt with the *NightZone* logo on the left breast. He was still barefoot, though, and he didn't venture beyond the top step.

"Hey. I thought maybe you'd bring my gun and truck back."

"Keep thinkin'," the sheriff said brusquely.

"Well, I made a bet with myself that it wouldn't be long before you'd be back."

"You win."

"Well, okay. Here you are." He glanced at his watch. "I got a little time, but not a whole lot. They won't let me work the train, but Mr. Waddell hired me in maintenance topside."

"Try not to screw that up," the sheriff said, and Estelle winced. Torrez moved to the bottom of the steps and looked up at his nephew. "Whose gun was that you gave me?"

"Whose gun?"

"Don't be stupid."

Quentin frowned and looked sideways at Estelle. "I don't know what you two want from me."

"For starters, let's keep it simple," Torrez said, his voice barely a whisper. "Where's the twenty-two rifle I gave you for your birthday? That rifle you gave me sure as hell ain't it, and don't bother wastin' my time tryin' to tell me that it is. I keep serial number records."

For a moment, Quentin hesitated. "I traded it off for the one you confiscated. The gun that you gave me? I traded it off."

"When?"

"When did I trade it, you mean?"

The sheriff said nothing, as intimidating as if he'd shouted in uncontrolled anger.

"A year or so ago, I guess. I didn't mention it to you 'cause I thought you might be angry that I did that."

"Why would I give a shit what you did?" Torrez said. "Who did you trade with?"

Quentin fell silent. He stood with one butt cheek on the old two-by-four railing, most of his weight leaning back against the door frame. "Look," he said finally. He held up a hand but didn't continue.

"Quentin," Estelle said, "just tell us what actually happened. We're going to find out one way or another. Save yourself some time and trouble."

For a long moment he stared at the flaked paint of the steps. "I don't want to get nobody in trouble," he said.

"You're in it already," Torrez snapped. "You want to stonewall this thing, all right. You know I don't *never* give up, so have at it. And when we come for you, it won't be for a polite little chat on the front steps."

Quentin shrugged, and for a moment, Estelle was afraid that the young man was going to call his uncle's hand.

"The gun you took belongs to Rolando Ortega. He and I hunt together sometimes."

"You went to school with Rolando, didn't you?" Estelle asked.

"Yes, ma'am. I mean, he was a couple or three years ahead of me. But him and Rafael and Maddy...we've all been together a long time. And now we're all workin' up on the mesa. How cool is that."

"Where's the gun I gave you?" Torrez asked.

"Look, I told Rolando that it's going to take me a while to finish up the stock work on his gun. So in the meantime, I loaned him mine. The one you gave me."

"I want to see it."

Quentin shrugged. "Then the guy to talk to is Rolando."

Torrez took a long, deep breath. "You still lyin' to me?"

"No, sir."

"You going to work with us on this?"

The young man looked puzzled. "Means what? I told you what the deal was."

"You don't need to tell Rolando that we talked."

"All right. That's easy enough."

"He rides the train topside?"

"As far as I know."

"Do you?"

"Sure. They let us ride for free. It's a long rough ride by road."

"Play this straight with us, and maybe I'll talk to the judge about gettin' your truck back."

Quentin grinned. "*Maybe* you will. What's that mean?"

"Just what I said." He pointed at the motorcycle. "And don't be ridin' that on the highway. The tag is expired."

The young man bent at the waist, both hands clapped in prayer, and intoned, "Yes, High Sheriff Uncle Robert."

Torrez raised a single index finger, aimed at his nephew. "Don't be a wiseass. And if Rolando don't have that gun, or tells us a different story, we'll be back."

Quentin bowed again.

Chapter Thirty

For several miles as they drove out beyond the airport, the sheriff said nothing. Estelle saw that he was obviously fuming, eyes narrowing now and then, glaring out at the vast prairie as if the answers lay there.

Finally, he seemed to relax a little. "It's just a loose end," he said, and Estelle wasn't sure if he was talking to himself or to her.

"The gun you gave him?"

"Yup. See, what would be the natural thing? Quent knows what we're after. If he *knows* that his rifle didn't shoot up the newspaper office, I figure he'd say so."

"But he didn't say anything about it."

"Nope."

"And even when that's tidied up, what do we have? If ballistics match, that's one thing. Then we'll be hot on a trail. But if they don't..."

"Then we don't got shit." He fell silent again as they turned south on County Road 14, a long, rough, graveled ribbon that cut down through the western side of the county, skirting mesas and boulder-studded arroyos.

"He could be a good kid if he half tried," Torrez said abruptly. "He's going to have to learn to stay off the sauce."

"Is that a recent thing?"

The sheriff scoffed. "He's been drinkin' since he was ten years old. Gotta have that *cerveza*." He glanced over at Estelle.

"You ride him pretty hard, Bobby."

Torrez made a face that looked as if he'd bitten into something sour. "Well, somebody's got to. His mother won't. His grandma tries, but she's a soft touch most of the time. Now that he's moved into his own place, who the hell knows? You gotta remember…" and he paused. "You gotta remember that I had a younger brother killed while ridin' with a drunk. So yeah, I guess I keep an eye on Quentin, maybe more'n I should. But that's the way it is."

"Maybe Maddy will be a good influence on him."

Torrez offered one of his rare laughs. "Don't hold your breath." He slowed as a dust cloud approached, the billows engulfing a lumbering road grader pulling a pickup truck. Low-angle morning sun blasted through the cloud and bounced off the bright yellow of the grader, creating art that as quickly drifted away. The operator raised a couple fingers in greeting as they passed.

"Twelve million," Torrez said.

"What is?"

"That's what Waddell gave to the county as a down payment on pavin' this road."

"I hadn't heard about that."

"He don't want the dust."

"I can understand that."

"Twelve million is a start. Won't do the whole thing. Bottom half, maybe, just oil and stone."

Rafael Gonzales had seen their dusty approach down the county road, and he stood at the ready by the gate.

"Good morning, Officers," he said with a welcoming smile. "You're out and about early."

"Yup. Where's Rolando Ortega workin' this morning?"

"I think…I *think*…that he's working down at the new

pavilion. But I'm not sure. Let me check." He stepped away from the sheriff's vehicle and juggled clipboard and handheld radio. A voice that sounded like a ten-year-old responded.

"Tracie, where's Orlando workin' this morning?"

"Just a minute." In less than that, she added, "He's out with one of the field crews."

"I thought he was. But where? At the new pavilion? I have a couple of guests who need to speak with him." He looked at Torrez, then looked heavenward as he waited.

"Just a minute."

The second voice was instantly recognizable. "Rafael, they're working in that rough country behind the pavilion. We don't want guests down there just yet. Who do you have?"

"It's Sheriff Torrez and Undersheriff Guzman, sir."

"Oh, well then, put him on, please."

Rafael reached out and handed the radio to Torrez. "It's Mr. Waddell, sir."

"I figured."

"Morning, Robert. Look, if you and Estelle are up for a little scrambling, you can find the crew out beyond the train stop, around that gigunda rock museum we've got out there. They're working on laying the power cables for the new pavilion. I gotta show you the renderings of it. I mean, really swank."

"We'll head that way."

"Who are you looking to talk to?"

"Rolando Ortega."

"One of the best I've got," Waddell said. "Look, do you need me for anything just now? I've got a conference call with the university folks in California, linked up with another university group in Brisbane."

"Go for it. We'll just wander around. Don't need no guide."

"I bet you don't," Waddell said affably. "I'll be tied up for an hour or so, maybe less. If you're still on-site then, let's do brunch."

The sheriff's reply was not much more than a mumble, and then he handed the radio back to Rafael, who pointed to a modernistic sculpture that marked the train stop. At the terminus of its run, the locomotive would edge up to that sculpture until bumpers touched. "If you park over by the stop, sir, it's a pretty easy walk around the end of the mesa. There are a bunch of surveyor flags over there, and you'll see the crews."

"Rafael, thanks," Estelle said.

"Have a great day."

"He's such a personable kid," Estelle said as they headed across the parking lot. Her hope was to coax some complimentary, or at least agreeing, comment from Torrez, but he didn't indulge.

Nosing the Expedition under a carefully trimmed juniper, he pointed ahead. "They'll be right through there."

The hiking was more a question of rock skipping as they worked their way around the east end of the mesa, following a trail of blue surveyor's flags. "It's going to take some work to establish a civilized trail through all this," Estelle said. Torrez had paused on a truck-sized boulder, scouting the route. He looked up toward the mesa rim, where the natural process of mass wasting brought the rocks to the bottom, in all sizes and shapes. In another few yards, they heard voices. By the time they reached the work crew, they were completely out of sight of the parking area, the train stop, or the entry building and gate. What they saw was the magnificent sweep of the prairie toward the east and south. Although Estelle knew every ranching family in the area, not a single building was in view.

There was just enough breeze to set the scrub brush, the acacia, the junipers, and burr oak whispering.

"Hey, there!" a voice greeted them, and Logan Barnes waved a hand. Barnes had traded a long career with the State Highway Department to join the *NightZone* crew, and the work appeared to agree with him. Lean and agile, he picked his way across to them. "You come back here in four months, and it'll be a different place." He stopped, shook hands with both officers, and then stood with his hands on his hips, admiring the view. "Something, ain't it?"

He'd gotten too much sun, and both ears were red and peeling around the margins. "What we're doing right now is flagging a route for the power and water." He shook his head in dismay. "Just no good way, and Waddell wants everything out of sight, out of mind."

He turned quickly back to Torrez. "But you wanted to talk to me about something?"

"We need to talk with Rolando Ortega."

"Well, shit. He didn't come in today. They should have been able to tell you that in the office. Who'd you talk to?"

"I think it was Tracie, topside," Estelle said. "But we spoke with Miles, too."

"Well, that explains a lot. Waddell, he don't know that sort of thing, and Tracie is one of our younger generation space cases." He grinned and shifted his dark blue ball cap on the red stubble. "No, Rolando didn't make it today, and that sort of thing ain't going to work for us, not if he keeps it up."

"He never showed up at all?"

"Nope. Can I help you with something?" He lowered his voice. "The kid in trouble, somehow, with you all?"

"We just need to talk with him, Logan."

"I'm kinda surprised he skipped today. You know, he's a moody kid, but a hard worker. And he's got a genuine affection for this crazy place. He was concerned for a while about those folks who bought the land north of us. Not too many kids are concerned one way or another about view shed, but you know, I think he is."

He shifted position and stretched out a hand toward the north. "There's one spot…just one…where if you know where to look, you can see the locomotive going in and out. Right through that sort of pass right there, about five hundred yards out? Past that grove of scrub oak and that thicket of acacia? Only place you can see it from here.

"And I think that's a nifty idea. You get a bunch of bird-watchers sitting around out here, and that little glimpse of the train, quiet as it is, kinda acts like an alarm clock, if you know what I mean."

"You said that Rolando had a concern about that?" Estelle asked.

"Well, no, not about the train or anything. But he was wondering what kind of development those folks were thinking about. Over there?" He pointed farther north. "The whole side of that rise is theirs, and on over into them foothills beyond. I can see his point. Get more development, and it's sure to be an eyesore. Can't help but be."

"It's hard to stop development," Estelle said.

"That's what they say, and that's exactly what I think, and you know, it's what I told Rolando and the rest of the boys. Look, I remember years ago when those vandals tried to stop *this* development by cuttin' down power poles. Remember that?"

"Of course."

"And where did that get 'em? I mean, killed the one kid, right? And what did they accomplish? Here *NightZone* is, and here it is to stay." He shrugged. "I suppose Rolando is at home. You have his number?" He had his cell phone half out when Estelle shook her head and reached out to touch his arm.

"We'll drop by. No big deal."

"But he shoulda called us, you know. Can't just skip work and expect to keep your job."

"You've been working this site since…"

"We got the aerial photo blowup, and now we're flagging the route from topside. Been out here in the rocks all week. Started last Monday." He grinned, showing lots of space for additional teeth. "Gettin' a backhoe or excavator out here is going to be a trick, don't you think?"

"Not if you got a Skycrane," Torrez replied.

"You used to hunt this country, as I recall."

"Used to."

Logan grinned at the taciturn reply. "Maybe that's where Rolando got off to. He's a huntin' son of a gun, that kid. Still, he's supposed to be here." He jabbed an index finger toward the ground. "You want him to call you?"

"We'll work it out, Logan," Estelle said. "Thanks for the heads-up."

"And watch your step goin' back," the man cautioned. "We had a time with the snakes on this hill. Killed a dozen or so already." His face lit up in a broad smile. "You ever see those signs like they got at some of the state and federal monuments around? *'Respect the rattlesnakes' privacy and stay on the trail?'* Something like that, anyway. Waddell's going to have to buy a whole batch of those for posting. And bird-watchers aren't too keen about watching their feet." He mimed holding a pair of binoculars to his eyes as he looked skyward. "You folks be careful."

Only lizards regarded their passage back through the jumble of boulders and scrub, and when they reached the parking lot, the locomotive and its four cars had just drifted to a stop, the engine's custom-made bumper/cow catcher ever so gently nudging the spring-backed stop.

To Estelle's astonishment, she counted forty-one people disembarking. A quick count tallied eleven who were obviously Asian, two couples flinging excited German back and forth, with the rest comfortable in either English or Spanish. An impressive collection of cameras and binoculars adorned all but the seven young women who wore *NightZone* shirts, arriving for the day shift. Quentin Torrez disembarked from the lead car. Rolando Ortega was not in the group.

"Not too long ago, I used to hunt this country," Torrez muttered. He had moved into the spotty shade of a juniper to watch the tourists arrive. "Could hike all day and not see a single person. Now we got trains running through it."

"Or at least *a* train," Estelle added. "Do you know where Rolando is living now?"

"I do. There's a problem with that, though."

"I can see that."

"We don't got anything on this guy," Torrez said. Once inside the Expedition, he sat silently behind the wheel, staring off into space. "We don't got much, anyway." He shrugged and tapped a slow rhythm on the steering wheel. "He borrows a rifle from my nephew. That don't mean he used it to strafe the newspaper building." He lifted one hand. "He owns a motorcycle. That don't mean he rode over to Thompson's property with it." He turned and looked at Estelle. "He's in that taekwondo class, but that don't mean he kicked Thompson over the cliff."

Estelle was surprised at Torrez's defense of the young man, since the sheriff had spent days convicting his nephew on far more speculative evidence. "And now he's upset enough about something that he skips work without a phone call or excuse," Estelle said. "Before we go any further down the road with this, I want to talk with Maddy again."

"Might as well while we're here."

Tracie was still on deck, and her voice was just as chirpy over the phone as it had been earlier on the radio. "Oh, Undersheriff Guzman, hi. Did you find Rolando?"

"Good morning, Tracie. Thanks for pointing us in the right direction," Estelle said.

Apparently Tracie was satisfied with the unanswer, because she bubbled, "No problem."

Actually, there are lots of problems, Estelle thought. "Is Maddy available?"

"Just a minute, please. Let me check." Shortly she returned to the phone. "So, actually, Maddy won't be in today. There's a note on the board that she called early this morning. I mean, she normally doesn't come in for the breakfast run anyway, 'cause she works afternoons and evenings."

"I'll catch her another time then. Thanks." She switched off as Torrez started the Expedition. "It's sort of like dominos, isn't it?" she said.

Chapter Thirty-One

Bustos Avenue crossed the village of Posadas east-west, and once clear of the village eastbound became County Road 19, a wandering, dusty path that cut through the flat scrubland, featureless save for a handful of arroyos that carved some character into the prairie.

On the southern horizon, Estelle could see the hump of the mountain of crushed stone that marked McIlhenny's Sand and Gravel enterprise, but the hard sunlight didn't reflect off a single ranch house roof. "Bleak" was the word that came to mind to describe eastern Posadas County.

A quarter of a mile after the pavement of Bustos Avenue gave up to the gravel, it gave up to the pretentious name *Camino del Sol,* which in turn became just plain old County Road 19. The CR19 dust generator passed the abandoned drive-in theater whose towering screen had long since been pummeled to rubble by the winds, then skirted by the remains of Valerio's Mobile Home Park—neither a park nor home to any trailers.

The Ortegas liked their solitude, Estelle thought. Just beyond the remains of the mobile home park, a tiny, tidy adobe nestled in a grove of stunted elms. Once home to a hardscrabble rancher and his schoolteacher wife, the place had been abandoned for years after their deaths until Juan Ortega recognized a good deal. He purchased the old Hocking place, cleaned out the dust, lizards, rattlesnakes, and mice, and settled in with his patient wife and their three kids.

Rolando Ortega was the youngest of the three, just twelve years old when Juan Ortega drove his aging pickup up into the Oria National Forest on top of Cat Mesa, and settled in with two unopened fifths of cheap bourbon. He'd made it through half of the second bottle before his system said, "Enough." Woodcutters discovered his nearly embalmed corpse the next day.

Estelle clearly remembered the almost serene expression on Juan Ortega's face, his head leaning against the door frame, the empty whiskey bottle on the passenger side floor, the half-finished one cradled between his legs.

Rolando's mother, Alva, took the death of her husband with philosophical equanimity. Maybe it was just relief. Although neither Alva nor the children bore visible bruises, hearsay claimed that Juan was quick with his fists. Estelle had spent some time sorting through department records and could find no complaints against the man. She'd seen him often enough at Posadas High School sporting events, where Juan's eldest son, Lolo, lettered in three sports.

Daughter Cindy Ortega wasn't such a standout, but managed to graduate and found a job in Albuquerque, clerking in a jewelry shop in Old Town that featured Native American crafts. As far as Estelle knew, Cindy had never returned to Posadas County.

Rolando, the youngest of the three Ortegas, drifted along at half-throttle or less, content to hunt, ride his ATV, and watch cable television. He'd tried rodeo work until a bull had stomped him. He tried a weight-lifting program for a while until the monotony of that bored him. During his sophomore year, he'd become friends with a middle school student named

Quentin Torrez when, entirely by chance, the two boys played hooky on the same day, seeing the perfect October weather as a chance to blast around the county on their motorcycles. Their paths crossed up on the mesa by the abandoned Consolidated Reservoir, where they spent a companionable hour assassinating frogs.

Sheriff's Deputy Thomas Pasquale had surprised the two kids there and sent them home with a handful of stern warnings: stop skipping school, stop trespassing, stop shooting their twenty-twos in a spot where bullets were sure to ricochet off wet rocks.

Pasquale might as well have saved his breath. He wrote a most entertaining report on the incident that then crossed the undersheriff's desk. Undeterred by their brush with the law, the two youngsters continued to be driven by the spirit of adventure. Soon enough, there wasn't a back road or trail in Posadas County where the two hadn't raised dust.

Miles Waddell's development in southwestern Posadas County was an attractive nuisance, but fate opened the correct door, behind which Rolando found himself an entry-level maintenance job that paid more than he'd ever known.

Undersheriff Estelle Reyes-Guzman admitted to more than a touch of anxiety as she and Sheriff Robert Torrez drove out County Road 19. Helping to keep the community's children on the straight and narrow until they became responsible adults and made productive lives for themselves was a fundamental charge for law officers. Of course it was the parents' responsibility and one of the easiest responsibilities to ignore.

As little as Bob Torrez talked about it, Estelle sometimes wished she could adopt the sheriff's simple philosophy. If a person breaks the law, arrest him or her. Period. Don't lose sleep over it. Don't waste time or money on fancy programs that tried to do the parents' job.

Torrez slowed as they reached the Ortegas' driveway.

Someone was certainly home. Three vehicles were parked this way and that: an older model, much-faded brown Oldsmobile Ciera; a massive, blocky Chevy C-10 short-bed pickup from the mid-sixties; and a diminutive Hyundai sedan with a back fender adorned with duct tape holding the left taillight assembly in place.

"The Olds belongs to Alva," Estelle said. Now retired from a bookkeeping service in Posadas, Alva Ortega kept busy with a few accounts managed from home. "The truck is Rolando's. The Hyundai is Maddy's."

"He ain't at work, the girl is shacked up for the day, and you gotta wonder," Torrez mused. "Hey?" he muttered, and pointed. A hundred yards up the road, near an optimistic stand of acacia trying to grow in the bar ditch, a vehicle sat with its hood up. An older model Ford Explorer, a liberal coating of Posadas County dust disguised any shine from its silver paint job. "What's she doing out here?"

"I have a feeling that maybe old habits die hard."

"She wasn't a cop long enough to develop old habits," the sheriff scoffed. He accelerated the Expedition on up the road and stopped window to window with the Explorer. Lydia Thompson sat relaxed behind the wheel, not looking the least bit stranded—and not the least bit intimidated by Torrez's glare. She looked tired, Estelle thought. Lydia took off her sunglasses, and the dark circles under her eyes said she hadn't managed much sleep.

"Your truck broke?"

Lydia smiled. "No, it's fine." She nodded toward the Ortegas'. "Maybe from down there, it looks to them like it is."

"What are you doing here?"

"My mistake. I thought this was a county road, open to the public." Lydia regarded Torrez, not defiant, but certainly unperturbed. She lifted a small pair of expensive binoculars. "Pretty good view." She was parked at enough of an angle that she could look out past the raised hood. She frowned. "I thought that your nephew and Miss Lucero were an item," she said, and glanced at Torrez.

"It ain't my week to keep track of his romances," Torrez replied, and Estelle thought that he managed to sound much more disinterested than he really was.

"Right now, Maddy and Rolando Ortega have an argument going that's heating up pretty good. And they're both supposed to be at work, aren't they?"

"So you're just sittin' here doing your own private surveillance."

"Well, Sheriff Torrez, why not? Someone needs to. Maybe with what you're learning"—she raised a hand, fingers spread, then raised the other, webbing the ten fingers together—"and with what I'm observing…"

Estelle leaned forward. "You haven't been able to hear what they're arguing about from here."

"No. But it's interesting watching the dynamics." She clasped both hands and rested them on the steering wheel. "Rolando is one of those guys who can't stand still when he's arguing. He yells something, then stomps out of the house, walks a few feet, then turns around and comes back for another round. He can't just hold still. Maddy won't follow him out into the yard. She stops on that little front porch. Then they both go inside and go at it again."

"And the mother?"

"Haven't seen her. Maybe she's inside, maybe she's out and about with some friend. That might be her car that's parked there." Lydia pointed a crooked index finger at the two officers. "I've seen Maddy and Rolando together up at *NightZone*, though. More than just a little friendly."

Torrez said nothing.

"I'd have to wonder how that sits with your nephew, Sheriff." Lydia almost smiled. "Seems like there's potential for an old-fashioned triangle going on."

"You've caught on to a lot for someone who's just spent a few days here," Estelle observed.

"Back when I was a trooper, that's the part of law enforcement that fascinated me the most," Lydia replied. "Getting to know the people, all the sordid little secrets, all the sore spots. Every little town had them." She flashed a smile. "And in New York, with a village about every six miles, that's a *lot* of sore spots." She nodded toward the Ortegas'. "That's a sore spot down there, guys."

"Tell me why you're here, Lydia," Estelle said, cutting off the sheriff. "And let's cut to the chase. Tell me why you think that Rolando Ortega had anything at all to do with your husband's murder."

"You're here, so you must think so, too." Lydia squinted into the distance. "Rafael Gonzales likes to talk." She shrugged and turned to look at Estelle with a half-smile. "The sweetheart at the gate?"

"When did you interview him?"

"First thing this morning. I was out wandering—and it's great country for that. I walked across the mesa and then down the paved road, trying to clear my head. He met me at the gate." She smiled. "I got the impression that he thought I should be curled into a helpless ball, using up half a ton of tissue. I told him I was too mad to cry, that I'd save that for later. He seemed to understand that. Anyway, one thing led to another."

"That 'other' being Rolando? Or Rolando and Maddy? Or Quentin?"

She nodded. "I sat down on the bench by his little gate hut there, and offered an ear. It turns out that Rafael doesn't need much prompting. He'll talk about anyone and everything."

"And somehow that led you out here."

Torrez shifted with irritation, but he remained silent, letting Estelle guide the conversation.

"Mr. Waddell's crew has developed an amazing sense of

loyalty to that project. That's obvious. And it's not just the generous wages they earn. On top of that, or maybe because of that, they're uneasy about how the land that borders them to the north is going to be developed. *NightZone* is one thing, way up on top of the mesa. But Rafael claims that most of the mesa crew believes that my husband wanted to develop that land into some sort of subdivision. We know what that means, right? Roads, lights, stores, dust. Everything Waddell *doesn't* want."

"And you're thinking that maybe Rolando took the notion to confront your husband? That he followed him over there?"

"Well, *someone* did, Estelle."

"But not necessarily from *NightZone*."

"That's right. It could have been someone just passing by on the county road. It could have been someone down from Albuquerque, someone with an issue. It could have been anyone. What's most interesting is that Rolando was bitching about the development to Rafael. He told more than one person that he was going to talk to my husband to find out his plans."

"That doesn't sound like something Rolando Ortega would do, Lydia."

"My thoughts exactly. I can hear a kid saying he's going to kick someone's ass, but I *can't* imagine someone like Rolando being Mr. Diplomat."

"He would have to know that he could easily get a job with your outfit, with all the building going on."

"Maybe, on down the road, if he thinks that far ahead. He's what, twenty-one or so? He's just a kid. We're not talking long-range, rational thought here. We're talking impulse. He's smart enough to know he's got a good thing going with Waddell, and doesn't want it threatened."

"So you're thinking that Rolando saw your husband over there on the property, and maybe hopped on his motorcycle, or into his truck, and drove over to talk to him."

"Could have."

"And yet *you* were in the neighborhood all the time, Lydia. He never talked to you? Rolando didn't? You're half of the outfit."

Lydia smiled at that. "You're kidding, right?"

"No."

"I don't think Rolando Ortega thinks that way, Estelle. I saw him outside the dining room before all this happened, said hello, and watched him try to stammer a reply. Nice blush he's got, I'll say that."

"You think Rolando might have kicked your husband over that cliff? Saw the easy opportunity and took it?"

"I could imagine that, yes. And today, Rolando skips work. Why does he do that? Maddy skips work, and the two argue. So what's going on?"

"If he did something as impulsive, as irrational, as kicking a man over a cliff, why would he draw attention to himself by then skipping work? Why not just business as usual?"

"Exactly. He's maybe kinda panicky. Maybe he's packing, and Maddy is trying to talk him out of it."

Torrez muttered something to himself and then, looking hard at Lydia Thompson, said, "You're going to stay right here." He looked across at Estelle. "We ain't here to push them into anything. Rolando has a rifle that I want to see, and that's it. That's it. Let's see if we can collect it just on our say-so, without the warrant." He looked across at Lydia. "You stay put, or better yet, go on home."

He pulled the Expedition into gear and continued on to a spot where the bar ditch was almost nonexistent and swung the heavy vehicle around.

Even before they reached Lydia Thompson's vehicle on the return, they saw her out of the Explorer, pushing the hood closed.

"We're going to have to keep an eye on that one," Torrez said. Lydia offered them a two-fingered salute as they passed.

Chapter Thirty-Two

Music coming from the Ortegas' home was loud, loud enough to seep through the old adobe walls. Twenty-six years before, when the Hockings lived here, the place had been storybook neat. Despite the prairie's best efforts to take over, the place was still tidy. Torrez stepped to the front door, avoiding a cardboard carton of empty oil cans. There was no doorbell, and he rapped on the door frame. The music stopped abruptly, and he rapped again.

Maddy Lucero opened the door and peered through the fly screen. Her eyes were a little puffy and red, and for a long moment, she looked at the two officers without saying anything.

"I need to talk with Rolando," Torrez said.

"Just a minute."

Torrez stepped back away from the arc of the screen door and turned at the sound of a vehicle on the county road behind them. Lydia Thompson's Explorer glided to a stop near the driveway.

"If she gets out of that vehicle, go explain the facts of life to her," the sheriff said. "I don't want her bargin' in here and gettin' people more excited than they need to be."

He turned as the door opened again. Rolando Ortega looked

as if he'd spent the night and day hiding in a dark, cramped cellar. He squinted in the bright sunlight, looking first at Torrez and then Estelle.

"What?"

"Good morning to you too, Rolando," Estelle said pleasantly. "We tried to contact you up on the mesa, and were told you hadn't come in to work today."

It wasn't a question, and for a moment Rolando seemed to debate with himself about what to say. Finally, he settled for, "Yeah, so?"

"I need to see my nephew's rifle," Torrez said.

"His what?"

"His twenty-two rifle. He's got yours for a stockin' job, and Quentin says that he loaned you his until he's finished."

Rolando's thick eyebrows caterpillared toward each other. "That ain't illegal, is it?"

"Nope."

"And what's she doin' here?" Rolando nodded toward the road where Lydia Thompson now sat in her parked Explorer.

Without missing a beat, Torrez said, "She was wonderin' what you and her husband were talkin' about the other day."

Rolando would not have made a good poker player, Estelle thought. She took the opportunity to add, "You rode your motorbike over there, Rolando."

"Yeah, so?"

"You and Mr. Thompson had a chat about his plans?"

"He talked about it some. Mostly he was tellin' me not to ride my bike around there, especially when they started work." He shrugged, his expression going clever. "I saw him hackin' around over there, and I thought maybe it was one of them guys who removed the surveyor stakes on him. So I stopped by."

"You and he talked some?" Estelle asked.

"Well, sure. You know. Time of day and stuff like that."

"Right at his car?"

"Mostly. He showed me some stuff."

"Like..."

Rolando's eyebrows twitched again. "Hey, look, I can talk to whoever I want. I don't need to pass on what the...what the conversation was about."

"Nope, you don't," the sheriff said. "You might be about the first person in the county who feels that way."

Rolando tried a weak laugh.

"I need to see that rifle," Torrez said.

"Well, I guess. If it's okay with Quentin."

"Tell me where it is and I'll go get it."

Rolando forced a humorless smile. "You want in my home, then come back with a warrant." *Too much television*, Estelle thought. The kids didn't know much else, but they all knew enough to demand warrants.

"Can do that."

"Yeah, you would, too. You'd warrant your own mother, wouldn't you? I've heard the stories."

"You ain't my mother, and yes...I would."

Looking resigned, Rolando nodded at his truck. "It's right over there in the window rack."

Rolando started to turn that way and the sheriff reached out a hand. "I'll get it."

The young man held up a set of keys. "It's locked. I got it."

Torrez stepped forward quickly until he was within easy grabbing distance behind Rolando. Estelle followed them toward the truck. The lock was stubborn, and Rolando worked the key for a moment before the door yawned open. Slipping the small rifle out of the window rack, he turned and handed it to Torrez.

"You want to think some more about this." The sheriff held the rifle without much interest beyond dropping the full magazine and jacking back the bolt to expel the loaded round from the chamber. "I need to see Quentin's gun."

"That's..." Rolando started to say, but Torrez's glare cut him off.

"No, it ain't."

"What do you mean, *it ain't*?" Rolando mocked. "That's the one."

"One six zero," Torrez said, and then recited the last five digits of a serial number, as familiar with it as he was with his own birthdate. "Quentin's gun is a Ruger, and that's the serial number. This is a Marlin." He reached out and passed the rifle he held to Estelle.

"What, you're takin' that too?"

"Yep. And unless you start showin' some sense, you're goin' with it." He was reaching for his handcuffs when Rolando held up both hands.

"All right, all right. Just back off some." He shook his head in disgust. "I'll get it." He stalked off toward the house.

"Hold it right there," Torrez snapped, but Rolando Ortega waved a dismissive hand over his shoulder. The sheriff reacted quickly, covering the distance between himself and the young man in just a few steps. He clamped a hand on Rolando's upper arm, spinning him around. Almost as if he expected it, Rolando used the momentum to rotate and lash out, this time a foot coming up in a fantastically quick and hard kick that caught Torrez on the side of the head, the blow only partially blocked by the sheriff's left arm.

Off balance, Torrez stumbled to one side as Rolando broke away and darted toward the front door. Estelle reacted to her left at the same time as she drew her Taser. The screen door slammed against the wall, and the young man disappeared inside the house.

"Hold it," Torrez barked at Estelle. Then he saw that it was a Taser in her hand and not her service automatic. "This don't need to escalate." His own automatic had been partially out of its holster, and he jammed it back in. He caught motion out of the corner of his eye and turned to see Lydia Thompson half-way up the driveway.

The sheriff's bellow could have been heard downtown. "Get the hell off this property," he roared, and Lydia stopped short. He turned to Estelle. "If she takes another step, arrest her ass."

They heard thumping inside the house, and Estelle distinctly heard Maddy Lucero, her voice high and strained, cry out, "Rolando, stop it."

"They ain't never going to," Rolando shouted in reply.

He slammed out through the screen door, a rifle at high port. No details of the weapon registered with Estelle, but the young man's intent was clear.

"You want this rifle?" Rolando shouted. At the same time he snapped the gun to his shoulder, the weapon looking small in his big hands. Too far away to use the Taser, Estelle froze. The rifle spat three times in rapid succession, and Estelle saw one of the sheriff's shirt buttons blown into bits. Even as she instinctively drew her own automatic, Rolando's rifle shifted slightly and spat twice more. A ballpoint pen in her left breast pocket exploded and something stung her under the chin. Estelle wheeled to the side, bringing her own gun up. At the same time, Torrez roared out a single word...Estelle heard it as "Down!" and the twenty-two fired once, instantly followed by two heavy, unbearably loud reports from Torrez's forty-five.

Rolando cried out a single, almost bleating "No!" and his rifle fired yet again, although the muzzle had reared skyward as the young man staggered backward on the small porch. Torrez fired a third time, and Rolando's head snapped back and hit the doorjamb. He twisted sideways and fell in an awkward heap.

His service automatic extended, Torrez advanced across the yard and stepped up on the porch. With the toe of his boot, he nudged the rifle farther to one side, then spun around as Maddy Lucero appeared in the doorway.

"Freeze right there," Torrez commanded.

"I'm not..." Maddy cried, and Estelle reached the screen door in three strides and pulled it open.

"Is Mrs. Ortega inside?" Estelle asked. Maddy didn't seem to notice as Estelle maneuvered the young woman's arms and then snapped on the handcuffs.

"She went out with a neighbor," Maddy whimpered. Her unbelieving gaze locked on Rolando's shattered form, and then she allowed herself to be led out to Torrez's Expedition.

"We need you to wait here while we sort this out," Estelle said gently.

"I was trying to talk to him," Maddy wept. "Really, I was. I didn't know..." Her voice trailed off. "Is that...?"

Estelle looked toward the driveway and saw Lydia Thompson pushing herself to her feet, right hand pressed to the side of her head, blood streaming down to soak her blouse and trousers.

"Sit," Estelle commanded, and when the woman was clear of the SUV's door, she slammed it shut and raced across to Lydia, reaching her just as Lydia sank to her knees.

"That bastard," Lydia said.

"Move your hand," Estelle ordered, taking Lydia by the right wrist. "Let me see."

The twenty-two slug had grooved her cheek just in front of her right ear, ripped through the tragus, that little knob on the front margin of the ear that protects the ear canal itself, and then skipped on to punch through the antihelix fold at the back of her ear, exiting through her hair without touching the skull.

"Can you walk over to the sheriff's truck?" She helped Lydia to her feet and they made their way to the back of the Expedition where Lydia could sit on the back tailgate ledge. "Let's get something on that." Estelle yanked open the big first aid kit that was bolted to the side panel. She slipped the packaging off a sterile four-by-six pad and pressed it gently to the young woman's head. "Hold that like that." The radio up front had come to life, with chatter from half a dozen directions as Torrez worked his handheld. "The ambulance will be here in just a minute or two."

Lydia grimaced as she regarded Estelle. "You're bleeding."

"Yep." With an index finger, Estelle rubbed the two small holes in her blouse, the one marked with black ink from her pen. "It's my chin, I think." She found another pad and dabbed the blood away. "You'll stay right here." She looked hard at Lydia. "Do...not...move...from...this...spot."

"Yes." The wound that had torn Lydia's ear was a superficial mess, but the shock was significant.

Estelle turned away and headed for the porch, even though she knew that there was nothing that could be done for Rolando Ortega. As she approached, Torrez looked at her critically. "You all right?"

"Yes. Just a nick." She reached out a hand and placed three fingers against Torrez's chest where the three rounds had stuck his shirt and then were stopped by his vest. The group could have been covered with a playing card.

As if she had put it off as long as she could, she turned slowly and looked down at Rolando. The first two rounds from Torrez's forty-five had hit him in the center of the chest...and he hadn't been wearing a ballistic vest. Still, he'd managed to fire the gun at least once more, a wild shot skyward, before Torrez's third round hit him just above the bridge of his nose.

"Oh, Rolly, Rolly, Rolly," Estelle murmured. She knelt and rested a hand on the young man's shoulder. His vacant eyes stared at the porch floor, the puddle of blood, tissue, and brains spreading under his head.

"I called the state," Torrez said. "And Taber is on the way." The sheriff twisted his head, working the kink out of his neck. "That pup kicked pretty hard."

"I think he had practice," Estelle whispered.

"The Thompson woman all right?"

"Nicked ear. She's lucky."

"And she shouldn't have been here."

"But maybe we're lucky in that, Bobby."

Chapter Thirty-Three

Lieutenant Edward DelFino set his coffee cup down carefully, pressing to make sure that the thermal cup's lid was firmly in place. He kept the cup well away from the paperwork. He made an exaggerated effort to make sure that his fingers were well clear of the cup before drawing his hand away. "You're sure you don't want anything?"

"No, thanks," Undersheriff Estelle Reyes-Guzman said. She knew that the lieutenant had made the offer out of simple courtesy, but it also established that he was running the show—even though the small conference room was just across the hall from the Sheriff's Department dispatch, just a few steps from Estelle's own office. DelFino's demeanor was almost apologetic.

Breta Baca, DelFino's partner, was wearing civilian clothes, her long blond hair secured in a tight bun at the base of her skull. Officer Baca was tall and willowy, and despite the tape recorders now in operation, favored old-fashioned yellow pencils and a yellow legal pad. Her facial structure was angular, almost severe, and her plain blue blouse and black slacks kept her appearance formal. She reminded Estelle of the second grade teacher who had tried to cope with Francisco and the other students before fleeing at midyear to take up a career with airport security.

For a small department such as Posadas County, without its own Internal Affairs Division, it was standard procedure to turn over the investigation of an officer-involved shooting to a disinterested agency—in this case the New Mexico State Police. Standard procedure, yes. But still an uncomfortable thing to have to do.

Sheriff Torrez had secured the chip from the Expedition's dash cam and made sure it was given to investigators, then turned over the rest of the investigation into the fatal shooting to them—essentially putting himself on standard three-day administrative leave.

A cart holding the thirty-two-inch television and its companion computer now rested near the end of the table.

"Undersheriff Guzman, we've met several times over the years, have we not."

"Yes, we have."

He managed a thin smile. "Although in less uncomfortable circumstances."

It wasn't a question, and Estelle didn't reply. It was difficult to think of the moment of Rolando Ortega's violent death as an "uncomfortable circumstance."

"And you know Officer Baca."

"Yes, I do."

"Good. So," DelFino said, "I've read your preliminary deposition, and the statement from both Lydia Thompson and…" he hesitated and shuffled papers. "Esmeralda Lucero." He let the papers drop and leaned back. "As well as the sheriff's brief statement." *In twenty-five words or less,* Estelle thought.

DelFino's thin, hawk-like face was sober, and his blue-gray eyes were complemented by his black uniform. "So. Why don't you tell me what happened." He tented his index fingers so the tips touched his nose. "And why don't we start with the reason that the three of you went out to Mr. Ortega's residence in the first place."

Estelle did so, keeping the recounting as unembellished as possible.

"So the Thompson woman didn't actually go out there with you?"

"No, she did not."

"What was she doing out there?"

"She told us that she was doing some surveillance on the Ortegas. Unofficially, out of personal curiosity."

"Did she think that Mr. Ortega had something to do with the death of her husband?"

"She may have. I don't know."

"But she took it upon herself to do a little recon."

"Yes."

"She's a former police officer, I'm told."

"Yes. The New York State Police."

"Both she and her late husband."

"Yes."

"That's impressive. Have you confirmed their employment with that agency?"

"No."

DelFino frowned. "Why not?"

"I had no reason to. I had just met her, and she was not a suspect in her husband's death."

DelFino waited a moment for Estelle to expand her answer. When she didn't, he said, "You had no reason to believe that she might have been involved in the death of her husband? Statistics say that her involvement was likely, don't they?"

"As we both know, statistics can say just about anything you'd like them to say, Lieutenant. But no. I had no reason to suspect her of involvement."

"And somehow, Mr. Ortega came under suspicion related to the death of Kyle Thompson."

"That's correct."

"You had hard evidence?"

"No. We had evidence that the firearm Mr. Ortega used in the shooting might have been the same one involved in a drive-by shooting earlier at the newspaper office. We went out to the residence to collect that gun. Our intent was to perform ballistic tests on the rifle."

"The sheriff tells me that the rifle in question was actually his own at one time." When Estelle didn't respond, DelFino's eyebrows arched. "Is that true?"

"Yes."

"That's sort of odd. How did it come to be in Mr. Ortega's possession?"

"It's my understanding that Sheriff Torrez gave the gun to his nephew on the boy's birthday three years ago. Quentin Torrez then loaned the gun to Rolando Ortega."

"Mr. Ortega tried to surrender *another* rifle to you and the sheriff yesterday? *Not* the one that the sheriff gave his nephew a number of years ago, and that was then loaned to Mr. Ortega—the rifle that the sheriff suspects was used in the drive-by. Do I have that right?"

"That's correct. He suspected it *could* have been used. Without an evaluation of the firing pin strikes on the casings, we couldn't be sure. I believe you have seen the results of our first tests."

"And the firing pin strikes, at first glance anyway, do match the ones from the drive-by—at least the ones left behind in the school superintendent's vehicle." DelFino frowned. "What evidence do you folks have that the superintendent's Navigator was used in the drive-by?"

"One of the victims of the newspaper shootings caught a glimpse of the vehicle. His description is consistent, and it appears that the superintendent's vehicle was apparently taken from the school lot, perhaps used and then returned to the school lot. And the twenty-five fired casings were found inside."

"You say 'it appears...was *apparently* taken...*perhaps* used.'"

He made a rocking motion with his hands. "Some slack there, Undersheriff."

"Certainly."

DelFino frowned. "Let me ask you something. You've been around for a lot of years. You've been involved in some high-profile cases. I've never had the pleasure of working with you, but some of my colleagues have. In fact, a recent retiree from the State Police tells me that 'if Undersheriff Reyes-Guzman says it's true, then you can take that evidence to the bank.' That's high praise."

He leaned forward and moved his coffee cup half an inch to one side. "Do *you* believe the superintendent's Navigator was the drive-by vehicle? That the cases found inside it were the ones from the weapon used in the drive-by?"

"Yes."

"Putting the onus on the rifle owned by the sheriff's nephew and loaned to Mr. Ortega."

"Perhaps. Until ballistics confirmed the connection, there was no concrete evidence. Supposition, based on circumstances."

"But no evidence against the nephew himself, somehow. This Quentin Torrez. Although it appears that his actions— showing you the wrong gun, and so forth—could be considered conspiracy of a sort. Trying to protect a friend."

"That's possible. But understand that we have no reason to believe that the rifle that Mr. Ortega used on the assault against us was at any time in Quentin Torrez's possession during the time of the shootings. Evidence supports the idea that Mr. Ortega acted alone. It's possible that Quentin Torrez had no idea of Mr. Ortega's intent."

DelFino supported his head with a fist on each side of his face as he read one of the depositions. "And that's the rifle that was used in the shootings yesterday."

"Yes."

"The three of you are most fortunate." He didn't wait for an answer, but reached down the table for several large plastic evidence bags. He opened the first and spread Bob Torrez's civilian shirt out on the table. Then he opened the second and withdrew Estelle's uniform blouse. "Three," he intoned, touching the holes in Torrez's shirt. "Two." And he indicated the rents in Estelle's uniform blouse. He looked up and nodded at her. "Good argument for vests, no?"

"Yes."

"Your deposition puts Mrs. Thompson about thirty-five yards behind you and the sheriff, out in the driveway." He pulled the scene drawing from the sheaf of papers. "You and the sheriff were standing approximately ten feet apart, and twenty-three feet from the home's front door." He traced the dotted lines on the diagram with the button of his ballpoint pen. "So what happened?"

"Mr. Ortega surrendered a twenty-two rifle to the sheriff, and when Sheriff Torrez said that it was the wrong gun, Ortega grew impatient and turned to go back into the house. He said he was going to get the correct gun. At that point, the sheriff caught up with him and grabbed him by the arm. The sheriff had his handcuffs out. Ortega tore loose from the sheriff's grip and spun around with a violent kick that struck the sheriff in the neck."

"Now that puzzles me on several levels," DelFino said, shuffling papers. "The sheriff is a big man…six feet four inches, the paperwork says. Ortega himself was no midget, maybe six two, six three? But that's a hell of a kick. You say in your deposition that Mr. Ortega is a member of a taekwondo class here in town. That sort of kick?"

"Yes. Very fast, very hard."

"And then?"

"And then the boy dashed into the house."

"The two of you didn't follow?"

"No. I had my Taser in hand, and the sheriff told me to put it away…that he didn't want things to escalate."

"Those were his exact words?"

"No. I believe he said, 'This don't need to escalate.'"

"But events *did* escalate. And that's where I'm confused. Why did the sheriff grab Mr. Ortega in the first place? You said that the young man turned to go back into the house. And the sheriff grabbed him. Who was holding the...the bogus...rifle at that point?"

"First the sheriff, and then me. He had examined the serial number, and then handed the rifle to me."

"And during that quick examination of the rifle that the sheriff made, right away he knew, somehow, that it was the wrong gun?"

"Yes."

"So the kid turns to go back into the house, and the sheriff grabs him. And at that point, the kid spins around and lets fly with some fancy kick that strikes the sheriff on the head."

"Correct. It appeared to connect immediately below the sheriff's left ear."

"Why would the sheriff grab the young man? Or attempt to?"

"I think that the sheriff wanted to go into the house with Mr. Ortega. He would have wanted to be able to inspect any other firearm that Mr. Ortega might have. A few moments before, when Mr. Ortega walked over to the truck to retrieve the first rifle, the sheriff went with him. He stayed within reach."

"Circumspect."

"Yes."

"So the two of them walk to the truck...just a few feet away in the driveway."

"Yes. Mr. Ortega reached in, lifted the rifle from the window rack, and handed it to the sheriff. The sheriff removed the magazine and ejected a shell from the chamber."

"Let me understand this. You have a kid...well, a young man, whom you may have suspected of being a felon at this point. And here he is, you say, handling a loaded firearm?"

"Yes. And that's why the sheriff accompanied him to the truck, and was within reach, was in control of the situation."

"So how did he lose that control?"

"The sheriff handed the rifle to me, and as he did that, Mr. Ortega turned away from him and strode toward the house. He said something like, 'Okay, I'll get it.' The sheriff commanded him to stop, but the young man didn't. By then, he was several paces away. The sheriff immediately caught up with him, and grabbed him by the upper right arm."

"Was he still holding his handcuffs?"

"I believe that he was."

"Now, in your deposition, you say that just as the sheriff grabbed Mr. Ortega, the young man spun around with a powerful kick. Was there warning that was going to happen?"

"None. Grab, spin, kick with the right foot."

"Now I have a question." Officer Baca's voice was nasal, and an edge made her sound whiny. "At what point in this whole confrontation did you acquire your Taser, Undersheriff Guzman?"

"A second or two after the kick. I dropped the rifle to the ground and drew the Taser."

"You didn't fire it?" Officer Baca asked, and DelFino watched Baca with what appeared to be amused curiosity.

"No."

Baca's thin eyebrows puckered. "Whyever not, Undersheriff Guzman?"

"The distance was rapidly increasing, and even as I brought the Taser up, Mr. Ortega had reached the screen door into the house, and that formed an effective barrier."

"You were never close enough to use the Drive Stun feature?"

"No. A contact tase wasn't a possibility."

"So let me get this straight. The two of you allowed Mr. Ortega to dash into the house, leaving the two of you standing outside in the yard."

"Let me dive in here," Lieutenant DelFino interrupted.

"Mr. Ortega managed to make it into the house, despite being ordered by the sheriff to halt. The sheriff is off balance, maybe even a little stunned, by the surprise kick to the head or neck. The screen door and the rapidly increasing distance made using the Taser impractical. That's the gist of it. Am I right?"

"Yes."

"Let's focus on one instant," DelFino continued. "Mr. Ortega was in the house long enough that Sheriff Torrez had time to tell you to holster your Taser so that the confrontation would not 'escalate.' Would you say that Torrez was obviously concerned about a possible escalation?"

"I think he was."

"And why would that be?"

Estelle closed her eyes for a moment, replaying the scene. "Rolando Ortega has a considerable temper, Lieutenant, and in this case, I really think that he felt cornered. Sheriff Torrez has the reputation as something of a bulldog."

"He doesn't give many breaks, does he?"

"No, sir, he doesn't."

"Have there been times when you saw yourself as something of a tempering influence?"

"Yes."

"So a few seconds went by after Mr. Ortega disappeared into the house. Neither one of you chose at that point to charge after him."

"No. That would be like trying to corner a badger, Lieutenant."

DelFino smiled, and Baca frowned. Did the young woman know what a badger was, Estelle wondered.

"You think he was in badger mode, then?" DelFino asked.

"We may never know exactly what was going through his head, Lieutenant. I suspect that when it became clear that his ruse with the substitute rifle was not going to work, and when he saw the handcuffs in the sheriff's hands, that he knew he was trapped, and responded aggressively."

Baca coughed discreetly, then said, "Despite all your experience, you weren't able to defuse the situation, to talk Mr. Ortega down?"

"No. He didn't give us the opportunity."

"Explain that." DelFino shot her a quick glance that might have been one of irritation.

"He dashed into the house, and when he reappeared, he held the rifle at high port. The time that passed was so short that the rifle must have been near at hand, and already fully loaded. When he burst back out through the screen door, he shouted, 'do you want this rifle?' But at that point, he did not hesitate. He immediately pointed the gun at the sheriff and fired."

"So for all intents and purposes, he came out through the door shooting." DelFino held both hands out, palms up.

"Essentially, yes."

"How exactly did that go down?" DelFino asked.

"He cleared the door, shouted 'Do you want this rifle,' and immediately fired three times."

"Fast?"

"Eighth notes."

"Show me."

Estelle reached out and slapped the conference table edge. "Bang, bang, bang. Like that. I heard the bullets strike the sheriff, and then he turned the gun, bang, bang," and she struck the table again, "and both shots hit me. One of them," and she touched the blouse pocket, "struck a ballpoint pen that was in my blouse pocket. A piece of plastic nicked me under the chin."

"And then the sheriff returned fire."

"No. Ortega pivoted a few degrees and fired once more. I believe that was the round that struck Lydia Thompson." Estelle reached up and pulled her own earlobe. "The shot ripped her ear."

DelFino waited, eyes locked on Estelle's.

"It was immediately after that shot...that *sixth* shot, that Sheriff Torrez fired."

"How many times?"

"Three."

"And in your judgment, what was the lapse of time between Mr. Ortega's sixth shot and the sheriff's response?"

"A fraction of a second." She reached out again and with two hands, drumming the cadence of the gunshots: the three pops by the twenty-two rifle, followed by two more, and then the sixth, followed by three quick slaps of the sheriff's forty-five.

"Just the six in total."

"No. The sheriff's first two rounds struck Mr. Ortega center mass, and he staggered backward a step or two, the rifle pointed upward, where it discharged again. The seventh time. That's when the sheriff's last round struck Mr. Ortega in the forehead."

"Had that third round *not* been fired by the sheriff, do you think that Mr. Ortega would have continued to fire? Even though obviously grievously wounded as he was?"

"That's impossible to predict, Lieutenant."

"The ME's initial examination shows that the sheriff's first two shots struck an inch apart, both exploding through Mr. Ortega's heart. One of the rounds broke the spine *behind* the heart." He looked up quizzically at Estelle. "That's extraordinary shooting, don't you think? Especially in a panic situation."

"The sheriff is an extraordinary shot, Lieutenant. And in the almost thirty years I've worked with Sheriff Torrez, I've never seen him panic."

Baca looked as if she wanted to break in, but the lieutenant interrupted. "Huh. So he *could* have placed those two shots wherever he wanted."

"It wasn't a situation where we had a planning conference, Lieutenant DelFino. In a situation like that, what is required is to put an immediate stop to the aggressive behavior. You're well aware of the theories behind the three-shot response. It is, in fact, part of your own training. Two shots to center mass to disrupt the flow of events, followed by a third shot to the head to terminate the situation."

DelFino nodded slowly, as if evaluating every word. Estelle continued, "As you well know, individuals have managed to return effective fire even when their heart has been blown to pieces. They may have five or six seconds, maybe eight or ten, to manage return fire, or return aggression of some sort. Fatally wounded as he was, Mr. Ortega was still on his feet, still brandishing a loaded firearm. The third shot to the head was clearly justified."

"Undersheriff Guzman," Officer Baca said while busily jotting something on her legal pad, "the question remains. Why didn't either you or the sheriff simply follow Mr. Ortega into the home and disarm him? Why did the both of you simply stand there and wait for him? In this case, wait for him to acquire arms and return on the offensive?"

"I like that word 'simply,' Officer Baca. Nothing that day was simple."

"The question remains."

Estelle took a deep breath. She knew nothing of Breta Baca's background, or how many times the woman herself had had to make such critical decisions. "For one thing," Estelle said finally, "the house was small and dark, and we were standing in the bright morning sunshine. We would have been essentially blind until our eyes adjusted. Mr. Ortega was obviously upset, and as I've already told you, it seemed prudent to wait, rather than pushing him into a corner."

"But you had a Taser in your hand, and never used it."

"That's correct. At first, I did have the Taser."

"And so?"

"The range was difficult, and the open screen door was in the way."

"When Mr. Ortega appeared for the final time, what was your first thought?"

"That perhaps he had acquired the twenty-two rifle that the sheriff had demanded from him, and would relinquish it."

"But he didn't do that."

"No."

"But you didn't fire your weapon."

"No."

"Did you draw your weapon?"

"Yes. But by then the situation was resolved."

"*Resolved,*" DelFino said. "That's a nice way to put it." He tapped the pile of papers into tidy order. "Had the sheriff not been there yesterday, how would you have handled this situation?"

"That's impossible for me to say, Lieutenant. Things happen because they are driven by events and circumstances."

"Would you have fired?"

Estelle shrugged, then for the tape recorder's benefit, said, "Impossible to say. As you know from your own experience, Lieutenant, we are trained to react to an armed confrontation in a manner that eliminates the threat. We do not shoot to wound, or disable. We shoot, if we have to, to end the situation. In this case, there is no way of knowing if Rolando Ortega might have been able to summon the final strength to fire his rifle again, or even several more times. He had already shot two officers and a civilian observer. The sheriff reacted as he has been trained to do."

"Undersheriff Guzman, it's my understanding that you have not seen the dash cam footage of the incident."

"No."

"Let's do this. I'd like to go back to the beginning, and this time, I want you to spin the whole narrative, without any questions or prompting from me or Officer Baca. All right? Beginning to end. Avoid explanations of *why* things went down the way they did. Just the *what.* All right? After that, I want to run the dash-cam footage. Is that agreeable?"

"Yes." She took a deep breath, then a sip of water, and began.

Chapter Thirty-Four

"Do you have time to speak with Miles Waddell?"

Estelle looked up as dispatcher Woody Ray appeared in her office doorway. He nodded deferentially. "He's out in the foyer and wonders if you can see him."

"Sure. Thanks, Woody."

In a moment, she heard the click of Waddell's boot heels out in the hall.

"If you don't have time just now, just tell me to get lost," the *NightZone* developer said. "I know your plate's full right now."

"Miles, it's good to see you. Come in." She folded several file folders whose contents had been spread across her desk. "You're a breath of fresh air in a couple of bad days."

"Well, thank you for that. Whatever I can do for you, you have only to ask. But look, let me get right to it, Estelle. I'm worried about Maddy Lucero. She's one of my best, and she's a wreck."

"With good reason to be worried, Miles. What has she told you?"

"She witnessed the shooting, as you know better than anyone else. She saw what Rolando did."

"Yes. We have her deposition."

"Christ," he breathed, and shook his head. "If you hadn't worn your vest—both you and Bobby. And Lydia..."

"But we did." She knew that her answer was curt, but the last thing Estelle wanted to do, even though she had high regard for Waddell, was wallow in the memory of the past forty-eight hours. When she had returned home the night after the shooting, exhausted from the adrenaline high and the unrelenting stress of the interviews, she still had had to face Francis. She returned home wearing the clean and pressed blouse that she kept in her office closet as a spare.

The other, with the two tears, complete with a splatter of blown ballpoint pen ink to mark one of them, was part of the package of evidence that the District Attorney would evaluate after receiving the recommendation of the two investigating State Police officers.

Earlier, at the emergency room, Francis had examined the pencil eraser–sized bruise in the middle of Estelle's chest, then stood for a moment with his eyes closed. Finally, he'd folded Estelle into a hug and the two of them had stood for long moments while the ER nurse discreetly tried to find something to do out of earshot. There had been nothing to say, but the following morning, when they both left for work—she to slog through the mounds of paperwork, he to work with Alan Perrone on Rolando Ortega's autopsy—the parting had been quietly painful.

Now, Miles Waddell thrust his hands in his pockets. "Maddy came back to work yesterday. Too soon, I think. She managed a few minutes with visitors, then she'd duck into the staff restroom. I could hear her cryin' when I walked by out in the hall. Carmine said Maddy's a basket case for sure. She's tryin' to hold herself together and not doin' much of a job with it. We finally sent her home."

"She's been down a tough road, Miles."

"Boy, I guess so. Is there anything I can do, do you think?"

"Be understanding. Be supportive. Give her space and time."

"All that I can do, and I know that Carmine is better at it than I am. She didn't come in to work today, though." He still had made no move to sit, but he leaned both hands on the back of one of the chairs as if he were going to use it as a walker. "I guess it's going to be kind of off and on for a while, huh?"

"I would expect so."

"Do we know what actually happened out there? I mean with Thompson?"

"No."

"Nothing?"

"Some guesses."

"But I mean, what happens now?"

"All the information garnered by the State Police will be turned over to the District Attorney, Miles. He decides if there is cause to turn everything over for Grand Jury action."

"Grand Jury? My God, looking to indict who?"

"To decide whether or not the shooting of Rolando Ortega was justified."

"You're joking."

"No."

"But the sheriff? I mean, my God, what else could Bobby have done?"

Estelle didn't answer for a moment, then said quietly, "Only people who haven't been there, who haven't been in that position, want to speculate, Miles."

He rubbed his belly. "This just turns my stomach. It really does."

"Any time there is a shooting, things get complicated, Miles."

"I guess so." He glanced at his watch. "I agreed—probably not the smartest thing I've ever done—but I agreed to sit down with Frank Dayan for a little bit this morning."

"Good luck with that," Estelle smiled. "You're certainly free to talk with Frank as much or as little as you like. We don't have that luxury, but you certainly do. He and I met for a few minutes yesterday, so he knows the basics."

"I don't imagine the sheriff has much to say at this point."

"I wouldn't think so, Miles. And I would imagine that Frank Dayan is smart enough not to try. I'll talk with Frank later today when I know what the DA is going to do."

"So, is there anything I should steer clear of?"

She shook her head. "Just stick with what you know, Miles. What you *know*. Don't speculate, don't go where you haven't been. Suppositions are generally counterproductive. Let things sort themselves out. Frank needs to do the same thing, but I can understand his urgency. He's got both his reporter and his editor down at the moment, so he's worried about them."

"They're going to be all right, though?"

"*Probably*," she said guardedly and shrugged. "Probably. That's as exact as I can be. In the meantime, any question Frank might have about the shooting, about the investigation, you'd be wise to refer him back to Lieutenant DelFino with the State Police. Frank should not be using you as a spokesman for law enforcement."

"Oh, absolutely not." Waddell nodded vehemently. "You know, I'm eager for things to return to normal, where our most serious threat is a tourist turning his ankle on one of our trails."

"That would be nice."

"But you're okay." He looked hard at Estelle. "You and the sheriff."

"We're okay. And Lydia is a lucky young lady."

"I guess." He shook his head in wonder. "She's staying with us topside, and I'm good with that. I mean, I expected her to beat a retreat back to the city, but she doesn't want to do that yet. So, for our part, we'll make sure she has her privacy, and we'll see how things progress."

Progress to what? Estelle thought, but she didn't voice the curiosity.

Waddell pushed himself away from the chair that had been his anchor. "You guys need anything? Anything at all?"

"The kids are coming back from Hawaii on Sunday. That's all I'll need."

"How about bringing them up for a fancy-schmancy dinner sometime next week?" He flashed a smile. "No strings attached. Ride the train out, relax over dinner, see the planetarium show, enjoy the night ride back to town. Get Bill to come with you."

"You drive a hard bargain, sir."

"You betcha. Will you do it? I even promise not to lean on the *maestro* about giving a concert sometime...much as everyone would treasure that."

"I'll do my best to persuade the powers that be."

He gave her a thumbs-up, even as he glanced at the clock. "And I promised Frank I'd stop by. Take care of yourself, young lady. I'm sorry you were caught up in the middle of all this."

She nodded and stood to accept his handshake that morphed into a hug.

She did not feel relieved, or jubilant, or celebratory. The pointless death of a young man had left too many questions unanswered.

Chapter Thirty-Five

Maddy Lucero had taken the step toward independence by renting a modest efficiency apartment in one of the two-story brick units a block from the high school. Built during the mining boom of the seventies, the three buildings were arranged in a horseshoe around a small, dusty, weedy common that featured an aging swing set in which only one seat of the three remained functional, a jungle gym, and a crawl-tunnel constructed from cast-off tires.

Maddy was standing outside her door, leaning against one of the metal roof supports, arms tightly folded across her chest. She watched as Estelle got out of the county car, crossed the graveled yard, and made her way up the stairs whose concrete treads were spalled so badly that the rusted metal framework showed through.

"The sun's nice," Maddy said by way of greeting. "For the past couple of days, I haven't been able to warm up." She nodded at the wad of tissues she clutched in one hand. "And I can't seem to stop the tears, so you'll have to forgive me." Her gesture was one of hopeless surrender. "Did you come to arrest me again?"

"Again?"

She laughed bitterly. "I call being handcuffed and put in the back of a police car being arrested."

"That was for your own protection, Maddy. And ours. We had no idea what was going to happen."

"Before you and the sheriff came out there, I tried to talk Rolando out of being such a dumb butt. I really did." She gestured toward the front door. "Let's go in, though. Lots of neighbors here."

The apartment was bright, leaning heavily on a Mexican motif, favoring Aztec and Mayan geometric designs rather than the more usual and traditional Santos and other nods to the Catholic faith.

A teakettle burbled on the kitchen range and Maddy crossed to the kitchen and selected a second mug from the shelf.

"Your choice," she said, and moved a boxed tea sampler forward within Estelle's reach. "The State Police said that they might want to talk with me again." She rolled her eyes and dabbed with the tissue. "They are extremely thorough, aren't they?"

"Yes, they are."

"They won't tell me how Mrs. Thompson is doing."

"She'll be fine, Maddy." Estelle tugged at her own right ear. "The bullet nicked her ear."

The tears came again. "But she'll be all right?"

"Yes." Estelle fished the tiny recorder from her pocket, switched it on, and set it on the table. Maddy looked at it and her face once more started to crumple. She took a deep breath. "Is this where you tell me I have the right to remain silent, and all that stuff?"

"You do, you know. You don't have to talk to me. You can call your lawyer and this goes back in my pocket. But based on what you told the State Police, I don't think you have anything to hide."

Maddy shook her head in resignation. "No. You go ahead. I'm so sorry about what happened that I'll do anything to make it right. But that's never going to happen, is it? Making things right, I mean."

"You can help us understand the 'why' of it all, Maddy."

She fell silent and took the moment to pour hot water in Estelle's cup. "I'm so sorry about Mrs. Thompson's husband. Rolando…Rolando, he knew about that spot on their land. He told me that he'd been over there lots of times, that it was scary. Just like straight down over the rocks."

"He told you that he'd had an encounter with Kyle Thompson."

Maddy nodded and snuffled into the tissue again. "He said once when he was over there, he stood in that spot and had this really powerful urge to jump. He didn't like heights 'cause of that. He said once he stood on the top bleachers of the football stadium over at the high school, and all he wanted to do was jump off the back railing."

She rewadded the tissue to give herself a dry patch. "I've never felt like that, but I've read that some people do, and I would think that it's a terrifying feeling. Then he saw Mr. Thompson standing right on the edge, talking about all the building he was planning to do. And so Rolando kicked him. He didn't *say* that's what happened, but that's what I'm thinking."

"Why would he do that, do you suppose?"

"I don't know. Some bizarre impulse is all I can imagine. I mean, I *can't* imagine. He said that Thompson told him once a few days ago to keep his motorcycle off the property, and he was mad at him for that."

"You two were arguing on the day of the shooting, Maddy. What was that about?"

The young woman didn't ask how Estelle knew, but said, "I was so mad at Rolando. I really was."

"Why was that?"

"See, he does things. I mean, he *did* things. Crazy things. He was mad at Mr. Waddell for not hiring Quentin on the train crew. He knew how much Quentin wanted that job, but then that stupid article came out in the paper?"

"The police blotter."

"Yes. And Quentin and Rolando were best buddies, and Rolando just thought it was stupid. So he did a drive-by, can you believe that? He *did* tell me that he'd done that, and I was so furious with him."

"But not enough to turn him in."

Maddy's eyes slammed shut, and then she said, "No. I should have, but I didn't, and that State Police guy said that's something the District Attorney would deal with. I mean, I *should* have told you guys, but I didn't. That's my fault, I know it is. But what's the point, I mean. Does Rolly really think that shooting out some windows is somehow going to change the newspaper's policy or something? I mean, getting his name in the paper was Quentin's own fault, after all. But then the whole town was in an uproar because Rik Chang and the editor lady were hurt. It *wasn't* just broken glass. I was petrified."

"But he commits the shooting with Quentin's gun, Maddy. Who's going to take the blame when it comes to that?" Maddy Lucero snuffled, and Estelle added, "You were dating Quentin, were you not?"

She nodded.

"And now you were dating Rolando."

The tears came again, and she reached out for the box of tissues that rested on the table.

"Kind of a triangle, don't you think?"

"What are you saying?" Maddy bleated.

"If Quentin is blamed for the newspaper shooting, that takes him out of the picture, no? Ballistics match his gun? Who does the finger point to?"

Maddy's black eyebrows puckered together. "You think Rolando did the shooting on purpose to get back at Quentin?"

"It's possible, isn't it?"

"Rolando doesn't think things through like that," Maddy

said, and Estelle was hard put not to laugh, and Maddy saw the shift in expression. "No, really. He doesn't."

"Apparently not. And when he has this brainstorm to go on his strafing run, he doesn't stop to think that there might be somebody working late at the newspaper office. Someone who might be hurt. He didn't think about that. And he didn't stop to consider that by taking the school superintendent's SUV that he was committing grand larceny auto?"

"That's what we were arguing about. He told me that he did that stupid stunt, I told *him* he should turn himself in for that, before things got any worse. 'Cause the cops were going to find him out, sooner or later. I mean, Quentin's uncle…he never lets go."

"Did you know about Rolando's plans for the newspaper shooting beforehand?"

"Of course not. If I hadda, I would have hit him over his stupid head with a frying pan or something. I only found out about it later."

"Was he here that night?"

"Yes."

"He stayed late?"

"About midnight, I guess."

Estelle carefully folded a napkin around the sopping tea bag. "When he left here, did you see where he went? What direction he went?"

Maddy shook her head. "I didn't watch him."

"Why didn't he stay with you?"

"He said he had something to do." She shrugged. "And we were workin' the next day, so…"

"You weren't at *NightZone* that night, then."

"No. My day off."

And there sat the superintendent's Navigator, Estelle thought, all by itself in the school parking lot, easy to see from the apartment.

"Just after your scrap with Rolando, over at his place? We

arrived and the sheriff asked to collect Quentin's rifle. Rolando tried to give him a different gun. Why would he do that?"

Maddy stared into her tea for a long moment. "'Cause if what you're saying is true, if he turned over that gun of Quentin's to the sheriff, it would be all over. That's what I think. You guys would just keep at it, and eventually..." She waved both hands over her head, as if trying to ward off the thoughts. "And then you'd find out about him kicking Mr. Thompson over the rocks." She gave a long, helpless shrug. "He didn't admit to doing that, but I really think he did. It's just so *him,* you know. All over, one way or another. I know that Rolly was getting frantic."

"Did he ever talk about Thompson with you? Did you have any inkling, any hint, about what he was planning to do?"

"No. And you know what? I don't think Rolando did, either. I think the opportunity presented itself, and boom. He kicked out, but he couldn't take it back." She wadded more tissue. "Just impulse." She looked up at Estelle. "Just like with you guys. The sheriff grabbed his arm, I guess to keep him from going into the house. I saw that happen, and off goes Rolando's hair-trigger temper, and he kicks the sheriff. And the sheriff had no choice, did he? I mean, when Rolly started shooting, he had to put him down." She was openly crying then, but ignored the tears.

Estelle reached out and turned off the microrecorder.

"What happens now?"

"Now, this gets written up into a formal statement. A copy goes to the State Police, a copy goes to the District Attorney, a copy stays in the Sheriff's Department files. The State Police will have more questions for you, some of them based on this... on what you've told me. It will be to everyone's advantage if you cooperate with them. Just answer their questions as best you can. There may come a point when it's suggested that you hire a lawyer. But you'll do fine."

Maddy Lucero closed her eyes, cradling her nose in the huge wad of tissue. "I don't think I'm ever going to be fine again."

Chapter Thirty-Six

When her phone vibrated, Estelle had been staring at the clock. Twenty-seven hours and a few odd minutes remained until the Gulfstream IV carrying Francisco, Angie, and the baby—this time in company with Carlos and Tasha—would touch down in Posadas, and thinking of that moment filled Estelle with both joy and apprehension.

Her sole souvenir of the shooting was the tiny bruise between her breasts, compliments of one of the twenty-two slugs that had whacked through her blouse and into her vest.

"I don't think I want to tell the kids," Estelle had said to her husband.

"Well, that's not going to work," Francis replied. "They'll read the stories in the newspapers and that makes it pretty clear exactly what happened. Let them ask, and then go with the casual shrug and a 'That's why we wear vests' explanation." He smiled down at her, but his dark eyes were pained. "You'll know what to say when the time comes."

If, if, if. She'd thought that through dozens of times, imagining what she would have missed had she and Bob Torrez *not* worn vests, or if Rolando Ortega had taken another instant and aimed for the head. No reunion on the airport tarmac, no sharing the triumph of careers, no participating in her children's or grandchildren's lives.

The awful experience of eight years before would flood back, that moment when Manolo Tapia had shot her with a nine-millimeter, and the bullet had struck her under the right armpit where the vest offered no protection. In less than a moment, her life had been in jeopardy, saved only by the skills of trauma surgeons—her husband included.

She knew there was no point in stewing, but that was easily said. The ruminations came unbidden and were resistant to interruptions.

Her phone vibrated, and for a moment, even though she recognized the number, she watched it turning circles on the polished desktop before picking it up. She'd come close to being outlived by an eighty-five-year-old.

"Good morning, sir."

"Is it?" His tone was rich with concern, and she smiled at the blunt, gravelly voice.

"I think there's potential."

"I'll take your word for it. Look, I know it's a little early, but I gotta have lunch. I'm starving, curious, and all at the same time, ebullient."

"That's quite a combo, sir."

"You bet. The State Police tell me that you all pretty much have things squared away."

"Getting close." That former Sheriff Gastner still had a line into the State Police hierarchy didn't surprise her a bit.

"That's good to hear. So how about it?"

"Lunch sounds delightful, in a dark booth far in the back of a dark corner."

Gastner laughed. "You're trying to avoid Frank Dayan."

"How could you possibly know that, sir?"

"You forget I have a long history with Frank. I know how he works. By the way, I drove past the newspaper office earlier this morning. The kid is back at work, wearing this sporty arm sling, camera in hand, headed out."

"Great news, as long as he's not headed my way."

"Probably going to talk a photo out of Sir Robert."

"I wish him luck with that, *Padrino.*"

"No Grand Jury, by the way. I damn near ran over Dan Schroeder with my wheelchair at the courthouse just now. I told Dan that if he tried to target Roberto with a Grand Jury investigation after a righteous shoot like that, he wouldn't be elected to dogcatcher, should the county establish such a position."

"I'm sure the DA was happy to hear your views, sir."

"Hey, when you're old and grumpy, you can get away with damn near anything. Anyway, I earned one of those weak Schroeder laughs, and he said no indictment would be sought."

"Great news. I'm glad you're in the loop, sir." She reached out and picked up the Post-it note that was first in the small pile by her phone, the one that listed Schroeder's number, the one that she had pointedly ignored. She stuck it to the phone itself, something to take care of after lunch.

"Oh, and I have some other news, too," Gastner said. "Too astounding to divulge over the phone. I'm having *way* too much fun, I can tell you that much."

"I wait with bated breath."

"Good deal. I'm out in the parking lot at the moment. Let's eat."

He was leaning against the front fender of her Charger when she walked outside, his walker folded and ready to stow in the back seat.

She returned his hug and then, with a still-beefy hand on each shoulder, he held her at arm's length.

"You're okay?"

"Yes."

"Bruises?"

She touched the center of her chest. "A little one, right there."

He grimaced and shook his head.

"So what's your news?" She held the door for him as he maneuvered into the low-slung sedan, and then she slid his walker into the back seat. Once behind the wheel, she looked at him and raised an eyebrow in inquiry.

"You remember who Colin Wheatland was?"

"Vaguely. He's the one who was accused of killing Josiah Bennett way back when."

"Good memory, and that's right. Josiah's son-in-law. They convicted poor Colin, and strung him up, but there was no proof he committed the murder, even back in those days." His grin was huge. "He is the one who purchased the Colt revolver from the mercantile. His signature is in the book. He forked over nineteen dollars and fifty cents for it, in two installments. That's why he signed, I think. Making payments."

"*Wheatland* bought it?"

"Yep. Irving is mailing me a copy of the page that shows Wheatland's purchase. How's that for a twist?"

"That's kind of neat." She started the car. "Now all you have to do is find out why Wheatland dropped his revolver and never reclaimed it. Why it lay out there for a century or more before you picked it up. And why it was fired twice before being dropped."

"See? Good stuff, right? And I've got my theories," Gastner said, and he rubbed his hands together in delight.

ACKNOWLEDGMENTS

Special thanks to Robert Rosenwald and Barbara Peters, along with their staff at Poisoned Pen Press, who have spent years of their valuable time supporting the efforts of beginning and veteran writers alike.

Thanks to "roadie readers" Laura Brush and Lif Strand. A writer could not ask for more encouraging and supportive readers.

ABOUT THE AUTHOR

Steven F. Havill lives with his wife of more than fifty years, Kathleen, in New Mexico. He is the author of more than thirty novels, taught in secondary schools for twenty-five years, and earned an AAS degree in gunsmithing in 2006.